Extraordinary praise for the Lily Connor novels

Earth Has No Sorrow

"Among the more unconventional of amateur sleuths . . . a richly textured story . . . Blake neatly juggles the theology and the police work." —*The Boston Globe*

"Following Blake's acclaimed first mystery, *The Tentmaker,* Texas-born Lily Connor, the Episcopalian priest who's human, intelligent and caring, returns in a superbly written and compelling novel set during the reflective period of Lent . . . Lily's quest for the truth takes her on a dangerous journey of both body and spirit that winds up with a heart-stopping climax and some disturbing revelations about the people in her life. The author exposes the very souls of her unforgettable characters with honesty, poignancy and wit. Rich settings and eloquent prose further enhance this most satisfying story, which will send new readers seeking the first in the series and leave those already hooked longing for the next addition." —*Publishers Weekly*

"Taut and thought-provoking, with an emphasis on character development and religious reflection." —*Library Journal*

The Tentmaker

"Shove over Brother Cadfael, and make room for Lily Connor in the vestry." —*Chicago Tribune*

"Blake has a gift for making her characters into real people, no small accomplishment in any setting, but especially noteworthy considering the temptations a parish mystery poses . . . There's good and evil afoot, to be certain, but not in the expected guises, and Blake's plot, which covers most of the seven deadly sins, keeps a reader guessing. As an exploration of spirituality and faith, the book succeeds on its own terms, rewarding the reader in the richness of its observations about the life of the spirit, one of the most interesting mysteries there is." —*San Francisco Chronicle*

continued . . .

"Put *The Tentmaker* on your list of books to read and add Michelle Blake to your list of new authors to watch."
—*The Washington Times*

"Lily is the most sympathetic heroine I've met in a long time, incredibly smart, literate, funny, and sexy—as well as (sometimes) insecure. And the church politics are so absorbing in their complexity, Trollopian in their wit. A terrific debut."
—*New York Times* bestselling author Alice Adams

"*The Tentmaker* deftly explores a shadowy world where nothing is quite as it seems. A well-crafted, haunting story."
—Margaret Coel,
bestselling author of *The Shadow Dancer*

"The hardest thing about creating a religious character isn't convincing us that [they are] smart enough to do the detective work: we all know how good they are at rooting out our hidden sins. What writers have trouble with is making us understand the mixture of doubts and certainties that led them to their clerical callings in the first place, and this is where Michelle Blake's Lily Connor makes such a distinctive entrance."
—*Chicago Tribune*

"This is superb entertainment, with multiple levels of pleasure, from a murder mystery to the mysteries of faith to the many meanings of love."
—Roger Kamenetz,
author of *A Jew in the Lotus*

"A wonderfully complex and interesting heroine in a well-written, thoughtful novel."
—Nancy Pickard,
award-winning mystery author

"One expects a mystery to be suspenseful, dramatic . . . and an absolute page-turner—Michelle Blake's *The Tentmaker* is all that. Rarer still, her novel is gracefully written, shows high intelligence and wit, and offers us an exact knowledge of a church milieu that would be fascinating even if her wealthy parish were not tainted by murder and corruption. A powerful talent, and I eagerly await for more."

—Stephen Dobyns,
author of *The Church of the Dead Girls,*
and the Charlie Bradshaw/Saratoga Raceway mystery series

"A debut novel that promises many good things to come."
—*The Cleveland Plain Dealer*

"A sensitive, deliberate debut, much in the manner of Blake's model, Dorothy Sayers."   —*Kirkus Reviews*

"Blake's writing is graceful, often elegiac, and her characters hum with humanity. Her examination of the divisive issues facing an influential religious organization in a fast-changing society gives a rich background to an entertaining mystery."   —*Publishers Weekly*

"This well-put together . . . mystery offers an in-depth look at the Episcopalian world and is sure to appeal to crime-fiction fans with an interest in the religion."   —*Booklist*

"Like Father Andrew Greeley, Michelle Blake manages to pull us not only into a good twisting mystery, but into the fascinating tensions and politics of a troubled congregation. She wields a fine double-edged sword."   —Craig Holden,
author of the highly acclaimed thriller *Four Corners of the Night*

"*The Tentmaker* is a fabulous amateur sleuth tale that centers on individuals questioning their beliefs. Though the story line is entertaining, this novel clearly focuses on Lily, an intrepid, complex character who hopefully will take her 'tentmaking' skills to future parishes and mysteries."

—*Midwest Book Reviews*

"Like Chesterton's Father Brown, Lily is a pretty good priest for a detective."   —*Boston Magazine*

The Book
of Light

Michelle Blake

BERKLEY PRIME CRIME, NEW YORK

If you purchased this book without a cover, you should be aware that this book is stolen property. It was reported as "unsold and destroyed" to the publisher, and neither the author nor the publisher has received any payment for this "stripped book."

This is a work of fiction. Names, characters, places, and incidents either are the product of the author's imagination or are used fictitiously, and any resemblance to actual persons, living or dead, business establishments, events, or locales is entirely coincidental.

THE BOOK OF LIGHT

A Berkley Prime Crime Book / published by arrangement with the author

PRINTING HISTORY
Berkley hardcover edition / May 2003
Berkley Prime Crime mass-market edition / May 2004

Copyright © 2003 by Michelle Blake.
Design by John Murello.

The quotations from Francine's notes on pages 89 and 90
are from *Q Parallels,* by J.S. Kloppenborg.

All rights reserved. This book, or parts thereof, may not be reproduced in any form without permission. The scanning, uploading, and distribution of this book via the Internet or via any other means without the permission of the publisher is illegal and punishable by law. Please purchase only authorized electronic editions, and do not participate in or encourage electronic piracy of copyrighted materials. Your support of the author's rights is appreciated.

For information address: The Berkley Publishing Group,
a division of Penguin Group (USA) Inc.,
375 Hudson Street, New York, New York 10014.

Visit our website at www.penguin.com

ISBN: 0-425-19690-9

Berkley Prime Crime Books are published by The Berkley Publishing Group, a division of Penguin Group (USA) Inc.,
375 Hudson Street, New York, New York 10014.
The name BERKLEY PRIME CRIME and the BERKLEY PRIME CRIME design are trademarks belonging to Penguin Group (USA) Inc.

PRINTED IN THE UNITED STATES OF AMERICA

10 9 8 7 6 5 4 3 2 1

In memory of my father

TWB

1910–2001

1

LILY LEANS BACK IN HER CHAIR AND REMEMBERS, AT the last minute, not to put her feet up on the desk. Sometimes the combination of nonchalance and cowboy boots confuses people. She's new at the job of campus chaplain, and she doesn't want the weeping undergraduate seated across from her to get the wrong impression.

From the chaplain's office, at the top of a hill on the Tate campus, Lily can see streets and trees and houses spread out below, with the Boston skyline in the distance. In late afternoon in mid-October, the setting sun shines on the underside of the bright maple leaves outside her window, so they glow with a sort of burning bush effect. She watches as the light flares and fades, while she waits for the undergraduate, Annie Kim, to get a grip. Soon, Annie is mopping her face with a Kleenex.

"Better?" asks Lily.

"Yes," says Annie. "Better. Thanks."

"I know homesickness," says Lily. "I'm from Texas, and when I first moved up here, I missed it, and my dad, a lot."

"Is he still there?" asks Annie. She leans forward and tosses the Kleenex into the trash. She's beautiful, Korean American, with dark brown eyes and thick black hair that seems to have been chopped off with a pair of pinking shears to a weird length, just below her ears.

"Yes," says Lily. In a way, that's true. And she doesn't think this is the time to explain that her father is in a grave in Benton, her hometown in the hill country. She's about to ask Annie if she has other people to talk with, but she's interrupted by a knock on the closed door.

Annie gathers her down vest and shoulder bag and stands. "You want me to let them in?" she asks.

Lily shakes her head. "Just a second," she calls out toward the door. "Do you like your roommate?"

Annie squints and looks out the window.

"No," says Lily. "Okay. Do you have other friends?"

The young woman nods, hesitantly.

"And you'll make a lot more," says Lily. "But it's tough at the beginning. It's tough for everyone. Some people are better at hiding it. Come by any time—I'm here Monday, Wednesday, and Friday. And come to services, too. It's a good place to meet people."

Annie smiles. "Thanks."

The person knocks again. "Just a minute," Lily calls out, impatiently this time.

But Annie is already on the other side of the room. "Thanks a lot," she says. And with that she opens the door.

Lily doesn't recognize the woman in the doorway. So she stares blankly, trying to think of one more thing to say to Annie, who is edging her way out into the hall. The woman in the doorway says, "Hi, Annie."

Annie halts for an instant. Then she says, in a brightly cheerful voice, "Hi, Professor Henderson. See ya." Then she is gone.

Lily focuses on her new visitor. She knows the face is familiar but doesn't know why. This is only her second week on the campus, and so the woman could be any of the twenty or thirty Tate people Lily has met and should recognize—being, after all, a priest, someone who's supposed to be good at recognizing people.

But the face calls up something else—a scene from her past, martinis, chapel, the small green quad of Cambridge Theological Seminary.

"Sam," says Lily, her mouth finding the name before her mind understands—this is Samantha Lamb-Henderson, who lived in Lily's dorm in seminary ten years ago.

"Do I look that different?" Samantha asks, after Lily's hesitation.

"No," says Lily, and stands. "Actually, yes. But then I probably do, too." She thinks one reason she feels confused is that Sam reminds her a little of the student who just left. Though she's not Asian, Sam is small-boned and olive-skinned with thick short hair that used to be—back in their seminary days—jet black, straight and shiny. Now her hair is short, almost boyish, and almost entirely white. Sam looks much older, thinks Lily, and she also looks taller. Then Lily sees that she has on high-heeled boots under her wide-leg black pants. She wears a long black cardigan—cashmere, Lily guesses—and a gray silk T-shirt.

"You look the same," says Samantha. "Precisely the same as you did in seminary. Same jeans, same boots,

same braid. You never had to try—you always looked so—
healthy, Texan, all-American."

"All-American?" Lily echoes.

Samantha lingers in the doorway. "I just found out you
were here, on campus, and I came over immediately. Is this
an inconvenient time for a visit?"

"No," says Lily. She motions to the chair vacated by
Annie. "It's a good time. I'm trying to figure out what to do
about— How have you been?" She immediately regrets the
question—she doesn't want to hear the string of successes.

Sam has become a big star in the small world of Biblical studies. Her last book, on the Gospel of Thomas,
crossed over into popular culture—or, at least, into the
New York Times Book Review. Meanwhile, Lily has plod-
ded along battling the church's conservatism and her own
skepticism and everybody's biases—hasn't written a book
or appeared on a radio show or put forward a new theory of
Biblical studies, hasn't done much of anything.

Sam spares her. She says, "Fine," and then asks, "What
to do about what?" She doesn't sit. She wanders the room,
studying the books on the shelves.

Lily wishes Sam would light somewhere. The floating
around is making her nervous. "Never mind. It just occurred to me I probably shouldn't talk about it—a minor
student dilemma. It's just that I'm so new and so temporary, I feel a little useless."

"Why temporary?" Samantha asks and sits on the edge
of the chair.

"Did you know Jim?" asks Lily.

"Jim?"

"Jim Hurston."

Samantha shakes her head, thoughtfully. She looks like
an intelligent bird.

"He's been chaplain here for the last four years. He was at Harvard Divinity School the same time we were at CTS. We took some courses together and got to be friends, and we've kept in touch. Anyway, his dad died recently, and now his mother's sick, so he's gone home to Virginia to get her settled in a nursing home. He asked me to take over for him until after the holidays."

"So you're only here until January?" asks Samantha.

"Yes," says Lily. "What about you? What are you doing here?"

"I've been transplanted," says Samantha. "From California. Tate's decided to start a full-fledged Department of Religion, and I'm their first hire."

"When did you move? Are you settled yet?"

Samantha shrugs—an elaborate gesture with both hands raised, palms up. "As settled as I'm going to be for a while, I suspect. I had a difficult year, and then, with the move—I don't seem to be getting much done."

Samantha doesn't look very healthy, with deep circles under her eyes and an uneasy red blush across her nose and cheeks. But she is still beautiful in a ravaged, old-world way—beautiful and weird, thinks Lily. "What are you working on now?" she asks. She's feeling more generous.

"I've been editing the new volume of sayings, with the Jesus group, in Chicago. My assistant and I have just returned from Greece, and I did a bit of research—nothing much. She's quite interested in Q. Any opinions on that subject?"

"Q?" Lily asks and laughs. "My opinion is that it existed. Matthew and Luke used it as a source. And the manuscript was eventually fed to a camel."

"You could hardly feed a leather scroll to a camel," says Samantha.

"Good point," says Lily. "Maybe it wasn't a scroll. Anyway, it's a little too hypothetical for me. I tend to be mired in the day-to-day muck—like where to send a homesick student or what to tell the Christian evangelicals when they ask me to speak at their meeting."

"What did you tell them?" asks Samantha.

"I told them I didn't think they would like what I had to say."

Samantha gazes out the window behind Lily, at the roof of the Tate library. "It's a sweet campus, isn't it? Not much of a library. Although, we have Harvard now, so I suppose it's a fair trade." She shifts her gaze back to Lily. "I stopped by to see if we could get together sometime, for dinner, lunch, a visit. What do you think?" When she finishes, the blush across her cheeks is more noticeable.

"Sure," says Lily. "Do you remember Charlie?"

"Charlie Cooper? Is he still around here?"

"He's a brother at the Society of Saint Peter. You want to include him? We could all get together, maybe for dinner. But I'm not sure—" Lily looks down at the calendar on her desk. "It's hard for me to tell what's going to be a good time. I haven't quite figured out my schedule."

"Let's make a plan, and if it doesn't work, we can change it," says Samantha. "I've been without company for a while. Since I embody the Department of Religion, I have no colleagues. A couple of women in the Philosophy Department have met me for lunch, out of pity, I think. No one's too thrilled to have me on board."

"Why not?" asks Lily.

"Oh," says Sam, "who knows." She gives a modified version of the elaborate shrug. "I suppose—well, no, in fact I know—the only reason they started this new Department of Religion is that they received a substantial endowment, and there was quite a bit of infighting over the money. What a surprise." She widens her eyes in mock wonder. "The two other departments that have been teaching religion courses thought *they* should have gotten some of it—or all of it. I suspect that's true, but it's too late now." Samantha walks to the door, then turns and leans against the frame. "It's good to see you again."

For an instant, Lily wants Sam to go away; then the feeling passes. "You, too," she says.

"Why don't you and Charlie come to my apartment next Friday, around seven? It's across from the Porter Square subway stop. MTA stop. You know what I mean. The Red Line. We can have drinks and walk somewhere nearby for dinner. I still make excellent martinis, and I still can't cook."

Lily hopes her smile looks amused and genuine, even though she doesn't feel amused. Being around Sam at the end of a long day is hard work.

"I'll drop off directions sometime next week. Is that all right?" asks Sam.

"Sure," says Lily. "Just slip them under the door."

"Or perhaps you'll be here," says Sam. "We could have coffee."

"Who knows?" says Lily. "I'm learning the job as I go."

Sam starts to leave, then turns around. "Are you seeing anyone?"

"Yes," says Lily, startled into honesty. She's usually close-mouthed on the subject of Tom Casey.

"Can you bring him? I'd love to meet him."

"Okay," says Lily, wondering how she's going to talk him into this one.

"And listen, that student, Annie Kim, is in my New Testament class. I like her. She's smart—and serious. If you need any help—I know it's confidential—but if I can do anything, let me know. And—do you mind calling me Samantha? Everyone does now. Samantha Henderson."

"Sure," says Lily.

They say good-bye and Samantha disappears around the corner. Lily can hear her boots on the stone floor of the chancel, then the heavy front door of the chapel open and close slowly. She leans back in the fancy chair—a black fabric machine with levers and knobs and even a couple of pedals—and puts her feet on the desktop. A more complete picture of Sam in seminary is coming back to her now— the dark, diminutive beauty, the vodka martinis in the dorm room, the shrouded history, the bursts of articulate brilliance, the moody silences. And now, the great success.

Lily closes her eyes and feels exhausted.

2

"I don't know," says Lily. "It was strange to see her. We liked her back then, right?"

Charlie laughs. They're sitting at a table in their favorite Indian restaurant, overlooking JFK Street in Harvard Square. Through the glass wall, Lily sees Venus and, below it, the new moon grazing the rooftop of one of Harvard's dormitories.

Charlie and Lily have been best friends since seminary. In a New Testament seminar on Mark, they discovered they were both converts, raised Catholic, confirmed in the Episcopal Church during college. They even look a little alike, tall and thin with dark hair and dark eyes. Charlie's face has always seemed to Lily the face of an ascetic—hollow-cheeked, aquiline—while hers is still the face of a small-town Texas girl—almost heart shaped, wide-eyed with thick lashes and thick, arching brows. Still, they look enough alike and have spent so much time together that strangers sometimes mistake them for brother and sister.

"Who's we?" he asks. "I liked her enough. She was sort of intimidating—you know, the brilliant, moody type. It seems to me you had mixed feelings, too."

"What do you mean? Was I jealous of her?"

"Lily," says Charlie. "This is a bizarre conversation. Why are you asking me what you used to feel about someone you knew better than I did?"

The waiter appears with water and a basket of crisp bread, and Lily orders—their standard order, *raita* and *saag* and *aloo gobi* and fresh mango chutney and nan.

When they're alone again, Lily asks, "Did you think of Sam and me—I mean, Samantha and me—as friends in seminary?"

"She always had this black hole around her. I had the feeling anyone who got too close would get sucked in. So I didn't think of you as friends, exactly. But not exactly *not* friends, either."

"Okay. I feel clear about that then," says Lily. The sky has turned black now; there's no light on the horizon, and through the glass she can feel that the air is colder, that winter is coming. "We had that seminar together, and she lived on the floor above me during—what?—our second year. And I used to go up there and drink martinis sometimes, on Friday evenings, I think. I seem to remember going to evening prayer a little—"

"Drunk?" asks Charlie.

"Buzzed," says Lily. "A few times. But we didn't hang out together."

"You thought she was cool—that's what I remember. She was older and stylish and smart. You've always been a sucker for the small, mysterious types."

"I know. It's as if I pick the thing farthest from
and worship it."

"I don't think that's so unusual," says Charlie. "And
didn't she have this whole other life in her past? You liked
that, too."

"Yeah," says Lily, as another piece of the puzzle floats
back into place. "She married her professor at Oxford and the
two of them wrote that book. Although she didn't get
credit—at least that was her story. And he was, what? A jerk?
He tried to keep her from leaving the country. Remember?"

"No," says Charlie.

"I don't know. It's just that I hadn't thought about her in
years, but when she came in today, it was as if she wanted
something from me, as if this was supposed to be a big re-
union. I felt like I'd let her down."

"She said she was lonely. She probably wanted you to
have dinner with her immediately, tonight. I don't think
impulse control was one of her strong suits."

"What do you mean?" asks Lily. She can hear her own
voice; it sounds louder and higher-pitched than usual.

"Lily," says Charlie. "Get a grip. She's a colleague.
You'll see her a couple of times. She'll make new friends.
You'll leave Tate. It'll be over."

Lily breaks off a piece of flatbread and dips it in the
onion relish. Of course, Charlie's view seems right. "I
guess I'm glad she's there, in some way," she says, while
chewing. "At least I know someone." But it's still there, on
the edges of her thoughts about Samantha, the mild sense
of dread she's felt since she saw her in the doorway.

FOR LILY, EATING INDIAN FOOD IS A RITUAL THAT RE-
quires some concentration. She has to be sure she has all

the right flavors and textures on her plate—the cool *raita,* the hot *saag,* the sweet mango chutney, the saffron rice, the nan, the lentils. So by the time she has her plate ready, she's too hungry to tell Charlie anything. They pass dishes and eat in silence. Lily has forgotten Samantha and is thinking about calling Tom at the police station to see if he wants to meet her at a pseudo country-western bar near their building on Commonwealth.

She likes the jukebox there, at Dale and Roy's—not Evans and Rogers, but the gay couple who owns and runs the bar. It's a mix of new country, which she doesn't care much about except for a few songs by the Dixie Chicks and Emmylou Harris, and traditionals like Patsy Cline and Loretta Lynn and Merle Haggard—some of them songs her father listened to when she was little and some of them songs she listened to herself during college and graduate school. And some she still listens to late at night when she's feeling homesick and missing her father.

She's not drinking these days, or she's not drinking very often—a beer now and then, because she doesn't much like beer, so it's not so hard to have just one. Tonight is one of Tom's late nights—he's a crime photographer, an officer in the ID division at police headquarters on Tremont. On days he has morgue duty, as he did today, he usually stays late to finish up paperwork. So if she calls him soon, she can catch him before he leaves, and they can meet. And she can have a beer.

Charlie is telling her about the grapevine he and some of the brothers planted last spring. "It was supposed to be this sort of Biblical exercise," he says. "You know, let's see what a grapevine really looks and feels like, since there are so many of them in the Bible. But it's mostly been a pain in the ass."

Lily nods and looks interested, but she's a lot more interested in her plans for the rest of the evening. "Don't let me forget to call Tom before we leave," she says.

"I'll try," says Charlie. "How are you going to talk him into this dinner with Samantha?"

"He won't mind," she says.

"Right," says Charlie.

There is something irritating about being known well, Lily thinks. And there's something nice about spending a lot of time in a place like Tate where people don't really know you, so they think of you as someone up to the job, who doesn't lie to herself about small things and sometimes large things.

"Also," Charlie says, mopping up his plate with a piece of nan, "I wouldn't get too involved with her."

"You just said I was making too big a deal out of this. That I should relax."

"Yeah," says Charlie. "Relax and don't get involved. The last thing you need is someone else to be taking care of. She sounds like a perfect candidate. You're only there a short time. Just try to stay out of trouble."

"Try to stay out of trouble?" she asks him, a bright, hard edge to her voice. "That's a great idea. Why didn't I think of that? Try to stay out of trouble. Just give me a minute while I write that down—"

"Okay, okay," says Charlie. "But you've got to admit you do have a way of getting involved in—whatever."

"In trouble. Yeah, I know." She eats in silence for a few minutes. "So, anyway, will you come to dinner next Friday?"

"Oh, I guess," says Charlie. "I just—I'm not that interested in seeing her again. Maybe you should go on your own."

"What will I tell her?" asks Lily.

"Tell her I live in a monastery and I'm not allowed to have martinis in single women's apartments."

"She's not an idiot," says Lily. "In fact, I think she's pretty good company most of the time. I just wasn't prepared for her this afternoon."

"You think Tom will come?" asks Charlie.

"If Tom comes, will you come?"

"Yes," says Charlie. "If Tom comes, I'll come."

"Then he's coming," she says.

Charlie rolls his eyes and tears off a piece of nan.

3

DALE AND ROY'S IS PACKED WITH BU STUDENTS AND would-be Texans and a handful of homesick Westerners, a few of whom Lily knows. The jukebox is blasting some horrible country rock that makes her think it was a mistake to come here, but then she sees Tom leaning against one of the tall round tables—there don't seem to be any stools— near the jukebox, and she feels cheered up. He's stocky, almost her height, with curly brown hair, long over the collar of his ancient leather bomber jacket, and the face of a former altar boy, which he is. He's totally out of place but looks, the way he always looks, totally at ease.

Tom has changed since she met him. Back then, she thought he didn't look like a policeman, too slight and sensitive, more like a photographer. But he's put on some weight, and something else, too, confidence, maybe—

Charlie says it's because Tom's in love. Lily says it's because he eats more than he used to.

When Tom sees her, he grins and waves her over. As she reaches him, he puts his arm around her shoulder and kisses her on the mouth, then yells into her ear, "I fought for this table, so we can't move until tomorrow morning."

"That's okay with me," she says. "Have you got any quarters?"

"No, but I've got lots of dollar bills. You want a Coke?"

"I think maybe I'll break with tradition and have a beer," she says, keeping her voice light and casual while calling out over the din of Garth Brooks and a pack of guys in polo shirts about two feet away.

He pulls back and looks into her eyes.

"What?" she says.

"Are you okay?"

"Yeah. This wasn't the best day I've ever had, but it wasn't the worst. I just haven't had a beer in a long time, and I thought maybe it would be fun to—oh, never mind, get me a Coke."

"I'll get you a beer if you want," he says. "I just wanted to be sure you felt okay about it. Up to you."

"No, you're right. Get me a Coke. And give me a couple of dollar bills."

"Okay," he says, reaching into the front pocket of his jeans. "But don't lose this table. It won't be long until a couple of guys over there fall off their stools, and then we'll have something to sit on." He heads for the bar.

She looks at Tom's longneck Bud, watching beads of moisture run at a leisurely rate down the side of the bottle. Here's the weird thing, she thinks—Tom, who could drink as much as he wanted, who doesn't drink often and doesn't notice if most people (except her) do, will nurse that same beer all night, and might even leave some of it sitting there in the bottom of the bottle when they leave.

But Lily—who started controlling her drinking years ago and stopped drinking altogether for a while, about eighteen months ago, after a serious foul-up brought on by a night of bingeing on sangría and filched Glenlivet—would, if she'd had a beer, have to time it just right so the alcohol lasted up until the very second they left the bar. Because if she had ordered a beer, she wouldn't be able to stand there after it was gone, watching everyone else drink theirs. In other words, people who don't have drinking problems don't seem to much want to drink, and people who do have them and can't drink, want to. Ha ha, she thinks.

When she sees Tom start back to the table, she takes the dollar bills and goes to the jukebox. She finds some new additions—Kris Kristofferson and Rita Coolidge singing "Loving Arms" and "Whiskey, Whiskey," Jerry Jeff Walker's "L.A. Freeway," Gram Parsons and Emmylou singing "Hickory Wind." She puts in the money, pushes the buttons, but the pleasure's gone out of the evening. She tasted that beer all the way there on the subway ride. Now she just wants to go to bed, but she'll have to pretend for a while, at least. She'll have to act like a normal person.

IT'S HARD TRYING TO HAVE A SERIOUS CONVERSATION over the music and guffawing going on behind them. Lily and Tom shout general news about the day, until Tom gets to morgue duty, the four-year-old boy who had apparently drowned in the bathtub but had a deep purple bruise along his right shoulder. When he tells her, he stares across the table at the jukebox, as if trying to make out the words on the lighted console.

Lily mentions Samantha but doesn't go into detail. She doesn't feel like yelling the whole thing, and it feels stupid to gossip about someone after hearing the story of the child. For a while, Lily didn't want to hear those kinds of stories from Tom's work. Then she thought, what kind of priest am I that I can't take hearing about real life? And what kind of lover am I if I can't take hearing about his day? Who else does he have to tell? Now she's used to it, as used to it as she wants to get.

When the Rita Coolidge songs start playing, Lily has trouble concentrating. They make her feel nostalgic, but she's never sure what this kind of nostalgia is for—is it for Texas; or her country-music, heavy-drinking college days; or her father, her childhood, and that vaporous sense of well-being she imagines being wrapped in back then? Whatever it's about, she now feels as if she's drifting away from Tom and the bar and the boozy laughter. There is something she's left behind, something she needs to find again, but she doesn't know what it is.

BY MIDNIGHT, THE AIR HAS TURNED COLD AND SHARP. Lily and Tom walk together up Commonwealth toward their apartment building. In the stillness, Lily listens to the sound of her cowboy boots on the sidewalk, and thinks of the sound of Samantha's boots on the floor of the chancel.

"Do we have anything planned for next Friday night?" she asks. Her arm is hooked through Tom's. The collar of her barn jacket is flipped up, so she can't really turn her head to see him without poking herself in the eye with a corner of the collar.

"Not that I can think of," he says. "Why?"

"You know the woman I told you about, Samantha

Lamb-Henderson, the one who went to seminary with Charlie and me and is teaching at Tate—?"

"Yeah," says Tom. "I remember."

"She's asked us to dinner—you and me and Charlie—next Friday. She lives in one of those big apartment buildings off Mass Ave, across from the Porter Square T-stop. Actually, she asked us for drinks, and then we'll go somewhere in the neighborhood for dinner."

"Do you want to do it?" Tom asks.

"I think we should," says Lily.

"That doesn't answer my question. Do you want to?"

"Not that much. But she doesn't know anyone, and she seems lonely. And when we talked today, I just felt sort of, I don't know, sorry for her. Which is weird, because she's famous and stylish and seems to have everything and to have done everything. But she really wants us to come."

"Is this someone you want to save? Because it seems to me things have been going pretty well lately, and you don't need someone to save right now."

"God," Lily says and laughs, a sharp, harsh sound in the cold air. "You and Charlie. She's the last person in the world who needs me to save her. I want to go, but I don't want to go by myself. And Charlie says he'll come if you'll come."

"Oh, I get it," says Tom. "If I don't go, you go on your own. But if I go, you have Charlie and me to go with you."

"That seems to be the deal," says Lily.

"So, if you want me to go, I'll go. But let's make it early, and short. I may have to work Saturday morning."

"I thought we were going hiking."

"We are. This will just be for a couple of hours. Guberman has a wedding. So I said I'd work for him if he can't get anyone else."

"What do you mean he has a wedding? He's getting married?"

"Guberman's gay."

"He could still be getting married."

"No—he has a job. He's shooting the wedding for a cousin or something."

"So you said you'd work for him?"

"If he couldn't get anyone else."

"That means you're going to be doing it. Once people find someone who says yes, even if it's a limited yes, they stop looking."

"Not necessarily."

"So you're working on Saturday."

"Probably."

"But you'll go to dinner on Friday?"

"Yeah."

"Great," says Lily. "Early and short." Then she adds, "Thanks," and squeezes his arm.

They arrive at their building, and Tom finds the key on his massive key chain, a brass, horseshoe-shaped piece of metal with knobs on both ends. He has a key for his office door, for the front door of his building at police headquarters, the locker where he keeps all his equipment, the dark rooms, his apartment building, his apartment, the dark room in his apartment where he keeps his other camera gear, the small mailbox in the apartment building's lobby, his car, his bike lock, the front and back doors of his parents' house in South Boston, the front and back doors of his sister's house in Wenham, Lily's apartment (on the floor above his), and a few other doors Lily doesn't know about or remember. But she likes the size and sound of the collection. For some reason, they remind her of her father, not because he carried a lot of keys (there weren't that many locks in the entire town of Benton) but because he used to joke that you could tell how important somebody was by how many keys he carried. "Me, I don't have but two," he would say. "And I don't know where they are half the time."

Lily and Tom get their mail and head for the elevator. As he presses the button, Tom asks, "Your place or mine?" and moves his eyebrows up and down, just slightly.

When he first moved in, last year, Lily used to worry that she would get sick of hearing him make this particular joke, but she never has. Maybe it's because she loves their arrangement so much, with her apartment one floor up and directly over Tom's (and with a slightly better view). And she loves walking into her own apartment, just the way she left it in the morning, with no one else's dishes or towels or records or books.

"Mine," she says. "Better view."

4

LILY AND TOM AND CHARLIE ARE SUPPOSED TO MEET under the large clock in front of the Harvard Coop. It is one week later, Friday evening, almost cold now, the dusk a dark blue sky and a sharp wind. Lily gets there a few minutes early, so she can see Charlie approaching down Mass Ave from the monastery on Brattle, past the Body Shop and the CVS, and at the same time see Tom come up out of the T-station and look for her across the street. She notices how his face relaxes when he catches sight of her.

"Okay," says Charlie, as they walk together back down Mass Ave, toward Samantha's apartment. "You got us into this. Fill us in. What should we expect?"

"Charlie," says Lily. "You're treating this as if it's some kind of punishment. We're going to meet a seminary buddy for a quick dinner. It has to be short, because Tom has to work tomorrow."

"Actually, I don't. But we can pretend I do. That's okay with me. I'll be our excuse to get out early."

"What about Guberman's wedding?"

"He got someone else to work for him."

"That never happens," says Lily.

"Yeah. You said that before."

"So," says Charlie. "What should we expect?"

"You should expect a woman in her late fifties, early sixties, very elegant, probably dressed in black. I bet she'll offer us champagne or white wine or martinis. I bet the apartment will be fancy, but sort of academic fancy, lots of leather-bound books and armchairs—" Lily stops and thinks about how she's characterizing Samantha, how she's getting into the game of making fun of her before they've even gotten there. "God, Charlie. I don't know. She may serve Boone's Farm and cheese cubes."

"I doubt it," says Charlie.

"I hope not," says Tom.

Lily notices how fast it turns from day to night now, in mid-October, as if the darkness is rushing toward December, its kingdom. She feels a tug of dread and sadness. Maybe in her old age, after all, she'll return to Texas, where there is not much winter to speak of, where the sun is king year-round.

Tom and Charlie are talking about the Red Sox, who lost their shot at the playoffs over a month ago. The two sound like a parody of Boston baseball fans—it was the media that killed them; it was Little; it was the Yankees. It's never the Sox. Normally, Lily would be joining in, but now she understands that some of her dread is less about winter and more about this upcoming event. She does feel responsible for getting the group together, even though it wasn't her idea. As they approach Arlington Street, the

dread becomes full-blown anxiety, a desire to turn around
and forget the whole thing.

THE APARTMENT FEELS COLD AND ODDLY EMPTY, EVEN
though there's plenty of furniture. Lily's first impression is
that everything has been set down in one place and never
moved, maybe never used. In the living room, a long, dark
leather couch hunches against the windows, and two
matching armchairs face the fireplace. There's a heavy ma-
hogany table in the dining room, ringed with matching
carved chairs. On the glass coffee table, a small stack of
books, all the same size, and a marble ashtray look as if
they're glued in place.

Samantha's assistant, Francine, who is joining them for
the evening, introduces herself and shows everyone the
white wine and gin and vermouth and martini shaker.
There is also some kind of melting cheese on a cutting
board and a plate of water crackers. Or Lily thinks they're
water crackers—she's never been sure what water crackers
look like. Samantha pours herself a glass of wine and starts
the tour of the apartment—a sprawling four-bedroom place
with two fireplaces and a complex layout that leaves Lily
wondering how they will possibly find their way back to
the front door.

Francine trails along behind, turning off lights as they
leave rooms, closing doors behind them. She looks too
young to be anyone's assistant—small and boyish, with
chopped-off red hair and at least four or five studs in her
right ear. There's something concentrated about her, as if
her whole being is focused on some essential task. But she
seems, at the same time, calm and competent, and after a
few minutes, like the more mature member of the pair.

Twice, she mentions to Samantha that they have a reservation. Twice Samantha ignores her, the second time stopping in front of a single photograph on a black enamel bedside table in her room.

"Here we are at graduation," she says. Lily finds herself staring at a photo of a group of seminary graduates, among them her twenty-four-year-old self and Samantha.

"Wow," says Lily. "I haven't seen a picture of graduation in a long time." Her own face in the picture looks a little sad, she thinks. She can barely remember the day. Her father was there, and they went out with Charlie's family afterward. Did Samantha come along? She can't recall.

When they finally get back to the living room, the food, glasses and liquor are put away, and Francine is standing near the door with her coat on.

"Do we have to leave?" asks Samantha.

Francine's face never changes. "Yes," she says, for the third time. "We have a reservation."

They walk, since the place is only a few blocks away, Samantha in front between Charlie and Tom, and Lily behind with Francine. At the restaurant, Lily finds herself trapped on a plush burgundy banquette between Charlie and Francine. Lily keeps trying not to look at the pierced ear, but she wants to ask Francine if the ones highest up didn't hurt a lot. That question feels a little premature. Francine is pleasant but contained—the opposite of this version of Samantha, who, as the night progresses, becomes more relaxed and self-assured and bordering on garrulous.

Tonight Samantha wears black again—wide-legged pants with a cream silk T-shirt and a black cashmere cardigan. She wears a pink silk scarf wrapped around her neck and she looks younger and healthier than she did the first day Lily saw her. Also, Lily can see Samantha's enjoying Charlie and Tom, and she has a pang of guilt about not wanting to come. From now on, she will quit worrying about Samantha—although an image of that picture on the nightstand stays with her. Still, Charlie's right. After she leaves Tate, she'll probably never see Samantha again.

Lily can get jumped by claustrophobia in tight spaces, and since the time, two years earlier, when she found herself locked in a box-like room for more than twenty-four hours, it's gotten worse. But she's doing all right on the small banquette until Samantha orders a bottle of wine for the table and Tom gets a beer and everyone's drinking, except Lily, who sips her tonic water and fixes her face in what she hopes is a convincing expression of enjoyment.

After they've ordered, Samantha begins to tell Tom about the months she and Francine spent in Greece last spring. Lily turns to Francine. "How do you know Samantha?" she asks.

"I was a graduate student at Stanford—I became her teaching assistant—and, let's see—then she hired me as her research assistant. After I graduated, I stayed on, because of the work she's doing." Francine has a soft southern accent—Virginia, or Maryland.

"What work is that?" asks Lily.

Francine takes a sip of wine. She's nice enough, Lily thinks, but hard to talk with. Francine speaks slowly, and Lily has the feeling she's editing each statement, as if to be sure it doesn't contain errors or indiscretions.

"Not much at the moment," says Francine. "The move, and settling in, and teaching in a new place, have taken up a lot of time."

"But what was she working on that interests you?"

"The Gnostic gospels, mostly. That's my own field."

"Oh. Samantha said you were interested in Q."

From across the table, Samantha interrupts and says to Lily, "It's hopeless to try to get information from Francine. She should have been the PR person for Los Alamos. Every book is top secret. I sometimes think she's disappointed when they're published and the secret gets out. Aren't you?" she asks Francine, in a teasing tone.

"No," says Francine, looking directly at Samantha. There is a moment of silence, and then the appetizers arrive. Everyone makes appreciative remarks, trying to erase the moment of discomfort.

"Do you like Cambridge?" Lily asks Francine, after Samantha returns to talking with Charlie and Tom.

"Not yet," she says.

"How come?" asks Lily.

"It's—small," says Francine.

"Compared to what?"

"Compared to the world."

Lily laughs. "Yeah, I know what you mean. It's pretty provincial."

"It's not really fair for me to judge Boston, though. I haven't seen much of it. I shuttle between Tate and the Annenberg."

"The Annenberg?" asks Lily. "The library at Harvard? What's there?"

Francine stares at the painting on the wall opposite their booth—a huge, green-and-yellow pear on a deep purple background. She's editing again, thinks Lily.

"They have a good collection of transparencies," says Francine. "There's a room devoted to manuscript research."

"Transparencies?" Lily asks.

"Photographic reproductions of manuscript pages," says Francine. And then she adds, "Have you ever been to Greece?"

"No," says Lily, wondering if she missed a segue.

"I'd never been out of the country, and I felt, when I got there, as if I'd been there before. As if I literally recognized it."

Lily nods. This is the longest speech she's heard from the young woman since they met, and the quasi-intimate revelation feels especially important.

From across the table, Samantha breaks in again. "You miss Greece because you fell in love there."

"Did you?" asks Lily.

"Yes," says Francine. "With the country."

"We met some wonderful people," says Samantha. She reaches behind herself, takes the bottle out of the bucket, and pours the rest of the wine into her and Charlie's glasses, then replaces the bottle, upside down, in the bucket. "Can we get another one?" she asks Francine. Then she turns to Lily. "There was this delightful young man, a graduate student in Biblical studies, who was off to Athos to take monastic vows and translate ancient texts. Nickolas." She says it with a perfect Greek accent and a slight brandishing of her wineglass.

Francine looks at Samantha for a moment and says, "Lily and I were talking about the library, and it reminded me to remind you to call about my card."

Lily can tell Samantha is not done with Greece, but she answers Francine, a glint of mischief in her voice. "Thank you. I'll try to do it Monday."

The waitress removes the appetizers and the entrées appear, causing another round of delight. The food is decorated, but not so that you can't tell what it is—on one plate, stick-thin french fries stand up straight, held together with a twist of onion; on another, three different colors of squash, from pale yellow to bright orange, surround an island of lamb and arugula.

Samantha refills her glass from the new bottle, then gets busy tasting everyone's food and making sure everyone tastes hers. She's taken on a kind of Auntie Mame quality; Lily finds herself pretending Samantha doesn't exist.

"So how come you switched from the Gnostic gospels to Q?" Lily asks Francine.

Samantha looks at Francine and smiles, eyebrows raised. "That's top secret, isn't it?" Lily can see Samantha's had too much to drink, and although she is still beautiful and lively, all the edges are blurred. There's something a little bit dangerous about her liveliness, as if it might slide into hysteria.

Francine looks across the table at Samantha and says, "Yes."

5

SATURDAY MORNING LILY LIES STARING OUT THROUGH the highest panes of the tall window by her bed. The window faces southeast, and she has hung the sheer white curtains a couple of feet down from the top of the frame, so she gets morning sunlight falling across her pillow in the spring and the fall. But it is still too early in the day for the direct light, so what she sees is a bright blue sky and the white blur of the sun behind the curtains, lower down. She hears Tom snoring, lightly, a contented sound. They have just made love and he has fallen back to sleep, a pattern she has not only grown used to but come to appreciate. It gives her time to herself in the morning.

She's thinking about the crème caramel she had for dessert, and about Samantha's face across the table, flushed and slightly swollen. By the end of dinner, Lily still hadn't decided about Francine. This morning, she thinks that she likes Francine, and that her diffidence has something to do with her strange, caretaker-like relationship with Samantha. After the exchange about Q and secrecy, Samantha ordered another bottle of wine, at which point Francine said she didn't want any more wine and thought everyone was probably ready for coffee and dessert. So Samantha ordered a bottle of champagne, which Francine refused to drink. That meant Charlie and Samantha had it to themselves.

Over dessert, Lily talked more with Francine about Greece. The young woman described a sailing trip they had taken along the shores of Athos, a sacred peninsula on which no women are allowed. As Francine began to describe the view of the monasteries from the boat, Samantha's voice rose above the restaurant murmur. Lily looked over and saw Samantha leaning close to Charlie, talking loud, repeating herself, saying, "Something so valuable— beyond your dreams. People have only imagined that it existed. It's so, so valuable—" Lily saw Charlie move away from Samantha, then move forward and place a hand on her shoulder. Francine was already up and walking toward them. The young woman put her mouth very close to Samantha's ear and whispered for a few seconds. Samantha's face went slack. Charlie talked about something, Lily can't remember what, while Francine paid the bill and got Samantha to her feet.

Lily also can't remember exactly how they all said good night. It seems to her that Samantha never spoke, that Francine spoke for her, and then led her down the sidewalk toward her apartment. Lily thinks of another restaurant scene, from when she was a little girl. She was visiting her mother, somewhere in California, and they were eating on the terrace of a restaurant with six or seven of her mother's friends. Suddenly her mother's boyfriend stood up, got Lily's mother to her feet, and left the restaurant. Neither of them ever turned around or noticed Lily or said anything to her. One of the other adults, a stranger, drove Lily home after dinner. The house was dark, and the door was locked, and when the stranger tried to walk around to the back door, he set off a loud alarm. Lily can remember the noise, and the smell of night-blooming jasmine, although she didn't know what the scent was at the time. Eventually, someone came to the front door and let her in.

She never sees her mother's face in these memories. She can't recall what her mother looked like back then. And since she hasn't seen her in almost twenty years, she doesn't know what she looks like now. It's odd, thinks Lily, but her mother's presence in the images from Lily's past is a physical blank, a space taken up by an indistinct person who moves and talks and leaves restaurants, but has no face.

The sun reaches the edge of the curtain rod, and she feels the first warmth on her cheek.

"What's Q?"

She rolls over and sees Tom, propped on one elbow, watching her.

"I thought you were asleep."

"I woke up."

"Q," says Lily. "You mean as in the Q source?"

"I don't know what I mean. Charlie and Samantha started talking about this thing called Q, and I felt like an idiot, sitting there eating my chocolate mousse with a spoon. The weird thing was they were so into it, this Q thing, and I couldn't tell what it was. "

Lily laughs. He kisses her shoulder.

"Q is not something you can talk about in bed," says Lily.

"What? You mean it's dirty?"

"No," says Lily. "If it were dirty, you *could* talk about it in bed. What I mean is—what I mean is, I need tea."

"Okay, how about I bring us breakfast in bed. Then you can tell me about Q."

"Deal," says Lily.

He leans over and kisses her on the mouth, a long kiss, then gets out of bed, finds his boxer shorts on the floor, puts them on, and goes into the kitchen.

"HERE'S THE THING ABOUT Q." LILY IS JUST FINISHing the scrambled eggs and croissant.

"What?" says Tom.

She swallows. "Q doesn't actually exist—not as an object."

"Yeah? Then as a what?"

"It's a theory. It's—wait a second." She leans over and puts her empty plate on the floor, then gets out of bed and goes into her study to look for her copy of the Gospel Parallels. In a few minutes she climbs back under the covers.

She shows Tom the book. "In here, the first three gospels, Matthew, Mark, and Luke, are broken down into chunks in order to show the material they have in common. Look," she says, and opens the book. Almost every page is divided into columns, sometimes two, sometimes three, and each column contains passages of gospel material. She shows him a page with three columns. "This page shows that Matthew, in the first column, and Luke, in the third column, have the same material as Mark, which is in the middle. So they all three write about Jesus' forty days in the wilderness. See—the passages are a lot alike."

"Yeah," says Tom. "So?"

"So the general theory is that Luke and Matthew both had access to the Mark material—the earliest known source—and got some of their stories and sayings from there."

"I can see why this isn't bedroom talk."

"Why?"

"Because if you're lying down, you might fall asleep before the punch line."

"You asked."

"I know. I'm kidding. Go on."

"Okay," she say. "But here on the next page, there's a long section where Luke and Matthew share material that isn't in Mark. See, the middle column is empty."

Tom takes the book out of her hand and studies the two pages. "Are they exactly the same in these parts—the parts they share that don't show up in Mark—all the way through?"

"No—and Luke and Matthew each has his own concerns."

"Like what?"

"In general, Matthew cares more about fulfilling the prophecies in the Hebrew scriptures and Luke cares more about the outcasts, Jesus as the savior of widows and tax collectors. But that's not the main point here. The main point here is that there are whole chunks of material in Luke and Matthew that come from the same place, but don't come from Mark. So the theory is that Luke and Matthew shared a second source that wasn't Mark. And that source—that theoretical source—is called Q, which stands for *Quelle,* which is the German word for source."

"Catchy title."

"Yeah, well, the Germans thought it up. Long on theory, short on wit."

"Okay," says Tom. He hands her the book and leans over to put his own plate on the floor. "Let me see that again." He takes the book and studies the two pages while Lily gets up and carries the plates into the kitchen. When she comes back, Tom's going through the book, page by page.

"You're hooked," she says.

"How come they don't think that Matthew just saw Luke's book, or Luke saw Matthew's book?" he asks.

She stands for a minute, watching him. The sun is on his shoulders, his thick brown hair is curlier than usual, and he looks like a kid with a new video game, completely absorbed. She thinks about his mind, how willing he is to take in ideas. Who else would go to a country-western bar one weekend and lie in bed reading Gospel Parallels with her the next weekend? "Some people do think that," she says, as she gets back into bed beside him. "But most people don't."

"How come?"

"I can't remember," she says. She lies down and props herself on her elbow, so she can see him while he reads. "What was Samantha talking about just before the outburst last night?"

"When?" he says, still reading.

"When? When she started yelling in the restaurant."

He looks at Lily. "She started yelling?"

"You know what I mean. When she was saying something was so valuable."

He's reading again. He says, "Um," looks up, and says, "I don't know. Probably Q, but by that time I had stopped listening." Then he returns to the book.

There's a line of fine hair that starts just below his navel and disappears into his boxers. She lays her head there, on his stomach, in front of the book.

"You've been drinking dirty water," he says.

"Have I lost you to Biblical scholarship?" she asks.

"If someone found this thing—a copy of this source—what would it be worth?"

"It wouldn't be—you couldn't put a price on it," she says.

"Okay. Let's say you had to choose between me and the original copy of Q, which would you pick?"

She sits up and looks at him.

"Well?" he asks.

"I'm thinking," she says.

"And?"

"What would I do with a copy of Q?"

6

IRONICALLY, FOR SOMEONE IN HER BUSINESS, LILY likes to keep Sundays to herself. She needs to see a day stretch ahead of her, not broken up into chunks of time claimed by other people. And the plan works for Tom, because it gives him a chance to go to church with his family in South Boston.

Lily likes most of Tom's relatives—all seven hundred of them, at her last estimate—especially his mother, Marion, a tall, broad woman partial to floral prints, who doesn't think it's a good idea for Lily and Tom to be together, but doesn't let that keep her from adopting Lily into the family. Still, when she can, Lily stays home on Sundays and lets Tom go over to South Boston. It's too much for her every week, all those nieces and nephews. She's an only child raised by her father on a ranch fifteen miles from the closest neighbor. Sundays are her fifteen miles.

She hasn't been able to stay home this Sunday, though, the day after she and Tom talked about Q and drove up to Topsfield for a hike along the Ipswich River, because this Sunday she is leading the ten o'clock service at Tate. Just about the time she would normally be getting home from her walk to the river and back, she is climbing the stairs to the pulpit. Before beginning her sermon, she looks out over the congregation and spots Annie Kim, who visited the office the same day Samantha appeared. Lily hasn't seen Annie since that day, and she makes a note to herself to find the girl after the service and see how things are going. Lily doesn't feel good about that meeting—she didn't know what to offer the girl. She didn't offer much, if she remembers it right.

The gospel passage is high on her list of top hits: the story of Zacchaeus, the tax collector. She likes the idea of the little man up in a tree, trying to see Jesus. Lily thinks the reason Zacchaeus became a tax collector was so he could tax the pants off the guys he grew up with, guys who had made fun of him on the ancient Hebrew equivalent of the basketball court.

Lily talks a little about this, and then she talks about Luke's insistence that Jesus came "to seek out and to save the lost"—which is what he did that day on his way to Jerusalem. He sought out Zacchaeus in the tree and asked if he could stay at the tax collector's house. This blessing transformed Zacchaeus—the blessing of being given the chance to be generous. When Jesus gave Zacchaeus what he needed, Zacchaeus was able to turn around and give other people what they needed, to repay the people he had cheated—probably, says Lily, the guys who hadn't let him play basketball.

Jesus was an outcast himself, a child without a father in

a day and place where all men were identified as their fathers' sons. So he knew what it was like to be kept at the edge of the court. And that gave him a lot of power. It gave him the power to see other people on the edge and to know how they felt.

Luke knows this about Jesus; he tells story after story of Jesus blessing the widow, the leper, the Samaritan, the poor. In fact, Luke is the only gospel writer who tells the story of Zacchaeus. This was probably a story that Luke heard and chose to tell because it captures the essence of Luke's Jesus, the man who sought out the lost. And it captures the essence of what Luke wants us to do as Christians.

For an instant, Lily is distracted by a memory of her conversation with Tom the day before, about Q. Where did the story of Zacchaeus come from, she wonders. It's not in any of the other Biblical material she's seen. Did Jesus do or say any of this stuff? What am I preaching from? Then she thinks about the fine hairs just below Tom's navel. Color rushes to her cheeks. She takes a deep breath and scans the page of notes in front of her, desperate to find her place in the sermon.

But it's too late. She's lost her place and her interest. She's not used to preaching, and she hadn't thought much about how it would feel to be in the pulpit again. She improvises about a couple of students she's met at Tate, those who spent their summer building homes for people in the Dominican Republic. She says she sees this phenomenon—this seeking out of the lost—happening all around her, every day, when a teacher recognizes a student for who she is or sees a talent that others have ignored. Indeed, Lily says, the world is a place that is full of these blessings, but we have to look for them and we have to make them. Whatever, she thinks, as leaves the pulpit.

. . .

GREETING PEOPLE IN THE VESTIBULE, LILY KEEPS A watch out for Annie, but the girl never appears. She must have gone out one of the side doors or maybe downstairs to coffee hour. But once Lily's changed and gone downstairs herself, there's no sign of Annie there, either.

As she chats with other students and the few faculty who come to campus on Sunday, Lily's trying to figure out if she can possibly make an excuse to get out of the next event on her chaplain schedule—lunch with students and a psychology professor who has published a book about the role religion plays in college life. Lily has tried to read the book. The writing is flat and serviceable; she is bored before she's into the second sentence. As far as Lily can tell, the professor thinks religion *does* play a role in college life, although she couldn't make herself read far enough to determine *what* role it plays.

But when the man shows up—a little guy with a thick toupee and a jolly, anxious manner—Lily can't bring herself to tell him she won't be there. Maybe there's more here than meets the eye. My Zacchaeus, she thinks, and then thinks, let's not get carried away.

SHE ENTERS THE COOL DARK VESTIBULE OF THE CHAPEL, crosses the hallway, and unlocks her office door. The luncheon went well. Most of these students have read very little—including the Bible—but when they do read something, they have good insights. They are enthusiastic and genuine, though uncultured in basic ways. At least that's how they seem to her, with her Catholic school education, in which she learned, if nothing else, the great books of

Western literature—Willa Cather, Charles Dickens, J. Frank Dobie—in other words, what nuns in Texas considered the great books of Western literature.

She gathers her backpack and sermon notes, leaves the office, locks the door, then turns into the vestibule. At which point she runs into someone standing behind her, silently. Both women gasp—it's definitely a woman—and then Lily says, "Sam?"

"Yes," she says. "I'm sorry I scared you. I thought you saw me."

"Christ," says Lily. "I think my heart's stopped." She leans against the door and catches her breath. "Were you looking for me?"

"Yes," Samantha repeats. "Can we talk for a minute?"

"You want to walk me to the bus? Otherwise I'm going to miss the 4:20 and there won't be another one for an hour."

"What if I drive you home? I'm happy to."

"Okay," Lily says. She's expected some kind of apology for Friday night. She's also dreaded it, but now she feels calm, as if something inevitable is happening, as if she's watching the rain start to fall, and her without an umbrella.

Samantha is not wearing makeup, so she looks older, and tireder. She's wearing jeans and a black wool turtleneck, and she has a black nylon briefcase tucked under her arm. Lily adds, "But I live over in Brookline."

"I don't remember where that is," says Sam. "Across the river, right? How hard can it be to get there?"

"During rush hour, it's easier to get to Java. But it shouldn't be too bad now. And if you're willing—"

"I am," says Sam. "I'm parked right here, in the faculty lot." She raises her right hand and points east.

On their way, they pass a group of students standing

outside the admissions building. Lily knows none of them
well, but she recognizes two or three from the luncheon.
Lily smiles and waves, and only one girl waves back, a
small, self-conscious motion of her hand. This causes the
rest of the students to turn and look, and a few of them
raise their hands to wave at Samantha. One calls out, "Hi,
Professor Henderson." Samantha waves back cheerfully.

"Your students?" asks Lily.

"Students, advisees. Of course, I have no idea what to
advise them to do. But everyone's good-natured about it.
People are much nicer here than they were at Stanford,
about everything. And the students—I thought I would
miss the whiz kids, but these students are so much more
pleasant to teach."

"You like teaching?" asks Lily.

"I love it," says Sam, and she's obviously telling the
truth. When they reach the parking lot, Samantha begins to
walk faster. "There it is," she says, and points to a sporty-
looking red car.

It's a BMW, some kind of little roadster. "Wow," says
Lily. "This is quite a car."

"Yes," says Sam. "It's my pet. I would bring it into the
house at night if I could."

"Probably be a good idea," says Lily.

"I have a garage space, covered roof, locked doors."
Samantha presses a button on the key chain and the lights
flash on and off, the horn beeps, briefly, and the locks on
the doors pop up. It's like coming home to a Labrador
puppy, thinks Lily.

THE TRAFFIC IS WORSE THAN LILY EXPECTED. SHE
dreaded riding with Samantha, expecting her to be a sort of

madcap demon on the road, but she's not. She's a good driver, careful. Lily has the impression she's protecting the paint job. "So," she says, at a red light on River Street. "You just use Henderson now? You dropped the Lamb?"

"Yes," says Samantha. "It wasn't mine, you know. It was William's. Well, the Henderson is his, too, but Americans were confused by the hyphen."

"Are you two ever in touch?" asks Lily.

Samantha makes a sound in her throat, between a laugh and a groan. "No, thank God. He's a little crazy. Actually, very crazy. Paranoid, bitter, full of plans for revenge."

"Sounds like half the people I know," says Lily. She's waiting for the apology, or whatever Samantha has planned. Lily feels sure she has something planned. She's not a woman who does things for no reason.

"True," says Samantha. "But most people we know don't act on the plans. William began to believe himself."

"What do you mean?"

"When I finally left him, or was rescued from our house—but that is a long and complicated story. Let's just say that by the time I left, he had become a dangerous person, and he still is."

"Dangerous—physically, you mean?"

"Yes, physically, and in other ways, as well. He's still powerful, at least in our small, shared world of Biblical scholarship—well known and respected. A little thing like imprisoning your young wife wouldn't tarnish an academic reputation in Oxford. First things first."

They are crossing the BU Bridge. A few sailboats are still out on the river, even though the light is fading. Lily feels herself being drawn into Samantha's story, and she wants to resist the pull. "Get into the far right lane, but don't turn yet," she says.

After a few more minutes of directions and maneuvers, Samantha clears her throat—the sound someone makes before she addresses a large, disgruntled audience. "I feel I owe you an apology," she says.

Lily doesn't say, "For what?" She stares through the windshield at the car in front of them, an old, blue Toyota with a crumpled fender and at least twenty bumper stickers, including KEEP HONKING/I'M RELOADING and EASY DOES IT.

"I have been drinking too much lately," says Samantha. "No, I have been drinking too much for a long time."

Lily glances at Samantha, whose face is composed. She doesn't seem uncomfortable, though Lily can feel her own palms start to sweat.

"In fact, I have always drunk too much, but now I'm getting old, and it's unbecoming. And probably dangerous."

Samantha doesn't seem to need a response, so Lily nods once and keeps listening.

"I'm sorry about Friday night. I wanted it to go well. I like Tom. And I've always been fond of Charlie. And you."

They are on Commonwealth, headed toward Lily's apartment.

"If I hadn't left Stanford," Samantha continues, "they would have made me dry out, I think. They couldn't fire me. But they would have had to do something. I missed an exam, once, missed a couple of classes, got drunk at department parties, went into the hot tub with my clothes on—very old-fashioned, nothing interesting. It's one of the main reasons I took the job at Tate. New place. New people. New habits. Not so much shame. But I see I've started off again in the same direction, and when I see the inevitable future stretch before me, I'm not sure I can stand it."

Lily has to decide whether or not she's going to say something about her own drinking and not-drinking, and she has to do it fast. With a lot of people, people she knows and people she can imagine, this wouldn't be a problem. But something about the force of Samantha's desire to reenter Lily's life makes her feel guarded. "Get into the left lane," she says. "You need to make a U-turn at the next light."

"Is that legal?" asks Samantha.

"I don't know. Charlie does it, and he's a monk."

"Also," says Sam. "There's some additional pressure. During the last couple of months something strange has begun to happen—to me, or to Francine, really, though we're both involved."

"I'm a little lost," says Lily. "Are we talking about drinking?"

"Yes," says Samantha. "We are. My intention had been to stop drinking when we moved East. But that plan has failed, and I believe one reason is this new situation."

Lily is, again, tired of Samantha, tired of her problems, tired of the energy required to be in her presence. "I think it's dangerous to glamorize drinking and not drinking," says Lily. "I mean, the reason we drink is because we want to, not because we have situations."

Samantha doesn't answer. After a moment of silence, she says, "I wanted to talk with you today because I need some help."

Aha, Lily thinks. She says, "Pull over here."

They stop in front of Lily's building. Unbelievably, there is a visitor's parking space right there, ten feet from the door. This never happens. Samantha parks and turns to Lily. "May I come up? I know this is a lot more than you bargained for, and I wouldn't ask if I knew where else to go."

Lily looks for her keys in her backpack, even though she knows exactly where they are—in the small zip pocket on the front of the pack. "Sure," she says finally.

7

SAMANTHA SITS ON THE SMALL BLUE SOFA IN LILY'S living room. Lily has switched on one bulb of the standing lamp at the end of the couch, but she hasn't turned up the heat or offered Samantha anything to drink. She thinks of Charlie saying to her, Stay out of trouble. It occurs to her she's not doing a great job of that at the moment.

Samantha holds the black briefcase on her lap, as if it were something alive that needed tending. "Thank you," she says. "I know you have a lot going on—can I have a glass of water?"

Lily nods and goes into the kitchen. She wants to be alone in her apartment, to take a walk, come back and shower, then see if Tom is home, make dinner, read. She wants to be able to breathe easily. She fills a glass of water from the tap. "Do you want ice?" she asks.

"No," says Sam. "Thank you."

Lily settles into the recliner, the one piece of furniture from the her childhood home, and glances out the window onto Commonwealth. The sky has gotten dark since they came in, and lights are coming on in neighboring apartments. Lily can see the couple in the apartment directly across from hers in the building next door; they have French doors between the kitchen and the balcony. The young woman is pregnant; the older man cooks elaborate meals every night, lights candles, pours wine. Lily has made up a story about them, which is that they were dating, she got pregnant, they married in a rush and the young woman now wakes up every morning thinking, Where am I and what have I done?

"I have something to show you," says Samantha. "I should try to prepare you for this, but I'm not sure how. I need an opinion. No—as I said earlier—I need more than an opinion. I need help."

Lily hesitates, then asks, "What kind of help?"

"Francine and I have received something in the mail. We're not sure what it is, we don't know where it came from, and we don't know why it's been sent to us. We need help making sense of it all. At least, I need help. Francine doesn't seem to think she does. I thought of you, of course, because of our friendship, and because I believe you've been involved in similar situations before."

"Like what?" asks Lily.

"Insoluble problems? Confusing circumstances? I'm not sure what to call them."

"Do you mean what happened last year, with Anna Banieka?"

"Yes. And then the death of the rector at St. Mary's of the Garden."

"How do you know about that stuff?" asks Lily.

Samantha shrugs, as if she can't remember. "The grapevine."

Lily feels unnerved, now. There is no grapevine connecting Samantha and her. But she also feels interested. Phrases from the dinner conversation come back to her, along with Tom's questions about Q, and the way Samantha clutches the briefcase.

"The problem is," says Samantha. "This must be kept between us, or among us, since Francine, of course, is included. I can't have anyone else knowing about this, not yet."

Lily nods. Her interest overcomes her discomfort.

Samantha opens the briefcase and hands Lily a cream-colored envelope, a standard document-sized rectangle.

The paper is heavy and rich, a kind of vellum, and Lily sees the package is addressed to FRANCINE LOETTERLEE, DEPARTMENT OF RELIGION, TATE UNIVERSITY. The postmark is from Washington, D.C. It's a double seal, with a cord wound around a button halfway down the back of the envelope, and glue on the flap, as well—although, the glue no longer holds. Lily unwraps the cord and opens the flap. Carefully, she reaches in and pulls out a single, black-and-white, 8×10 photograph and a piece of cardboard cut to the same size.

The light in the room has grown so dim that Lily can't see the picture well. She turns on a lamp that sits on the table beside her chair. The photograph shows lines of square Hebrew script on what looks like some sort of scroll; she sees a sewn edge on the right side. Lily can't decipher the words themselves, since the breaks between them are small and she hasn't read any Hebrew in a while.

Near the bottom, the letters are faded and illegible.

"What is it?" Lily asks.

"This manuscript," says Samantha—then she stands and walks around behind Lily's chair, leans over her shoulder—"contains standard Q material, very much what you would expect."

Part of Lily's mind is taking in what Samantha is saying; another part is scrambling ahead, trying to understand what she's holding in her hands. The writing is in two sections—a longer first paragraph and a smaller second paragraph. "Expect?" she asks.

"Point well taken," says Samantha. "Expect, if one were to posit the existence of such a thing."

"Such a thing being?"

"As I say, it contains standard Q material."

"And you have no idea who sent it?"

Sam smiles and shrugs her shoulders, then raises her hands, palms up, in a "who knows" gesture. "I have a guess—or, to be accurate, I have guesses."

"And they are—?"

"I would rather not go into that now, in part, because they are guesses. And because we have no way to determine whether or not the manuscript is authentic."

"Why you?"

"Do you mean why Francine? Presumably—if it is, let's conjecture, authentic—someone believes the world should know this material exists. And trusts her."

Lily leans back in her chair and glances, again, at the lights along Commonwealth. The sky is completely dark, and she sees her own face, superimposed over those lights, her eyes dark hollows in a white mask. Then she sees the face of the young pregnant woman in the window across the way. She is gazing out into the night, and Lily imagines she can see longing and greed and a broken heart in the tilt of the woman's head, the stoop of her shoulders.

The photograph in Lily's hands feels heavy and large, as if it had grown in the last few moments. If she believes her own eyes and what Samantha tells her—and for some reason she hasn't yet figured out, she does, in her heart, believe all of that—then this is an ancient version of Q, the missing gospel source.

Samantha points to the first group of lines, which fills the top half of the parchment column. "Do you read Hebrew?" she asks.

"No," says Lily. "A little. But I can't read this."

"Yes," says Samantha. "It's fairly typical. No periods, no commas, very little indication of units—paragraphs, chapters, passages. This is the do-unto-others page, after the Beatitudes." She runs her red fingernail under the first line of text. Lily winces. It's not the real thing, she tells herself. *"But I tell you, Love your enemies,"* Samantha reads, *"and do good to those who hate you. Bless the ones who curse you and pray for the ones who treat you badly."*

"That's what it says?" asks Lily.

"Yes, why?"

"Because," Lily begins, but she can't finish. Her voice is caught in her throat. This happened to her in the manuscript room of the British Museum, too, when she realized she was seeing Wordsworth's handwriting, Keats's death mask, the Gutenberg Bible. She had to sit down on one of the benches along the wall and let herself be overwhelmed. She had to weep. But she doesn't want to cry in front of Samantha. So she just shakes her head.

"Should I go on?" asks Samantha.

Lily nods.

"*When someone hits you on the right cheek*—which means backhanded, like this—" Samantha touches Lily's right cheek with the back of her own right hand. "Very insulting. Let's see—*offer them the other cheek, too. And when someone takes your cloak from you, let them have your shirt. Give to anyone who asks. And if someone robs you, don't ask for your property to be returned.*

"*And treat people as you want them to treat you. If you love the ones who love you, what credit is that to you? Even people who sin do that much. And if you only do good to the people who do good to you, what credit is there in that? Even sinners do that.*"

Samantha points to the beginning of the smaller second paragraph. The first few lines are clear, but the writing at the bottom of the column is so light Lily can't make out individual letters. "*You will become sons of your Father in heaven. Be merciful as your Father is merciful. Don't judge and you won't be judged.*"

Samantha takes off the glasses. "That's about all I can honestly read, although I'm always tempted to fill in the rest. Actually, I did fill in a little here." She points to a faintly visible line near the end of the second paragraph. "It looks as if the bottom of the scroll is in the worst shape. Mostly illegible. I'm guessing it says, *By the standard with which you measure, it will be measured back to you.*"

Lily stares at the letters—the words crammed together across the column, most of the clauses joined with a *vav*, a single vertical mark meaning "and"—no punctuation. But as she stares she begins to be able to make out the breaks, the clauses and sentences, the groupings of words. And then for a moment it's as if she can read the text without effort, as if the letters suddenly reveal their meaning through the written shapes. *"Don't judge and you won't be judged,"* she reads in a quiet voice.

"Yes," says Samantha. "It all makes so much sense, doesn't it, when you read it this way?"

"It makes perfect sense," says Lily.

8

Lily dreams of texts. Mostly she's trying to make out the message, in a dim light, with no help. And the writing shifts. When she thinks she's mastered one line, she goes back to the beginning and the words have changed. Toward morning, she dreams she's struggling to read a thick, tome-like book, open on a high pedestal. Then she's reading out loud to hundreds of people, and a man appears next to her. He's not tall, not quite her height, and bearded, and he smells of something she can't make out. In the dream it's her father, even though the man is dark-skinned and sturdy, nothing like her tall, clean-shaven father. But then Tom comes in, and everyone disappears.

Not too tough to decipher, she thinks when she wakes up alone and hears the rain against the windows. At least, not the ending. Last night, Tom came into the apartment and Samantha got the picture back into the envelope before

Lily knew what was happening. They talked briefly—Lily has no idea what anyone said—and then Samantha got up to go. Lily walked her to the door and said, "So, I'd love to hear more about this." She felt like someone in a drawing room comedy.

"Good," said Samantha. "I'm free tomorrow after class, around three. No, I may have to see a couple of students. Come to the office at four. I'll give you a cup of tea in one of our chipped mugs."

And Lily got through the rest of the evening in a weird, fugue-like state. She went for a long walk and then told Tom she thought she was getting a cold. When he said maybe the walk hadn't been such a great idea, she snapped at him about needing fresh air. He went downstairs to his own apartment and played Guster Goldfly, loud. She thought maybe he had moved the speakers up to the ceiling.

Now she lies in bed and stares through the windows above the curtains. From time to time, she can see fine glistening drops against the gray sky. She tries to focus on the day ahead of her, to walk herself through each event, imagine herself taking the T, talking to a student leader of the Campus Christian Movement, eating lunch in the coffeehouse at the bottom of the hill. Eventually she gives up. Her only task today will be to make it to four o'clock.

Mid-morning, she's in her office at Tate, supposedly listening to the student leader of the CCM. The group has been trying to get her involved since she arrived. She has been polite, firm, honest, but also impressed with their dogged determination.

At the moment, the young man is explaining why gay and lesbian students aren't allowed to be officers in the organization. Evidently, the Student Senate is challenging the movement's right to Tate funding and offices, given its discrimination against gay students. Lily tries to focus, even takes notes while he talks, but finds herself writing Hebrew words across the top of the page. *Cotev, cotevet*—conjugating the verb *to write,* the first Hebrew word she learned.

Unfortunately, this means she misses most of what the student says. He's a senior, thin, pale-skinned and dark-haired, sincere, a nice enough guy, she thinks. He wears a white dress shirt with the sleeves buttoned at both wrists. This detail makes Lily feel sorry for him, so she tries not only to listen but also to empathize, but she's having a hard time doing either.

"I'd just like to distinguish between not allowing them to be members and not allowing them to be officers," he's saying, at the end of a long speech explaining the group's policy.

"By 'them,'" says Lily, "I guess you mean your fellow students who identify as gay and lesbian."

"Right," he says. He doesn't seem to feel this as the reprimand Lily meant it to be. "We're not telling anyone they can't join the group. We're just saying they can't lead the group."

"Mr.—" She glances down at her notes.

"John," he says. "John Wickham."

"Mr. Wickham, I guess I'm not sure exactly why you're here."

"Because, see, you're the chaplain now. And we thought it would be good if you could, maybe, be on our side when we go before the Senate Committee on Student Affairs."

"No pun intended," says Lily.

"Right," he says, sincerely. That tone, his sincerity, along with the buttoned cuffs, finally gets Lily's attention.

"Here's the thing," she says. She puts down her notepad so she isn't distracted by the Hebrew letters. "Or, I should say, here are the things. First of all, I'm only an interim chaplain, so it's not going to do you much good to get me on your side, even if that were possible, because I'm not going to be around long enough to help you."

"Yeah. But see the hearings are next week—"

"Okay," says Lily. "Let me give you the second thing. The second thing is that I respect your tradition. I respect the fundamental wing of the Protestant community in this country, because I think that you guys are, often, less hypocritical than we are. I actually believe in a close and literal reading of Bible texts—within reason. And I think the liberal wing of the church doesn't do enough of that, doesn't check in with the Bible often enough. In general, you know your Bible a lot better than any of us."

He's sincere, but he's not stupid. He can hear that this is not, in the long run, going to lead where he wants it to go. So he barely nods when Lily takes a breath.

"But the problem here," says Lily, "is that you don't have any Biblical justification for these kinds of arbitrary restrictions. Does Jesus, anywhere at anytime, prohibit homosexuality?"

"No," he says. "But Leviticus—"

Lily smiles and raises her hands, palms out. "Don't start in on Leviticus with me. You know as well as I do that you wear clothes of more than one type of fabric and eat shellfish, so who tells you guys what parts of Leviticus you get to ignore and what parts you're called to uphold? Besides which, you need to make up your minds whether Hebrew scripture is a collection of wrong-headed legalisms or a list of honored laws."

"Then what about Paul?" he asks her. "Romans, chapter one, verses twenty-six to twenty-seven?"

"The men who 'burned in their lust toward one another'? More complicated, for sure. I would argue the use of the phrase 'against their natures' indicates heterosexual men lusting after other men, which would indicate to me a society going in for sensations in a big way—a decadent society practicing sex as one of many self-indulgent pleasures. But in fact I'm not sure what Paul meant. Let me ask you this: Do you let women be leaders in your group?" she asks.

"Of course," he says.

He's about to get self-righteous, and Lily would like to avoid that if possible, so she softens her tone. "And do you think it's okay for women to speak in church?"

"I see where you're going with this," he says. "But you can't throw out the whole Bible just because some of the things it prohibits are outdated."

"Outdated?" asks Lily. "So we're back to the earlier question. Who decides when these prohibitions have served their purpose, have become outdated? And if many of them have grown outdated over time, isn't it presumptuous to think that we are somehow living at the end of time, that those changes won't continue to occur? At what point will this process of growing outdated be over?"

"That's a good question," he says. "So maybe, eventually, all of it will be outdated? And what will we do then? Where will we look?"

"It is a good question," says Lily. "On the other hand, does it seem reasonable to believe there'll be a point in time when the Bible, and our perception of it, will suddenly cease to change? Or does it seem more reasonable to believe that our perceptions of the Bible will always be changing?"

He shrugs. "You're talking about extreme relativism."

"Absolutely," says Lily. "Do you know there's a historical, scholarly tradition, based on texts written during the same time the books of the Bible were written, or maybe even earlier, in which Jesus is believed to have taught Mary Magdalene many things he chose not to teach the male disciples? There's even a group of scholars who believe Jesus and Mary Magdalene may have had sexual relations. And there's another group that believes Jesus may have been gay."

"Just because there are people who believe that, doesn't make it true."

"No, it doesn't. People believe a lot of things because it fits into their own personal views of the world. And the problem is that a person can then go back and read the Bible, or texts from the same period, and find something to support almost every one of those claims."

"But texts from the same period aren't the same as the Bible."

"Not to our eyes. But who decided what was sacred scripture and what was Apocrypha? The human hand has shaped the Bible all along the way, from the first recordings of stories to the final editing process. It's still happening. The Oxford Annotated is quite a different text from the King James."

He's leaning forward now, his face slightly flushed. "So you don't think any of it's worth reading?"

"I think it's all worth reading. I hold scripture sacred. It's one of the three points upon which Anglican doctrine rests—scripture, tradition, and reason."

"Then how do you know what's true and what isn't? How do you know what parts to believe and practice, and what parts to leave out?"

"Christians have to find a way, a lens, if you will, through which to interpret this body of text on which our faith is founded. And now we get to the third thing. The third thing is that my lens—and in this I am not alone—is the two great commandments: You must love the Lord your God with all your heart and with all your mind and with all your soul, and you must love your neighbor as yourself. You must love your neighbor as yourself. And I don't see the word *straight* in there anywhere."

He nods his head a couple of times and stands up. "Thanks anyway," he says. He reaches across the desk to shake hands.

"I'm sorry," says Lily, after he turns toward the door. "I know I haven't been any help to you, logistically, at least. But you might think about what I've said. I can tell your faith is honest and well-intentioned, and I can't imagine you would willingly damage another student's life, or psyche, or future."

He puts his hand on the door frame. His shirt sleeves are too short, and she can see his wrist, thin and white. "What about my psyche?" he asks. "I believe what I believe just like you believe what you believe. You know, Jim may not agree with us, but he always hears us out. He meets with our group a couple of times a year and listens and gives us guidance. I just don't think—" He broke off and shook his head, staring out into the vestibule.

"What?" asks Lily.

"I don't think you're as open-minded as you think you are."

"You're probably right," says Lily.

He nods, not looking at her still, then leaves.

She sits and turns her chair so she can see out the windows behind her desk. A grassy lawn slopes sharply down from the quad, past the library, to the street below; the bright maple leaves hang limp with rain, dreary against the gray sky.

Conservatives, 1, she thinks. Liberals, 0.

9

SAMANTHA'S OFFICE—OR SET OF OFFICES—IS ON THE
second floor of Camden, the stucco building that houses
the philosophy department. At the top of the stairs, Lily enters a narrow hallway with a row of doors on the right. The
first door stands open and reveals a lounge, with two old,
mismatched couches, a watercooler, a small refrigerator, a
sink, a coffeemaker, stacks of paper plates and cups—the
usual detritus of a department gathering spot. No one is
there. Next door is a small office, tidy and cheerful, with a
poster of a rocky green island coast surrounded by brilliant
blue water, with GREECE printed at the bottom; a poster of
Erykah Badu in a vivid orange turban; a map of the world
with Africa and South America in the top half; and two
large windows that look out onto the tops of the trees,
bright yellows and reds against a darkening sky. The desktop holds a phone, a notepad, a canister of pens, a large

desk calendar, and a photograph in a Plexiglas frame: Francine leaning over the railing of a boat, with a green, rugged coast, like the one in the poster, in the background, except in this view an old stone building clings to an out-cropping of rocks along the coast, as if the building itself had grown out of the landscape.

Lily is almost half an hour early. She got so restless by three-fifteen that she couldn't wait. She wants to see the photograph of the manuscript again, to hold it in her hands and have Sam translate the words. She feels something like a physical pull, like the draw of food when she's hungry, like the draw she felt toward Tom. She hears a sound from the room next door—the legs of a stool scraping across a wooden floor—and walks into the hall and around the cor-ner to see who's there.

The door is closed. Lily knocks, but there's no answer. She hears the sound again, a scraping of wood on wood, a cough. She knocks again, louder, then turns the knob slowly. The door opens and Lily sticks her head in, expect-ing to see Sam at a standard issue desk.

But this room surprises her—while the first two spaces were mid-level university fare, this looks like a newly ren-ovated kitchen in an upscale condo, with white walls, a shiny wood floor, and two long rows of white file cabinets. A butcher-block worktable stretches the length of the room, and piles of what look like manuscript pages are stacked at regular intervals along one side.

Francine sits on a tall stool, back to Lily, bent over something in front of her. She doesn't turn or acknowledge Lily's presence, and there's a moment in which Lily feels as if she and Francine are in two different worlds. Then she sees the headphones attached to a tape player, and realizes Francine is, in effect, in another world. She walks around the end of the table, so Francine can see her; the younger woman holds a lens to her eye, something like a jeweler's magnifying glass, except instead of studying a diamond she is studying an 8×10 photograph. Lily feels a quickening of her heart. Her breath goes shallow and the hairs on her arms stand up.

As if the intensity of her response has traveled across the room, Francine looks up. Her face goes almost gray.

"Sorry," says Lily, trying to make light of the moment. "I didn't mean to scare you."

Francine still has the headphones on, but before she removes them, she opens a drawer in front of her and slips the photograph and the lens into it. Then she takes off the headphones and puts them and the tape recorder in with the photograph. The lens she drops into the pocket of her blazer. As Francine shuts the drawer, Lily hears a latch slip into place and notices that the drawers facing her, the two at the end of the table, have some sort of buttons near the handles.

On her own desk in the chaplain's office there's a lock system: none of the drawers will open unless the top drawer is opened, and it can only be opened with a key— that is, if you want to lock it, which Lily doesn't. She thinks the drawers have buttons similar to these, but she can't remember exactly what they look like. As she glances up, she finds Francine studying her, watching her study the lock system. A look passes between them—a form of acknowledgment, but Lily's not sure what they've acknowledged. The whole encounter has lasted only a few seconds, and when Francine speaks, her tone is neutral.

"Sorry," she says. "I thought I had locked the door. My fault. And I didn't hear you—obviously. Are you looking for Samantha?" Lily is struck, again, by the incongruities: Francine's little body housing such a competent adult.

"Yeah. We were supposed to meet here, but I'm early." Lily thinks about what to say next, and then before she can finish thinking, she speaks. "Listen, I know. Sam told me about the photograph. She showed it to me."

Francine nods as if Lily has just commented on the weather. "She should be back pretty soon. You want to wait in the lounge? You want coffee or anything?"

Lily still feels as if she and Francine are in two different worlds. "No, thanks. But I'll wait in the lounge and you can keep working. I don't want to interrupt."

"That's okay." Francine gets off the stool, pushes it toward the worktable, and heads for the door. "I'm ready for a break."

Lily follows her out of the room, without glancing at the drawer. In the lounge, Francine finds tea bags, makes Lily a cup of tea using the hot water dispenser on the watercooler, and starts a new pot of coffee for herself. They talk about Francine's commute from Porter Square. Francine has her back to Lily the whole time. As the hot water begins to pour through the filter into the glass pot, she turns and leans against the counter. "So, what did Samantha tell you?"

It takes Lily a second or two to make the switch from banter. "About the photograph?"

"Yes," says Francine.

"She said someone sent it to you."

"Did she explain to you what she thinks they are?"

"They?" asks Lily.

"It."

"Q material, in Hebrew. You don't agree?"

"Why?" asks Francine. The coffee is ready. She takes a white mug off a hook and fills it, then sits on the couch across from Lily.

"Because you said, what *she* thinks. What do you think?"

"Did I say that? That's weird. She's the expert." Lily notices that Francine's voice has lost the eerily detached quality, though her manner remains, as always, reserved.

"But it was addressed to you."

Francine is sipping her coffee, but her eyes open wide, and she glances at Lily over the rim of the mug. Then she sets it down on a battered oak table with a glass top that sits between the two sofas. "She told you quite a bit," she says.

"I saw the envelope." And then, because Francine's eyes seem to open even wider, if possible, Lily asks, "Are you surprised?"

"Yes, and no."

"I was," says Lily. "Why me?"

"She seems to think you can help us find out what's happening," says Francine. "And she thinks highly of you. She's always talked about you a lot."

Lily feels a small chill up her spine. "What do you mean?"

"About you two being friends in seminary. She doesn't make friends easily, so it meant a lot to her, that you two were close."

Lily doesn't say anything. Francine is watching her, though, and Lily notices again how little Francine misses.

"You haven't exactly stayed in touch, have you?" asks Francine.

"No," says Lily. "We haven't." She drinks her tea. The warmth comforts her. "But you haven't said—"

Francine sits facing the doorway, her eyes lowered.

Then she looks up and at that moment her face transforms. It's as if a whole mix of passionate feelings have surfaced at once—attachment, confusion, and anger.

"HAVEN'T SAID WHAT?" ASKS SAMANTHA. SHE'S wrapped in a black cashmere shawl, with a black leather briefcase slung over her shoulder. Her eyes look dark and sunken, as if she's been awake for days and is wearing extra makeup to camouflage the signs of her exhaustion. Without waiting for an answer, she crosses to the counter and sets down the briefcase. "Is this coffee fresh?"

"Yes," says Francine. Her voice has resumed its neutral distance. Then she adds, "Lily's here to see the photograph."

Lily hears a tiny hesitation between the words *the* and *photograph*.

"I know. I thought you were going to be gone all afternoon, or else I wouldn't have asked her to come. What happened to your doctor's appointment?" Samantha leans against the counter, a mug of coffee in her hand.

"Shit," Francine says, and glances at the large-faced watch on her wrist. "I completely forgot."

"Is it too late to get there?" asks Sam.

"Not if I take the car."

A moment of silence. "That's fine," says Sam. "Lily is thoroughly conversant with the public transportation system. We can get back to my apartment, and you can join us there later."

"Oh," says Lily, because that's all she can think of to say. "I'm not—I can get you back to your apartment, but I can't—I've got to be home tonight."

Francine has already stood up, rinsed out her mug, and hung it back on the hook above the sink. "Give me the keys," she says to Samantha. "I'll meet you back there, or I can come and get you here. Call me on the cell phone."

"They're in the pocket of the briefcase," says Samantha, then she turns to Lily. "See if Tom can join us. We'll all have dinner. I swear I'll behave." She raises her right hand in a sort of courtroom gesture.

Francine picks up the briefcase and leaves the room.

"I can't get him now," says Lily. "Anyway, we're not very spontaneous—he is, I'm not. But I need to go to the Women's Center, my other office, for a meeting." She's now claimed she has to be two places at once. "It just won't work tonight. We'll do it another time."

"Good," says Sam. "Tomorrow."

Lily is spared a response when Francine stops in the doorway. "What do you want me to do?" she asks Samantha.

"Meet me at home. I'll take the bus and have an adventure."

"That does sound adventurous," says Francine, the first ironic thing Lily has heard her say. She must be very angry, she thinks.

"She's very angry," says Samantha, after Francine leaves.

"Yeah," says Lily. "I thought so. She doesn't like it that you told me. Maybe we should put this off until later."

"That's ridiculous."

Now Sam sounds mad. If it weren't for the photograph, Lily would keep her distance from these two. She knows she should, but it's too late.

"Technically, though—" Lily begins, hesitantly.

"Yes, technically, they're hers, because they were addressed to her. But she came to me with them, she asked me for my help. She can't read half of it. She has no idea about what to do, what she's dealing with—" This time Samantha interrupts herself. She takes a long swig from the coffee cup. "Sorry. Feelings seem to be running high these days." She sits on the sofa facing Lily; she places her cup on the coffee table between them. Then she leans back and closes her eyes. When she opens them, she says, "We received a second mailing."

"Another photograph?"

Samantha nods.

"When?"

"Today. It came with this morning's mail."

"Can I see it?"

"Yes."

SAMANTHA TAKES OUT A KEY AND UNLOCKS THE DOOR of the workroom, where Lily found Francine. Once inside, Samantha takes a smaller key on the same chain and unlocks the drawers. It occurs to Lily that this is a flimsy security system for these photographs. Samantha opens the drawer into which Francine returned the photograph and the tape recorder, takes out the photograph, an envelope, and then one more identical envelope, and shuts the drawer. From her pants pocket, she pulls a small leather case, removes a pair of reading glasses with red frames, and puts them on.

She returns the photograph Francine was studying to its envelope, and then she puts the envelopes in some order— Lily assumes it's in order of arrival, since Sam seems to be studying the postmarks. She withdraws the first photograph from its container and motions Lily over. "This is the one I showed you," she says. Samantha puts the envelopes on her left and places the photograph on her right, never letting go of it.

Lily stands next to her, in front of the photo, but not touching it. She recognizes the shapes of the blocks of text.

"Can you read any of it?" Samantha asks her.

"Not really. I thought, yesterday, last night, that I could make out a few lines. But when I see it now—I think I was just reading along with you."

"Do you want to hear it again?"

"Please," says Lily. She listens and scans the lines as Samantha speaks. And she feels what she felt last night—something about Samantha's hesitations, her variations of words and phrases, makes the language sound as if it is being spoken aloud, as if she is hearing these things for the first time. When Samantha reaches the less legible writing, near the end, she pauses. "Shall I read what I think is here?"

Lily nods.

As she reads, *"Do not judge and you will not be judged,"* Lily realizes that these are the words the man was saying in her dream the night before. He repeated them, she thinks, and he was speaking to her.

10

"So, let's look at the second one," says Samantha. She moves the original to one side, opens the second envelope, and puts the photograph down in front of Lily.

The shape of the blocks of print is different. There is a smaller block, then short lines, as if it were a poem, then a larger block.

"What's that?" asks Lily, pointing to the short lines.

"The Lord's Prayer," says Samantha. "I'll read from the beginning, shall I?"

Lily nods.

"*Blessed—or lucky—are the eyes that see what you see. Many prophets and kings have wanted to see what you see and did not see it and wanted to hear what you hear and did not hear it.*"

Lily begins to be able to make out letters, and a word here and there. It's not the same as the phenomenon that happened the first time she saw the text; the secret gate to the text hasn't swung open. But she can distinguish the long straight *vav,* the final form of the *mem,* the word *melech,* "king."

Samantha continues. *"Father,"* she translates, "—though, as you know, this is *abba,* a sort of poppa sound, a child's word, not the usual language used to speak to God—*Father, let your name be honored and let your time,* or reign or power, *come. Give us our bread each day. Forgive our failures as we forgive those who fail us. And do not put us to the test."*

"Read it again," Lily says. "Do you mind?"

"No, I don't mind. *Father, let your name be honored and let your time begin. Give us our bread each day. Forgive our failures, because*—or as—*we forgive the ones who fail us. And do not put us to the test."* She looks at Lily. "Should I go on?"

Lily nods.

"Ask and it will be given to you. Search and you will find. Knock and it will be opened for you. Because everyone who asks receives, and everyone who searches finds, and for the ones who knock, the door is opened. Who among you would hand his son a stone when he asked for bread? Or would give him a snake when he asks for a fish? If you who are selfish know how to give good gifts to your children, how much more will your father in heaven give to those who ask?" Samantha takes a deep breath and leans away from the table

"Is that it?" asks Lily.

"Yes. That's all on this page."

"Aren't the last two lines illegible?"

"Almost, but not as bad as on the first page. We've made

out a number of letters, and, of course, we know the text. Or, I should say, we know how we expect the text to read."

"So," says Lily, "you don't know exactly what those last two lines say."

"No," says Samantha slowly. "Why?"

"It's just that your voice never changed," says Lily.

"What do you mean?"

"You didn't hesitate. It was as if you knew them by heart."

"I do," says Samantha. "Don't you? It is in the Bible."

Lily looks down at the two photographs, the two manuscript columns, side by side. "No, it's not. It's different in the Bible."

"Yes. You're absolutely right," says Samantha. "But this is the order in most reconstructions of Q." She pauses then asks, "What are you after?"

"Nothing," says Lily. "I'm just—I guess it's hard to believe all of this. I'm not sure I'm ready to trust that these things—that these photographs are of a real manuscript."

"Nor am I," says Samantha. "And I don't think we should trust that. But you can trust me."

"I know," says Lily. "Sorry." She doesn't know what else to say. She glances back down to the texts. "The letters look the same, don't they? I mean, it looks as if both pages of the manuscript were written by the same person."

"I think so," says Samantha. "And we're beginning to believe he was not, officially, a scribe."

"Meaning?"

"A scribe was a professional. They trained in the craft. They learned how to keep the nubs of the pens sharpened and to stay in the ruled lines. There were specific marks indicating a paragraph break, or an insertion, or an error. The marks varied from region to region, sometimes from school to school, but most manuscripts contain some markings—especially if the manuscript has been edited by other scribes—or copied."

"And?" asks Lily.

"There are no scribal marks. And, look—some of the letters are written differently each time they appear. Look at these three *he*'s—" She points to a letter like a square, inverted U, with a small triangle at the top of each corner. "Each one is slightly different. The first has a tiny triangle on the right corner, the second has a very large triangle on the right corner, and the third is almost balanced, as if this young man—it seems reasonable to assume it was a man, since we have no evidence of women scribes—were still practicing."

As Lily looks at the letters again, she begins to see the irregularities, and not only in the *he*. Also, she notices that the strokes at the top of the page are slender and graceful, whereas near the bottom they become heavy and awkward. "Why are these so fat and these so thin?"

"It looks as if he didn't sharpen the nub often enough. Or didn't do it correctly. And as the letters become thicker, you also see these spots, where the ink seems to have collected at the bottom of a stroke, as if he were, again, learning how to do this as he went."

"So you're saying the writer probably wasn't a scribe?"

"Not an experienced one, at least. Learned enough to write without a plethora of spelling errors, though there are a few. In general, he seems comfortable with written language, but not well-versed in formal writing. Francine calls him the fisherman scribe."

"Because?"

"Because the *pe*'s—see here?—look like little fishhooks.

And because she thinks the manuscript is written by one of the apostles."

"But that would mean—" Lily doesn't finish her sentence. She's not sure what she intended to say.

"I know," says Samantha. "She's been working very hard on dating the writing—finding any samples, photographs of texts from the first century. That's why she's been buried in the Annenberg. We haven't done anything on the second one, of course. I'm withholding judgment at the moment."

"I just don't see—"

"No. None of us does see," says Samantha. She picks up the first photograph and places it into the envelope. "But it's late, and you have many places to be."

Lily can tell she's being punished for having to leave and for refusing to have dinner. "You said you wanted me to help, but I don't see how I can," she says. "I wouldn't know where to begin finding out where these came from."

"You're rushed now, but when you have more time, and as I gain a better sense of what information will be useful, we can talk more."

"Can I see them again?"

"Of course," says Samantha. "We're all in this together now."

11

LILY AND SAMANTHA TRAVEL TOGETHER TO THE PORTER Square MTA station, then Lily stays on the train. After the Kendall stop, the train leaves the tunnel and approaches the bridge over the Charles. Neon blue evening sky, with a pale green strip below, shows through clouds in the west. The buildings of the skyline, especially the Prudential with its walls of mirrored glass, seem to glow from within.

Lily decides not to go to the Women's Center. She needs time to think. She gets off the train at the Boylston Street stop and calls Barbara at the center to tell her she'll see her tomorrow. Then she leaves a message for Tom, saying she's going to be late, that he should eat without her. Afterward, she crosses the street and enters the Episcopal Cathedral of St. Michael's and All Angels, arriving at Evening Prayer in time for the end of the psalm.

She drops her pack, quietly, kneels in an empty pew,

and prays for herself and Charlie and Barbara, for Tom and Samantha, for Francine, for Annie Kim and all the students in the Christian Movement, and a prayer of gratitude for the beautiful light on the river. When she raises her head, she sees her friend, ally, adviser, and confessor, the Right Reverend Lamont Spencer, stand and step to the pulpit to read the lesson.

"A reading from the book of Zechariah," he says. "On the twenty-fourth day of the eleventh month, the month of Shebat, in the second year of Darius, the word of the Lord came to the prophet Zechariah." It's the first of the night visions in the book of Zechariah, the word of the Lord in a series of dreams. "In the night I saw a man riding on a red horse! He was standing among the myrtle trees in the glen; and behind him were red, sorrel, and white horses." Lily closes her eyes and listens. She can see the trees (she makes them into lilac bushes, since she can't remember what myrtles are) in blossom, and the horses, and the man.

She has always believed in dreams. In the Bible, God speaks to people through dreams a lot. She dreamed of horses recently, maybe last night, but galloping horses, horses galloping over a desert, and the riders were brutal, riding over the sand toward a village, in order to steal something of great value. Then she was in the village, and the short man with the beard was in there, and she thought he was her father again. She doesn't remember any of the action, but now that she concentrates, she thinks the man touched her on her arm. Something about the pressure of his hand made her think of her father getting her out the door to school early in the morning, or navigating her through the barn, especially when the horses were out of their stalls (what is sorrel, she wonders) or down the church aisle on Sundays. Lily thinks that's when the man said, "Do not judge and you will not be judged." She is lost in the dream, trying to retrieve it, when the handful of people in the cathedral stands for the canticle.

She recites along with the others, but her mind is still in the images. By the time Spencer returns to the pulpit to read the gospel lesson, the dream has evaporated, as if she were pressing too hard on it with her desire. The vacancy leaves her feeling lonely.

"When the unclean spirit has gone out of a man," Spencer reads, "he passes through waterless places seeking rest, but he finds none."

This is from Q, she thinks. It must be. It's in Matthew and Luke, but not Mark.

"Then he says, I will return to my house, from which I came."

She imagines the scroll, but not in a photograph, in person. The leather is in front of her, and she sees the Hebrew letters clearly.

"And when he comes he finds it empty, swept, and put in order. Then he goes and brings with him seven other spirits more evil than himself, and they enter and dwell there; and the last state of that man becomes worse than the first." Lily thinks she knows the identity of the man in the dream. And if she's right, surely it means the manuscript is real—doesn't it?

LILY WAITS UNTIL THE CATHEDRAL HAS CLEARED BE-fore she approaches Spencer. He's been standing about halfway down the center aisle, chatting with some regulars. As he starts back up the aisle, he waves at her, and she steps out of the pew to meet him.

He hugs her and asks, "How have you been?"

"Good," she says, after a moment's hesitation.

"Oh, yeah?" he asks, stepping back. "You don't sound so sure."

Though Lily considers Spencer exceptional, he has his church-guy habits. This is one of them, this radar for unhappiness, a little extra energy when emotional need rears its head. It makes her want to smile and lie, which she does with everyone else, but not with him.

"I'm fine, considering I'm trying to do a job for which I haven't been trained."

"What—you mean being human?"

"Yes, that, and working as chaplain at Tate."

"That's right," he says. "You took Jim's job. You want to come backstage with me while I hang up my costume?"

"Sure. Let me get my stuff."

She retrieves her pack and follows him up the aisle, making a simple bow at the altar. Spencer presses on a section of the wall to the right of the chancel rail and it becomes a door to the sacristy. She follows him into the dim room; the marble countertops look cool and clean. She's not sure what she's doing here, not sure what she hopes to get from seeing him, but she's not willing to leave yet. She leans against the counter while Spencer hangs up his cassock and bows his head. He always prays before and after a service.

"You want to come on up to the office?" he asks when he finishes. "I've still got some calls to make before I go home."

She wants to go, but she knows if she does, she'll tell him what's going on with the manuscript. "No," she says. "I just stopped by to say hello."

He looks at her closely. "Let's sit here for a while then. Tell me about Tate." He sits in one of the straight-back chairs along the wall.

For an instant her heart takes a wild leap into the belief he already knows about the manuscript, and is asking her to fill him in on the details. Then she sees her mistake, sits beside him and says, "Everything's fine—on the surface."

"What's that supposed to mean?"

"The job itself is fine—although there's something lacking in my performance. My pastoral skills aren't what they used to be."

He looks at her without comment.

"I know. I know," she says. "I'm not doing enough parish work."

"I have a nice little job coming up at the first of the year—you know St. Margaret's, in the South End?"

"I know it, not well."

"They need an interim for next year. Are you interested?"

"Let me think about it," says Lily.

"You could think about it. Or you could just say yes, now, and that would save me a lot of trouble. This is a good match. You'll like these folks. They've been very active in the Urban Coalition. It's right up your alley."

She shakes her head. "I'm not sure I've recovered from St. Mary's. And I always neglect the Women's Center when I'm doing interim work. I don't think it's a good time."

"Don't say no, yet. Let me know by December. I'll look for other prospects, but I won't give it away before then."

Lily smiles and shrugs. "You're persistent. I'll give you that."

"One of my many charming qualities," he says. "How's everything else?"

"Do you remember Samantha Lamb-Henderson? Did you ever know her?"

"Is that the Samantha Henderson of Gnostic gospel fame?"

"That's the one."

"I know of her, but I don't know her. Is she at Tate now?"

"She is. She was also in seminary with Charlie and me, and I haven't seen her in a while. But she's—I don't know—sort of a difficult personality. It's hard having her around again."

"Can you steer clear of her? You'll only be there a short time, right? Isn't Jim planning to come back before Christmas?"

"After," says Lily. "I know. But she's lonely and troubled. She's drinking too much. I feel sorry for her."

"An excellent basis for a relationship," says Spencer, and glances at his watch. He looks at her more closely. "Is there more to it than that?"

"Yes—but it's complicated. I'll tell you more another time."

"Is that it—this woman from your past? No trouble with the university?"

"No," says Lily, and smiles. He's thinking of the problems she's had in other interim jobs, of her problems with authority, in general. "This time the institution and I are in good standing. It doesn't hurt that nobody seems to know, or care, where I am and what I do."

"I wish I could say the same." He puts his hands on his knees. "I've got to get these calls made."

"Right," says Lily. She's almost surprised, and almost hurt, by the abrupt end. "And I need to get home. Good to see you."

"You, too," says Spencer. "And when you want to tell me the rest, you know where I am."

. . .

LILY WALKS OUT INTO THE AUTUMN NIGHT AND stands at the top of the cathedral steps. The wind has picked up. She starts down the steps, but before she reaches the sidewalk, a group of young people appears across the street, emerging from the Common. They are all in black, some with leather jackets and leggings, some with long capes and tall hats. Their faces are white, and one of them carries a trident, or a pitchfork, also black, long and shiny. When they cross against the light, a car slams on its brakes and blares its horn. One of the young men, she thinks it's a young man, in a cape and pointed hat, flips the driver the bird and yells something, but Lily isn't sure what he says. They are walking toward her, and the man who yelled looks up at her on the cathedral steps, points, and says something to the others. They notice her and everyone begins to laugh. Then they round the corner toward Downtown Crossing and disappear.

It's the last night of October, she thinks. Halloween. But that's not as comforting as it should be. Having a secret cuts you off from the rest of the world. I have nowhere to go and no one to talk to. Even as she forms the phrases in her mind, they sound melodramatic to her. And, yet, that is how she feels.

12

FOR THE NEXT TWO DAYS, THE TEXTS ARE ALL SHE thinks about, no matter what she's doing or appears to be doing—interviewing candidates for a fund-raising, grant-writing job at the Women's Center; walking home, down Commonwealth; taking the bus to her office at Tate. The thoughts come in two forms. The first is a sort of non-thought—a visceral need to see the photographs again and to hear Samantha's voice translating the words out loud.

The second form comes when she's alone and the cravings—to see and hear the words—abate. These thoughts are clear and sharp edged, simple questions, most of which have been forming just below the surface of her consciousness for the past few days. It's as if she was in too much of a haze to ask them before, but now she needs some answers.

These two states of mind vie for attention when she's

awake. And at night the dreams keep her just as busy. She doesn't remember most of them, but the man's there a lot, the one with the long beard, and now there's a woman with him. The woman has blonde hair and red lipstick and big breasts and doesn't seem familiar, at least not when Lily sits up at two A.M., in her dark bedroom and tries to recapture what's just happened. What does Marilyn Monroe have to do with all this?

At a late lunch in the student center with Frank Cohen, the campus rabbi and leader of Hillel, on Wednesday, she forces herself to concentrate on what he's saying. He wants to talk with her about a possible forum on the violence in Israel and Palestine. He's a big man, with pale, damp skin, and Lily has the sense that he's more involved with his job than any of the other clergy on campus. The rest of them seem sincere but worn out. He seems revved up, as if this particular idea, the forum, might actually *solve* the problems between Palestine and Israel.

"So what do the other campus clergy say?" asks Lily.

Cohen leans back and lets out a deep sigh, then he waves the idea away with his right hand. "They're nice people, but terrified someone's going to get in an argument. Listen, no one around here has the—whatever it takes—to sponsor something like this. They're worried the Jews will be insulted, the Christians will be insulted, the Middle Eastern students will be insulted. This is supposed to be the academy, right? Anyway, I thought since you're new and not here for long, you might be willing to go out on a limb."

"Let me think about it," says Lily. "I like the idea, but the problem is I won't be around to clean up the mess, if there is one, afterward. And I don't want Jim walking into some turmoil I've helped to create."

"At least you've got a good reason," says Cohen. "These other guys. Makes me wonder—you know those bracelets, with WWJD printed on them. It scares me when I see them, because I think what they mean is, you know, do the soft thing, do the Hallmark thing. But Jews like me—people who have studied—know that world, the world of Palestine during Roman occupation, and let me tell you, that particular long-haired, kitten-hugging Jesus wouldn't have lasted a minute, much less thirty-three years."

"So how do you see Jesus?" asks Lily.

"I see him as a Jew," says Cohen. "He's a tough little Jew. Listen, that throwing the moneylenders out of the temple is not a metaphor. He believed he had been sent to reform the Jewish religion. Have you read Sanders?"

"E. P. Sanders? Yes."

"My point being, he wasn't a man to shy away from controversy, if you'll notice."

"That's true," says Lily. "And yet he talks a lot about forgiveness."

"You don't think forgiveness is controversial? What if just one of these guys, one of the leaders, said, 'Okay. I forgive you. Let's start new.' What would happen?"

"I suspect he'd be killed," says Lily. "Well, he was, wasn't he?"

"You mean Rabin? That's right. That's just what happened. And he didn't even—never mind. Anyway, think about this. You're probably right about the timing, on your part, at least. But you might talk to Jim about it when he comes back, tell him you think it's a good idea."

"I will," says Lily.

They clear their table, throw away their napkins and paper plates, and walk out into the cool, gray November afternoon. It's after three o'clock. Lily figures she should spend another half-hour in her office, returning calls and answering e-mail. Then she's free to visit Samantha's offices. She will be arriving unannounced this time—she and Samantha don't have plans to meet today—but the need to see the photographs overwhelms any considerations of politeness. It also overwhelms her desire for distance from Samantha and Francine. In other words, thinks Lily, my judgment is not too great at the moment.

When she arrives this time, Francine is at her desk, talking on the phone. Lily can hear her before she sees her, and Francine's voice sounds strained; she keeps repeating each thing she says, as if the person on the other end can't hear her very well. "I don't see how I can... No, I said I don't see how that's possible. You'll have to call me later, at home... Call me at the other number, at my home number."

Lily would like to linger in the hall, but an irritating sense of decency requires her to let Francine know she's there. When she steps into the doorway, Francine glances up and stops talking. The young woman looks startled, and her eyes are wide and glassy, as if she is almost in tears. "I've got to go," she says into the receiver. "No, now. I have to hang up the phone. I'm saying good-bye now. We'll talk this evening. Good-bye." She hangs up. "Sorry," she says to Lily. "My mother—she's not—she doesn't hear well."

It seems unlike Francine to offer personal information, but she's upset and rattled, thinks Lily. And something else, but I can't tell what it is. "I'm sorry," she says. "Is she older?"

"No," says Francine. "Well, yes. She's just—she gets confused."

"Is your dad still alive?"

"No," says Francine. "Are you here to see Samantha?"

"Sort of. I don't really have an appointment. I just had some questions, and I thought maybe I could look at the—" Before she finishes her sentence, she sees Francine glance out into the hall, as if checking to see if anyone's out there. "You know."

Francine nods. "Do you want to wait in the lounge? Have something to drink, if you like. I have to finish a couple of things here."

Lily doesn't want anything to drink, but she goes into the lounge and stands near the door, her back to the hallway, listening. She hears nothing from the office, only a metal drawer opening and closing, then the sound of Francine typing on the computer. Why am I doing this, she wonders. Because the photographs are mailed to Francine, and no one seems to know why.

Suddenly someone is behind her. She turns to see Samantha with her briefcase and black scarf, standing, watching, her head to one side, bird-like.

"Hi," Lily says.

Samantha smiles. "Can I get you something?"

"No, thanks," says Lily. "I'm just waiting for you."

"So I see. Does Francine know you're here?"

"Yes," says Lily. "But she's busy. She told me to come in here until you got back from class."

"Let me put down my things," says Samantha. "And I'll be right with you." She turns and goes into Francine's office. After a moment, Lily hears the door close.

Lily takes a few more steps into the lounge, then steps backward, once, twice. She can hear the women's voices, through the door, but not their words. She's afraid to go out into the hall. Being caught once is enough, especially being caught by someone to whom she's gotten used to feeling superior. I am really a prig, she thinks.

When Lily hears the door open again, she gets a paper cup and fills it with water from the cooler. In a few minutes, Samantha is standing in the doorway, smiling. She motions to the workroom. Lily throws the cup away and follows her.

13

As Samantha unlocks the door to the workroom, she looks over her shoulder and says, "I could flatter myself that you're here to see me, but I think we both know that's not the whole story." She lets Lily walk in before her, then closes and locks the door behind them. "You want to see them again, don't you?"

"Yes," says Lily.

"It's hard to get them off your mind. I find myself in a sort of trance state, teaching my classes, reading, eating, chatting, even driving, which I usually find utterly absorbing—they're always there—" She taps her forehead. "Just below the surface." She unlocks the drawers, then takes out the two envelopes and lays them on the wooden surface. "One at a time? Or both?"

"Both," says Lily.

"Did you have something specific in mind, something you're looking for?"

"Not exactly. I wanted to see the writing again, and to hear more about what you've found out."

"Found out?" asks Samantha.

"About the writing, about possible dates, sources, ideas of people who might have sent them—anything."

Samantha reaches for the first envelope and removes the photograph without speaking. Then she takes out the second photograph and places them side by side.

Lily stands beside her and feels the quiet rush of blood she has felt each time she's seen them. Together, the photographs transform each other; instead of seeming like lonely pieces of a text, they imply a completed scroll.

"They're not consecutive, are they?" Lily finally asks.

"Not if our reconstructions of Q are accurate. Of course, we don't know exactly what we have here. This might be an early compilation of sayings, predating the Q document. The source for the source, so to speak."

"So why these two?" asks Lily. "Why did the person send these two, in this order?"

"I have no idea," says Samantha. "The person himself, or herself, is such an abstract projection of suppositions it's difficult to grant him, responsibly, motive or thought pattern."

"But you said you have guesses."

"I have a few guesses, each one based on a different set of suppositions."

"Give me one."

"Let's do the writing first, shall we? I should say right away that without carbon tests on the ink, nothing's conclusive. And anything can be faked, by someone with enough skill and knowledge."

"But?" asks Lily.

"But the writing is consistent in interesting ways."

"Meaning?"

"Keeping in mind this is speculation, yes?"

"Yeah."

"We've found certain characteristics of the letters that tell us quite a bit. Look at the *vav,* here," says Samantha, pointing to a straight, vertical line, the equivalent of "and," used to connect clauses and phrases. "You see how close it is in size and shape to the *yod,* here?"

Lily sees the same vertical mark, but in an odd place, in the middle of a word in which, it seems to Lily, it doesn't belong, where there should be a different letter, the smaller *yod.* "How can you tell that's a *yod?*"

"It doesn't make sense otherwise. And it's the same throughout. But the point is, this tendency, first of all for the letters, in general, to be of uniform size and then for the *vav* and the *yod,* specifically, to be the same size, is consistent with the script of the middle Herodian period."

"Herodian period being when Herod was alive?"

"Not exactly. The entire period goes from about 37 BCE to 70 CE, because it includes the rules of Herod's descendants. But the first part of the mid-Herodian covers 4 BCE to 39 CE. And this writing is from that period."

"What else?" asks Lily.

"Look at the *he*'s, throughout," pointing to two instances of the same letter, the square, upside-down U, with small triangular marks at both corners. "You see how the entire letter seems to be connected, drawn from right to left without lifting the pen? And with those little triangles at the top? Of course, in this case the triangles are different sizes, but, as I told you, we think that's because the scribe was inexperienced. In any case, the triangles are from the same period. In the Hasmonean period, the period just before this, the horizontal stroke, that top bar, is drawn separately from the right vertical. But here—well, you see."

"So you're saying the writing is consistent with the writing from a certain period, and that period is from sometime in the first half of the first century?"

"What the script seems to indicate is that if this scroll is real, if this manuscript is authentic, then it was written sometime during, or just after, Jesus' life."

"And what would that mean?" asks Lily.

"I don't understand the question," says Samantha.

"No," says Lily. "It was a little vague. I'm trying to find a way to understand this. Maybe I was asking, what would it mean to me?"

"I can't answer that. But it's had a startling effect on me."

"Which is?"

"I've begun to consider going to church. Something I haven't done in many years."

"So you believe they're authentic," says Lily.

"No," says Samantha. "I don't believe anything. I only know what has happened."

"And if they're not authentic?"

"Then someone has gone to an extraordinary amount of time and effort and expense to trick me. And possibly to ruin me. At least, professionally. Since my professional life is all I have, to ruin me—period."

"But they were sent to Francine, right?"

"Yes, but let's not kid ourselves. There's no reason to believe Francine would be a target for such an elaborate hoax. On the other hand—"

"On the other hand," says Lily. "If it is real, then there's someone who might send these to Francine. The guy she met in Greece, Nickolas."

"That's possible. Although as far as we know, Nickolas is living out his novice year on Mount Athos, with little or no connection to the outside world."

"Do you know for a fact he's there?"

"Not for a fact. We haven't seen him on the island. And I'm hesitant to make any inquiries."

"Because?"

"Because, on the unlikely chance that the photographs are coming from Nickolas, I would rather not raise questions about him, where he is, what he's doing. I would rather no one thought about him at all."

"That makes sense," says Lily. "There are visitors, aren't there? Can't men visit the island?"

"Yes," says Samantha, slowly.

"So it would be possible for him to get visitors to mail the envelopes once they got home."

"I considered that. But you have to imagine the type of people interested in vacationing on the monastic capital of the world—scholars, members of religious orders, devout laymen. It wouldn't be easy to convince one of these people to participate in such a fantastic smuggling effort."

"But couldn't he tell them this is something for his family, or his friend, girlfriend, sister?"

"I suppose. Still, it's hard to imagine a visitor to such a place being willing to smuggle even a love letter off the island. And the idea that you could be sure the accomplice wouldn't open it—?" She shrugs, her elaborate hands-in-the-air, palms-up, who-knows gesture. "Also hard to imagine."

Lily has been looking down at the manuscript most of the time, waiting for the gate to open again, waiting for the meaning to appear through the words. That hasn't happened, but what she is noticing is an urge to touch the words. She reaches out and places her finger on the top line of the first photograph.

"And all of this would apply only if they're authentic," says Samantha.

"And if they're not?"

"That's a longer story."

14

SAMANTHA PULLS THE PHOTOGRAPH OUT FROM UNDER Lily's finger, gently, and replaces it in the envelope. "Assuming the texts are not authentic," she says, "then we have to think about the amount of time and energy that has gone into creating them. Animal hide acquired, stretched, prepared. Appropriate ink and writing tools—although the ink would only matter if we got our hands on the pages themselves. And they're mailed from two different places." Samantha puts the envelopes face up, side by side, above the photographs. One postmark is stamped Washington, D.C., the other is stamped Los Angeles.

"So, if they're fake, who would go to that much trouble. And why?"

"Again, I can only imagine it would be to discredit me. I appear to be pretending to have received authentic texts, to be ignorant of their source, to involve the scholarly community, the international community of archeologists and curators."

"And you appear to gain what?"

"Attention, a boost to a flagging career."

Lily notices the *flagging,* but doesn't take it up. "So this assumes someone who hates you—or Francine, I guess—so much that he, or she, is willing to spend an unbelievable amount of time and money to lure you into discrediting yourself? I don't see it."

"What don't you see?"

"It's too—baroque. It requires too much dedication."

Samantha is quiet.

"Who would want to do that to you?"

"You have no idea how many people dislike me."

"Dislike won't cut it," says Lily. "We're talking long-term, tortured hatred."

"Of course, you're right."

"So? Who's in that category?"

"My husband," says Samantha, "would top the list."

"Which husband?"

"Lamb-Henderson."

"I thought you were divorced."

"Actually, I never bothered. I left the country in a rush."

"Because?"

"Because I was afraid."

"Of?"

"I was afraid he was going to kill me."

"Had he tried?"

"I was never sure. Two things happened, one after the other, and I became convinced my life was in danger. When I look back on it now, of course, over the stretch of miles and years, I can't be certain."

"What happened?"

Samantha looks up and smiles at Lily. "You're quite re-lentless, aren't you?"

Lily blushes. "Sorry. Sometimes my curiosity gets the best of me. And if you want me to help figure this out, I have to know every possibility."

"I don't mind. It's just that I've never talked about it, and I feel embarrassed, I think, to have been involved in something so tawdry."

"Do you want to tell me?"

"Yes," says Samantha. "I do. But shall we finish up here first?" She nods, indicating the photographs.

Lily glances down at them. They look almost sinister, as if this new information has transformed them. But then, she sees the short, poem-like lines of the Lord's Prayer and imagines she is hearing the prayer for the first time, from a tough little Jewish teacher who has come to reform religion.

An hour later they sit together in Samantha's apartment. Lily had wanted to go someplace public and neutral, but Samantha said she couldn't talk comfortably if there were other people in listening distance. So Lily finds herself perched on the edge of Samantha's leather couch. She has refused the offer of something to eat or drink. She feels like Persephone: If she lowers her guard, she'll never be able to leave.

Samantha sits in the matching chair, sipping a glass of wine and sparkling water. She has put a plate of cheese—it's pungent; either very expensive or very spoiled, thinks Lily—and crackers on the table. But neither of them eats anything.

"So," Samantha says, for the second time. "I don't suppose you would like to chat about the weather before we begin this story."

Lily tries to smile.

"No," says Samantha. "All right, then. I married relatively young—just out of college, on my Rhodes year at Oxford—my first marriage, his third, though he was not much older than I was. That would have been a warning to most people, I know, but I knew so little of the world. His stories about both his ex-wives involved these terrible betrayals. That could have been a warning, too, of course, but I saw him as someone who had been wronged. It's hard to describe how naive I was then. In any case, I became his amanuensis. That was his word. We might call it secretary, or graduate assistant, typist, ghostwriter, researcher, cook, servant, concubine." She takes a sip of wine.

Lily finds herself looking into the fireplace, though there's no fire. It's too painful to look at Samantha.

"We wrote two books together. His name was on both. Only his name. When I challenged him the second time, he became violent." She drinks more wine. "Not overt violence. Not loud or visible. He would grab me around the arm and squeeze very tight and make me look at him. I had to keep my eyes on his eyes. It was some kind of test, to see if I was telling the truth, to see if I loved him enough. Honestly, I don't remember what he said. For months I had a series of deep blue bruises, the shape of his fingers circling my arm, just above my wrist." She touches the spot, lightly. "So I would have to wear long sleeves. Near the end, I could only wear long sleeves. Then he began to lock me in the bathroom. He would let me have my books and a chair. Then he would lock the door with a key and leave me there until he came home. One time he left for the weekend."

Lily glances up to see Samantha set down the glass and raise her right hand to her eyes, thumb and pointer each delicately resting on an eyelid. She lowers her hand and picks up the glass.

"I never think about this anymore. I was quite terrified. And yet I tried for the longest time to pretend everything was all right." She smiles apologetically. "I was young. Growing up, I was used to much worse. This seemed tame to me. I thought everyone has to live with something awful, and this is mine. As things go, it's not as bad as most."

Lily is watching her now.

"Finally, a colleague's wife came by on a day when William had locked me in. She rang the bell—I remember this part vividly—and I opened the bathroom window and called to her. She said, 'Are you ill?' and I said, 'No. William's locked me in.' And she said, 'Yes, I see. I'll just get the police, shall I?'" Samantha shakes her head. "The Brits, you know. No one acted as if anything were out of line. The police eventually came, and they got a ladder, and the colleague's wife—Adelaide Proctor—took me home with her."

Samantha finishes her wine and sets the glass down on the table. Lily looks into the fireplace again, until she can't stand the silence. "What happened then?"

"William came to their house. I could hear him having a drink with the husband downstairs. She stayed upstairs with me. When I heard his laugh, I went into the bathroom and vomited." Samantha gets up and goes into the kitchen. When she comes back, her glass is full.

"Sure you won't have anything?" she asks.

"Yes," says Lily. "Thanks."

"Let's see. I stayed with them for about a week. One day they were both out—the first time I was alone, really—he appeared at the back door. He must have been watching. I was in the kitchen. There was a window in the door, so I looked up and saw his face. He couldn't get in, and he didn't dare break the window. But I was transfixed. We stared at each other, and then he said, 'If you don't come back, I'm going to kill you.'" She shakes her head, again. It's as if she's hearing the story rather than telling it.

After a moment of silence, Lily asks, "Did you file charges?"

"No," says Samantha, and laughs, a short, harsh sound. "That would have been—there were these rules, you see? The Proctors were willing to help me as long as I behaved. Well, I've drawn this out long enough. I moved to Liverpool—I thought, I'll have to take a boat home, so I'll move to a port. I had no job and no money, but they loaned me enough to get a room." Her voice has become lighter. "I got a job as a typist and saved. I quite liked that job. After I had been there almost a month, someone blew out the flame on the gas heater in my room, when I was asleep. Fortunately, the smell woke me. I was hospitalized."

Lily glances at the wineglass in Samantha's hand.

"Yes, I know," says Samantha. "But I wasn't drinking. I didn't start until I moved back to the States. Then a week before I was to sail to America, a man pushed me into a busy intersection. These could certainly have been accidents. But I didn't think they were, at the time."

"Where is he now?" asks Lily. "Your husband, I mean."

"Yes, it's odd that this has all come up, because Adelaide Proctor called me two weeks ago. She was in New York visiting her son, and she found me in the office at

Tate. She said that William's never remarried. That he's retired. And that he's been traveling."

"Did she say where?"

"Yes, she did. She said she thought he was touring the States."

15

By the time Lily leaves Samantha's apartment, it's pitch black and the wind is blowing off the river, straight down Mass Ave. She zips her parka and turns up the collar, but that doesn't help much. She's supposed to meet Tom in Harvard Square, under the clock, and she's late, or she's going to be late by the time she gets there. So she walks fast, looking back over her shoulder to see if the 77 bus from Arlington might be coming, to rescue her from the wind and the time, but there's no bus in sight.

If what Samantha has just told her is true, then everything changes. If Samantha's former husband is that crazy, that obsessed, it seems possible, even likely, he would spend the money and time and energy necessary to involve her in a scandal. On the other hand, she thinks, why not just pay a student to say she slept with him or accuse her of plagiarism? Why this elaborate, expensive hoax? And behind all these thoughts is an image of the manuscripts, the sewn edge, the letters opening to reveal their meaning.

At the corner of Linnaean, she looks back once more and runs into someone waiting to cross the street. "Sorry," she says, barely glancing at the man, who turns out to be Charlie.

"Lily," he says. "It's me. What are you doing?"

Lily stops and stares at him. It takes her a few seconds to reenter the world of Cambridge, almost seven o'clock on a Wednesday evening. "I've just been—" She points vaguely behind her, away from Harvard Square. "And I'm going to meet Tom." She points down Mass Ave, toward Harvard Square.

"So we have our directions straight," says Charlie. "Are you taking some kind of drugs?"

"Yeah," she says, her awareness returning. "You know me. Can't get to Thursday without that Wednesday night pop."

"I'm going to the Square, too. I'll walk with you. It looks like you could use some help."

"I'm fine," says Lily. "I'm rushing because I'm a little late, and Tom's waiting under the clock. I'm afraid he's going to freeze."

"On the other hand, Tom's a pretty bright guy, so he might go inside."

The light has changed, so they cross the street together, facing into the wind.

"Jesus," says Charlie. "This is brutal. You're not dressed very warmly."

"No kidding. Why are you going into the Square?"

"I'm assisting at St. Tim's on Sunday. I told Doug I would stop by and go through the motions with him. Linda's down with the flu, and I'm not sure where every-

one else is. Anyway, he thinks of me as liturgically im-
paired, so he's making me do a run-through. You want to
come?"

"To watch you walk through the services?"

"No. To church, Sunday. He does a nice job."

"No, thanks. I have the day off and I'm going to keep it
off," says Lily. "How long will it take, tonight?"

"Not long. It depends on how many times he makes me
practice the solemn bow. Why?"

"I'm meeting Tom for dinner. You could come find us
afterward, if you want."

"Great. Where you will be?"

"Good question," says Lily. "We were thinking about
Rick's Kitchen."

"Understated, cheap, and you get used to the smell after
a few minutes. Sounds great."

"Okay. Meet us there when you're done. We'll eat
slowly."

"Sort of savor the atmosphere."

"I'm not much on atmosphere."

"That will be in your favor."

TOM AND LILY ARE IN A BOOTH AT THE BACK OF THE
long, noisy downstairs room. Lily's plate is empty; she has
started on Tom's french fries. She is also drinking a beer.
She ordered it nonchalantly. After Tom ordered his Sam
Adams, the waitress looked at her and said, "Beer?" And
Lily said, "Yes." Simple as that. Tom didn't say anything.

She hasn't had a drink in a long time, and the beers
came before the food, and she didn't eat much for lunch, so
she felt it right away, in a nice way, the muscles in her neck
and shoulders starting to relax, the shadow of Samantha's

story receding. She measures how much to drink by how much Tom drinks; she figures if her beer is at about the same level as his, then she's doing fine.

At the moment, he's telling her a story he heard at work that day. A young woman, visiting Boston, left her friend's apartment just before dawn, to catch an early train. As she rounded the corner onto Tremont, two young guys in an American, late-model car pulled over and asked her if she needed a ride. When she said no, one of them got out and tried to drag her into the backseat. She screamed and whacked him across the face with her backpack, which happened to have her laptop in it. Then she dropped her suitcase and ran, screaming, toward the police station, which she had noticed the day before as she explored the neighborhood.

"But here's the thing," says Tom, as he reaches for a french fry. "Do you want me to order more of these, because I'm not done yet."

"Sorry," says Lily. She lets go of the french fry she's holding and takes a sip of beer.

"Here's the thing," he repeats. "What she kept screaming at the guy was, 'I'm a writer, you asshole. Don't hurt me. I'm a writer.' She says she screamed it while she was running to the station, too. And it's the first thing she said to the guy at the desk. He said he thought she was turning herself in."

Lily laughs. "Who was that—Vicenzo?"

"Yeah, Vicenzo."

"Did she get her suitcase back?"

"What do you think?" asks Tom. "They don't sound like the kind of people who turn in lost property."

"No, I guess not. Did you meet her?"

"She was gone when I got there. But Vicenzo said she

was kind of nice, and pretty. She was pretty. I saw the photo. The guys whacked her pretty hard, here," he says, running his finger down the right side of his face, from his forehead to his jaw. "Anyway, he said she wasn't a nut case. She was laughing about it, about the writer part. It's funny what people do when they're in shock. You remember when you were in the hospital, after that thing out in Lester, and all you could think about was your boots?"

"My dad gave me those boots."

"Yeah," says Tom. "I know. But you had been locked in a box for thirty-six hours and all you kept talking about was those boots. I think it was kind of like that. The mind seizes on what makes most sense to us, what makes us who we are."

"What would you scream about, do you think?"

He looks up at her, and for an instant she's terrified he's going to say, "you." But he doesn't. "No telling. I guess I'd yell, 'I'm a photographer, you asshole.' No, probably, I'd yell, 'I'm a Catholic.'"

"Well, that might work," says Lily.

Tom glances at something over her shoulder, then smiles and waves. Lily looks into the smoky mirror on the wall behind Tom and sees Charlie headed toward their booth. He slips in next to Tom and scans the food on the table. "Anything left over for me, or should I order for myself?"

"Order fries," says Tom.

"Can I have something else, too?"

"Have whatever you want," says Tom. "Just be sure you include fries."

Charlie notices the beers, first Tom's, then Lily's, and raises his eyebrows. But he doesn't say anything. He signals the waitress, orders a cheeseburger special and a Coke, and turns back to the table.

"That didn't take too long," says Lily. "You must have remembered the steps."

"Doug was in a hurry," says Charlie.

"Who's Doug?" asks Tom.

"The rector at St. Tim's," says Charlie. "He's a great guy, just kind of a stickler for details."

"Unlike you guys at the monastery," says Lily.

"Good point," says Charlie. "Of course, they don't like to leave me in charge of liturgical details either."

Lily laughs, then takes a big sip of beer. She can feel Charlie watching her—they're probably both watching her, but she doesn't care. This is fun. When the waitress arrives with Charlie's Coke, Lily considers ordering one more drink, but she knows that would be the end of the pleasure. Charlie and Tom would both have something to say about it, and that would defeat the purpose. Anyway, this one has worked its magic; she feels a little lightheaded, definitely more relaxed than she's been in a while. In fact, she feels very lightheaded.

"I heard an interesting story today, too," she says.

"About what?" asks Tom.

"About Samantha Henderson's first marriage—well, only marriage. I think."

"What about it?" says Charlie. His food arrives, and everyone pauses to watch him put ketchup on the burger and fries.

Lily finishes her beer and notices she's having a little trouble picking up the conversation where she left off. Then she remembers she was talking about Samantha. A muffled alarm goes off somewhere near the back of her brain, but she ignores it. "About what a creep the guy was. He made her help him with his books and wouldn't give her credit. He got violent. In the end, he locked her in their bathroom."

"And what brought about this sordid confession?" Charlie asks.

"It's complicated."

Charlie looks up from his plate and narrows his eyes. "This doesn't bode well. Didn't I tell you not to get involved over there?"

"Too late," says Lily.

"What do you mean?" asks Tom.

"They need some help—Samantha and Francine. They're new, and this very weird and complicated thing is, like, happening."

"Like, happening?" says Charlie. "You've been listening to too many students. What weird and complicated thing?"

"They've received some mailings, some stuff in the mail, and it's hard to tell if it's authentic or not, but it could be, and if it is, it's—" The alarm was much louder now, too loud to ignore. "I shouldn't say anymore."

"It's that Q thing, isn't it?" asks Tom.

He does this, guesses what's on her mind. Usually it doesn't bother her, but tonight it's the last thing she needs. She isn't alert enough to fend off his instincts, and she's already said more than she should.

"What are you talking about?" says Charlie. "What Q thing? You mean Q, the source?"

Lily reaches for one of Charlie's fries. It's suddenly clear to her she should never have started this conversation. Why did she bring it up? Because it's the only thing on her mind, waking and sleeping; everything else is window dressing.

"So that's it?" asks Tom. "That's all you're going to say?"

"I'm sorry. That was stupid of me. I shouldn't have mentioned it, because it's not my information. I just—" She looks into the mirror behind Tom and Charlie and sees a man standing in the front door, scanning the row of booths, as if he is meeting someone. He's medium height, medium build, dark complexion, mustache, maybe Middle Eastern or Mediterranean, and he looks vaguely familiar. Just as Lily turns, his gaze reaches her booth, and they make eye contact. She turns back quickly, as if she had gotten a mild electrical shock.

"What?" asks Tom. "You just what?"

"Nothing," she says. "Do you know that guy?"

"What guy?" asks Tom.

"The guy in the doorway."

"There's nobody in the doorway," he says.

And when she looks in the mirror, the doorway is empty.

"I'm not going to spend all my energy fishing information out of you," says Charlie. "You'll tell us everything anyway, eventually. You always do."

"I wouldn't count on it," she says. "Not this time."

16

FRIDAY IS AN AUTUMN CALENDAR DAY, CRISP AIR, strong breeze, all the colors brighter, everything in motion. Lily sits at the desk, her back to the door, and watches students climbing the stairs past the library. A young woman in a short black skirt and black tights pauses on the steps to talk to a young man in a Red Sox cap and baggy jeans; as the girl reaches up to touch his face, she drops a folder and papers spray down the steps, across the lawn. Lily can't hear the young woman's shrieks, but she can imagine them. A few students chase the pages, but most watch as the papers skid past.

All the commotion is just a background for her thoughts. At this point, all of life is a background for her thoughts, which are more real to her than anything else, except the manuscript. She's still berating herself for even hinting at the existence of the photographs when she was with Tom and Charlie. At first, Samantha's insistence on secrecy was annoying, but now Lily understands that insistence. If these are pictures of a real manuscript, written in the first century, it's impossible to place a value on it. And there are people who would do anything to find it. And, she admits, she doesn't want to share it with anyone else.

So far, Lily can't figure out a way it makes sense for the manuscript to be fake. Samantha's ex-husband sounds crazy, and maybe dangerous, but Lily still doesn't see the point of going to so much trouble. On the other hand, if they are photographs of an authentic manuscript, where are they from, where has it been, who would have access? Nickolas is the obvious choice, but all of Samantha's doubts about that scenario are convincing. How could he get them off the island? And how could a young man, a novice, stumble upon this manuscript, hidden for two thousand years on an island filled with ancient manuscripts? And who was Francine talking to on the phone the other day? It wasn't her mother, Lily feels sure of that. Francine's face was not the face of a young woman talking to a senile mom. It was full of emotions—including fear, Lily recognizes for the first time.

Lily hears a noise behind her, turns the chair toward the door, and sees Francine standing on the threshold.

"Sorry," she says. "Am I disturbing you?"

It takes Lily a few seconds to make the transition from the Francine in her thoughts to the Francine in the doorway. "No," she says. "I was just thinking about you."

"I can imagine," says Francine. "We're a compelling subject these days." She steps into the room and hesitates.

"Yes," says Lily. "No kidding."

"Can I close this?" Francine asks, and points to the door.

"Sure, go ahead. And sit."

"Thanks." Francine sits in the wooden armchair on the other side of the desk. She seems more distant than usual. "Samantha asked me to deliver a message."

"Okay," says Lily.

"We received another delivery yesterday, in the mail."

Lily nods. She can feel blood rise to her face, sense the hair at the nape of her neck.

"This one, though, is a bit different," says Francine.

"Why?" asks Lily. "What's in it?"

"It makes more sense for you to see it. It's a little hard to explain."

"When?" asks Lily.

"We thought we might all meet somewhere public. Samantha suggested the Starbucks on Mass Ave, between Harvard Square and Porter Square."

"I'm confused," says Lily. "You want us to look at the manuscripts in a coffee shop?"

"Yes," says Francine. "I think it would be better."

"Why?"

Francine clears her throat. "I don't know if this is true or not, but it may be—there might be a man following me."

"What do you mean?"

"There's someone I've seen twice on the campus, once at the student center and once in the downstairs lobby of our building—he was walking into a classroom. But when I glanced in the classroom later, on my way down to the basement, it was empty. There was no class, and he was not there."

Lily doesn't answer immediately. She's remembering the man in the door at Rick's last night.

Francine takes her silence for skepticism. "I know. I understand what it sounds like. I saw him once more, on the

T. He rode with me from Porter Square to Davis and then I lost sight of him."

"What does he look like?"

"He's completely nondescript—medium build, dark complexion, maybe Mediterranean, Greek or Italian, or Yugoslavian. I can't tell. No beard, no mustache, jeans and sweater and a backpack. He could be anyone. But I don't think he is—just anyone, I mean."

Lily hesitates, then says, "I know."

"What do you mean?"

"I may have seen him, too, or someone like him. I think the man I saw had a mustache. But it was quick, and I can't be sure."

Francine's mouth opens slightly. Her face looks pale. "Where?" she asks.

"In a restaurant last night, with Charlie and Tom. But, honestly, I wasn't sure then, and I'm still not sure, the guy was looking for me—it was just a feeling."

Francine doesn't speak for a moment, and then she says, "Samantha shouldn't have brought you into this."

"Why not?"

"Because knowing about these photographs may be dangerous," says Francine. "It would appear that it is dangerous."

"Francine," says Lily. "You and I are guessing. Nothing has happened. We've only seen two dark-haired men—or one guy who wears a fake mustache sometimes." Lily realizes she's panicked at the thought of not seeing the photos again. If Francine decides it's too dangerous, she might talk Samantha into hiding the photographs away and not letting Lily see them anymore. That can't happen.

Francine smiles, at least, and Lily relaxes.

"I'll meet you at the Starbucks," says Lily. "We'll be surrounded by people. I'll look at the new arrival, and we can decide what to do next. What time?"

"Five-thirty," says Francine. "We'll already be there."

"Okay," says Lily and she nods encouragingly. "It'll be fine. The three of us can make a plan. Don't worry." And don't even think of leaving me out.

LILY IS ON AUTOPILOT FOR THE REST OF THE DAY. During lunch with the Catholic chaplain, a nice man with a round head and thick, springy hair, she has to ask him to repeat himself more than once. They are trying to plan services for the end of the term.

"It's always a bit of a challenge," he says. "Because of course they want the holiday services, but Advent generally starts during their reading period, and they're so preoccupied with studying, they don't really turn out in any significant numbers."

"Hm," says Lily.

"Would you like to do Advent services?" he asks her.

"Yes. Sure. What did Jim do?"

"Well," he wipes his mouth carefully, folds his paper napkin, and lays it across his empty plate. "Jim is not much of a liturgist. But since you're Anglican, and, I believe, Anglo-Catholic, is that right?"

"What?" she asks.

"Aren't you Anglo-Catholic?"

"Pretty much," she says.

He looks as if he would like to ask what that means, but he doesn't. He nods and says, "So I would imagine you enjoy the holiday liturgies. I do."

"Advent's my favorite season," says Lily.

"Yes," he says. "Mine, too. Except, of course, for Easter."

"I hate Easter," she says, then she notices his face. "Well, no, not hate. But I do prefer Advent."

"Good," he says. "Let's plan some services, shall we?"

"Hm," says Lily.

17

AT FIVE-THIRTY LILY WALKS INTO THE STARBUCKS. The place seems full. She finds Samantha and Francine at a small round table at the back of the shop, inside, away from the window. She waves, gets in line, orders a cup of tea, and joins them.

As soon as she sits down, she can sense the tension.

Francine leans forward and says, "He may have been on the bus with me on the way here."

"You didn't come in Samantha's car?" asks Lily.

"I had to stop by home," says Francine.

"Okay," says Lily. She's trying to sound calm and respectful, but part of her is feeling something like "sheezz." Then she thinks of the moment at Rick's, and she's not so sure. "Can you see this guy now?"

"No," says Francine. "Please don't look around for him. I feel better if he doesn't know we know he's there."

"He's where?"

"Wherever he is," says Francine.

Lily doesn't answer.

"Perhaps we should explain what we have in mind," says Samantha. "What we thought might be a good way to proceed from here."

"Sure," says Lily.

"We have brought you a set of copies of the photographs, as well as the translations and notes Francine has put together over the last week. We'll give them to you before we leave here."

Samantha keeps talking, but Lily has trouble concentrating on the rest. She is stuck back on the part about her having her own copies of the photographs, at home, to look at whenever she wants.

"Are you listening?" Francine asks.

Lily nods. "Could you just say that last part again?"

"After you have read the new material," says Samantha, "please find a place to hide these, but don't tell us where it is."

"How many copies did you make?" asks Lily.

"Each of us has one full set, and we will put an additional set somewhere safe, somewhere we won't return to again. That way there's less chance of our leading anyone to it."

"You seem more certain than you did earlier," says Lily. "I mean about being followed."

"Francine wants to err on the side of caution," says Samantha. "I can't disagree. Until we know for sure, one way or the other, we should assume we are being watched. And we should assume it's because of these photographs."

"Okay," says Lily. And as she says it, she realizes she's

grown more afraid over the last few minutes, as if Francine's fear is catching. "If we want to know for sure, we'll need someone to watch one of us for a few days. We need to get some help."

"No," says Francine. Her voice is louder than usual. "We can't bring anyone else into this. We should never have included you to begin with. I'm not willing to put anyone else in danger."

"All right," says Lily. She'll figure out a plan on her own, then. Maybe later Francine will be more receptive. "Can I see the new page?"

"Not here," says Francine.

"Where was this last one sent from?" asks Lily.

"Vancouver," says Samantha.

"This guy gets around."

"I know," says Samantha. "Or, as we speculated, it could also be one person asking other people to do the actual mailing."

"You said this one was different," Lily says to Francine. She nods.

"Different how?"

Samantha looks at Francine. "Perhaps we could let her read the translation now."

"No," says Francine.

"Please," says Lily.

"Yes," says Samantha. "Then we can discuss it together. I want to know what Lily thinks."

Francine shrugs once and nods, but it's clear she's not happy about it. Samantha reaches into her briefcase and pulls out a manuscript folder—a brown cardboard accordion case with an elastic clasp. She opens it, takes out an envelope, and hands it across the table to Lily.

"The translations are behind the photographs. The

pages aren't titled, but the one you want beings, *And he drove out a demon.*"

Francine stands. "I'm going to get a refill. Anyone want anything else?"

Lily and Samantha shake their heads. Then Lily opens the envelope. She leaves the photographs and takes out a sheaf of pages, which she scans until she finds the translation of the third photo.

> *And he drove out a demon that couldn't speak. He touched his finger to the man's forehead. When the demon had gone out, the man spoke, and the crowd was amazed.*

Lily reads the lines three times, then raises her eyes and looks at Samantha. "I don't understand."

"No," says Samantha. "Nor do we."

"He touched his finger to the man's forehead..." Lily reads out loud. "But that's not in any other text, is it?"

"Not that I have ever seen," says Samantha. "Read the rest."

Lily reads through the first paragraph.

> *But some of them said, "He casts out demons by Beelzebub, the chief of evil spirits." But he said, "A kingdom divided against itself won't stand, and a house against itself collapses. If Satan is divided against himself, how will his kingdom stand? If it is by the power of Beelzebub that I cast out these demons, by whose power do your sons cast out demons? They will be your judges. But if it is by the touch of—*uncreated? not-created?*—light that I cast out demons, then the time—*rule, place*—of God is here now.*

"What is this?" asks Lily. "What are we reading?"

"I don't know," says Samantha. They lean their heads close and speak quietly.

"Does this mean it's not authentic?"

"I don't think so," says Samantha. "Let's think. We have come up with one reason why someone might have gone to all this trouble to fake these pages—to lure me into making a fool of myself. I haven't come up with any other possible explanation. But if that's the idea, why make the fake manuscript unbelievable? Why use language that makes the text implausible?"

"But, 'not-created' light?" asks Lily. "It sounds like something from *Star Wars*."

"Yes," says Samantha, "I know. Even Francine has been stymied by that one. Read the rest."

Lily reads the second paragraph.

> *He who is not with me is against me. He who doesn't help me to gather, scatters.*
>
> *When an unclean spirit goes out of a person, it wanders through waterless country, looking for a place to rest. Not finding one, it says, "I will go back to the home I have come from." But when it comes, it finds the place swept and cleaned.*
>
> *[Impossible to decipher from here on. Probably reads, The spirit goes out and gets seven other spirits more evil than himself, and they enter and dwell there; and the last state of that man becomes worse than the first.]*

Lily reads through the page twice. Then she looks up as Francine returns with a fresh cup of coffee. The shop has gotten even more crowded over the last fifteen minutes.

Samantha asks, "What do you think?"

"I think the whole thing is out of my league," says Lily.

Francine looks back at her. "It's out of anyone's league," she says. "But it's ours now, whether we like or not. So we need to decide what to do."

"At the risk of sounding repetitive, I say we talk to someone else, an expert in the field, someone we can trust," says Lily. "At least we can get a better idea of the likelihood of this whole thing being a fantastic hoax."

"No," says Francine, and nods in the direction of Samantha. "To begin with, she *is* an expert in the field. Second, we don't show them to anyone else until we know more about what they are, where they've come from, and—please don't turn your head when I say this—until we know who the man is leaning against the bank window across the street."

Through an effort of will, Lily keeps her eyes focused on the two women at the table. "Is this the same guy who has been following you?"

"I don't know," says Francine. "It could be—same size and coloring."

"Can I get up to get some more tea and look?"

"If you can do it convincingly," says Francine. Lily can tell she does not have high hopes for this.

Lily stands, goes to the counter, and asks for a refill of hot water. The guy at the counter—a skinny blond with acne and a goatee—hesitates, then fills the cup. As she turns, she glances out the window. She can see a young man in a green parka a few sizes too small standing across the street, but his back is to her. Almost on cue, he turns to look at an ambulance wailing its high-pitched siren down Mass Ave. She stops suddenly and spills hot water on her hand. "Shit," she says, louder than she intended. A few people look up at her. She shakes the water off her hand, wipes her hand on her jeans, and glances out the window again, but he's gone. She starts to doubt herself, then shakes her head, almost imperceptibly. It was the man she saw in Rick's Kitchen two nights ago, the man who scanned the row of booths until he found her.

18

Tom is working until eight o'clock, so Lily has her apartment to herself. She left him a note on his door downstairs, asking him to call before he comes up. She doesn't want him to walk in and surprise her with the photographs and notes spread out on the dining room table.

The notes are mostly indecipherable to her. Francine seems to have tracked the history of each passage, where it appears in the gospels, who believes it's in Q and, if they believe it's in Q, where in Q it would probably be. Lily stares at a paragraph on the forgiveness passages, the "do unto others" section, which reads, in part, "In favor of Lukan order: Catchpole 1986: 303; Crossan 1983: 342; Grundman Lk 146; Guelich 1976a: 449–450..." It continues on in this vein for a few more lines and then adds, "The usual defense of Lukan order is based on the argument that it is less likely that Luke would have broken up Q 6:27–28,

32–33, 35c by inserting Q 6:29–31 than that Matthew would have rearranged and rationalized the material when he created the series of antitheses."

Okay, she thinks, I don't care. She feels shallow for wanting to get to the good stuff. But that's why she didn't stay in school and get her Ph.D. She likes the good stuff, the stuff about people, about herself, about faith and God and Jesus. You could probably argue that it's all about God, but that argument didn't make the usual defense of Lukan order any more interesting to her.

She lines the photographs up next to one another and scans the writing itself. She tunes her eyes to the details, the individual letters, the rectangular *he*'s, the long, straight *vav*'s, the slightly shorter *yod*'s, the final form of the *mem*'s at the ends of words. By the third photograph, the letters are more uniform, the thickness of the stroke more consistent. Yes, this seems to be someone learning as he goes. A person begins to emerge for her, a man determined to record these words, someone willing to learn a new profession in order to make sure these sayings are written. Or why not a woman? Samantha said there had never been any evidence of women scribes, but this may not be a scribe, not really.

Lily pushes her chair back and stands, staring down at the texts. Then she goes to the kitchen, gets a glass of water, and returns. But once she's back, she can't figure out where to put the water. What if it spills on the table? She returns to the kitchen, finishes the water, and puts the glass down in the sink.

The image of the water spilling has raised the question of safety. Staring down at the photographs, again, she tries to think of a place to hide them. Every place she thinks of in her apartment—the freezer, the toilet, inside a cushion, behind a print, in a record album—seems to have been used in a movie. If Hollywood can think of it, surely anyone else in the world could come up with it, too.

She considers taking the manuscript to her office at the Women's Center, but then she remembers the man across the street from Starbucks. She doesn't know what she believes is happening, but until she does know, she can't risk anyone else's safety. She can't drag Barbara into this.

She sits and tries to read through the notes on the text of the third photo. They're more of the same, up to the line that describes Jesus touching the forehead of the man with his finger. At this point, Francine has written, "There is no evidence of these words in any known text, although both Matthew and Luke use the phrase 'the finger of God' in the final sentence of this section—where our text reads, 'the touch of [ ] light.' We could speculate that the act of touching with the finger is a variation of 'the finger of God.' There is no precedent for the phrase 'not-created' or 'uncreated light.'"

What follows appears to be a concordance of all the mentions of light in Matthew and Luke. Lily scans the list of passages, then takes her Bible from the end table, where she keeps it for her morning prayers, and begins to locate and read each of the references. They are the familiar ones: hiding light under a bushel; letting your light so shine; the eye being the light, or lamp, of the body.

She thinks of the Gospel of John. John has a lot to say about light. She turns to the first chapter and reads,

> *In the beginning was the Word, and the Word was with God, and the Word was God. The same was in the beginning with God. All things were made by him; and without him was not anything made that was made.*

Or, she thinks, was not anything created that was created. Which could imply, I guess, that there are things that
are not created, that are uncreated.

John is a sort of stepbrother in the gospel family—
poetic, druggy, unreliable. Still, the most beautiful writer
of them all, especially in the King James version, which
Lily sneaks in for her personal use. And who's to say this
uncreated light isn't exactly what John was talking about?
Or it may have nothing to do with it.

She leans back in her chair and rubs her eyes, then rubs
her whole face, as if to bring herself back into the world.
She hears a noise, and she realizes she's completely forgotten to listen for Tom coming in downstairs. And then the
noise is louder, and then her front door opens and Tom's in
the doorway saying, "Hello, is anyone home?"

Lily stands so fast her chair falls over behind her.

"Whoa," says Tom. "What's up?"

"Nothing," she says. She picks up the chair and gathers
all the notes and photographs into a pile, which she then
begins to try to neaten. At least the photos are out of sight.
"I thought you were going to call."

"Why was I going to call?"

"I left you a note, downstairs, and told you to call before
you came."

"I came here first." He tilts his head and looks at her. "Is
this a big deal?"

"No. I wanted some privacy, that's all."

Tom goes into the kitchen and gets himself a glass from
the cupboard. Then he opens the refrigerator and fills the
glass with water from the gallon tap container she keeps on
the top shelf. When he gets to the sink, he pauses, noticing
her glass. Lily sees him lean forward, to get a better look at
what's left in the bottom. What he wants to do, she thinks,

is pick it up and sniff it for vodka fumes. He returns to the living room and leans against the back of the sofa. "So, like I said, what's up?"

Lily can't say, What do you mean? And she can't tell the truth. The silence grows until it's a third presence in the room with them. "I can't tell you."

"Why not?"

"Because, I promised I wouldn't tell."

"Promised who—Samantha?"

She hesitates. "Yes, Samantha."

"And is she more important to you than I am? Because, I gotta say, this thing is getting in the way. You've been weird for the past week or so, since she showed up. I'm guessing it's about this Q stuff, right?"

Lily nods.

"Is it dangerous?"

"Why would you ask that?"

"Because you seem afraid of something. And I'm pretty sure it's not me—at least, I hope it's not me."

"It's not you," she says. She sits down again at the table. "It's just that Samantha told me about this thing, and I promised I wouldn't talk about it. But now it's getting more and more complicated, and it looks like—"

"Looks like what?"

"It looks like someone may be following us. Although, I don't really think that could be happening."

"Why not?" Tom comes and sits at the table next to her, turning his chair to face her.

"Because it's too unreal. People don't follow people in real life. Do they?"

"Sure they do. I mean, not that often, but it's a pretty good sign that something's not right. Don't you think?"

Lily nods. She feels as if she's being pulled in opposite

directions with so much force that she's paralyzed, and that if the force keeps up, her mind might split.

"Why don't you just tell me however much you can, and I'll figure out the rest. Then we can talk about what to do next."

"Okay," she says, surprising herself. And she knows she's going to tell him the whole story, with all the details, from the beginning.

19

"JESUS FUCKING CHRIST," HE SAYS, HALF AN HOUR later. He is walking back and forth between the living room and the dining room.

"Nice mouth," says Lily. "I'm glad your mother's not here to hear you say that."

"I'm glad my mother's not here for a lot of reasons."

"What's that supposed to mean?"

"Can we stick to the subject?" he asks.

She's still at the table, the photographs and translations of each text spread out in front of her. "Okay," she says. "But sit down so I can see you."

He sits in the chair next to her and tips it back onto two legs. He keeps his eyes on her face the whole time. "So what do you think is happening? Do you think this thing is real?"

"The text, you mean—the book?"

"Yeah. The Q thing. Do you think these are pictures of a real—what would you call it?"

"Scroll, I guess. It's a scroll, on animal hide."

"Are these pictures of a real scroll from the first century?"

"I don't know. I don't have any way to know. But if they're not real, why would someone care enough to follow the three of us around town?"

"But what's your gut feeling—you know—have you had any dreams?"

She nods and looks out the window. "I keep dreaming about Jesus. And some woman."

"What woman?"

"I don't know."

"What does she look like?"

"She looks like Marilyn Monroe."

"Oh, yeah? You're dreaming about Jesus and Marilyn Monroe?" He sounds happy for the first time this evening.

She looks at him and then looks out the window. "I'm glad you think it's funny."

"What?" he asks. He raises his hands, palms out, as if to say, I'm innocent. "What? You tell me a story about an ancient scroll and a couple of Mediterranean guys shadowing you, you tell me you're dreaming about Jesus and Marilyn Monroe, and then you get mad at me for making a comment? Come on. You're lucky we're not halfway to McLean's by now."

"You think I'm crazy?" she asks him.

"I don't know what to think. I mean, no, I don't think you're crazy. But I can't tell what you really believe or don't believe is going on here. Do you think Samantha's flipped out? Do you think she created these things herself to get attention?"

"I have thought that, a couple of times."

"Why? What happened?"

"One time she was reading to me—" Lily pauses and finds the photo of the second installment of text. "And, you see down here, where it's so faint and blurry? You really can't read that part. But when she translated it for me, out loud, she just read right through it, as if she already knew what it said."

"You mean she could read the part you can't see?"

"Yeah."

"Did you ask her about it?"

"I did. But she said she'd been reading it closely for a while—although, I think they had only gotten it that day, maybe the day before. She said she was filling in, from what she already knew should be there."

"Does that make sense?"

"Yes," Lily says slowly. "It could. But all this time, they've kept the photos locked in a table in their offices at Tate. Not very secure. And I've never fully believed her idea about someone going to the trouble of having these photos made up, somehow, and sent to her, so that she would take them out into the world and get charged with perpetrating a hoax. Too iffy, and too elaborate."

"What else?" asks Tom.

"In this last photograph, the latest installment, there are these two phrases that don't exist in any other Biblical text I've seen. And this raises a whole other set of questions."

"Such as?"

"Such as, if someone is faking these, why make them less authentic by throwing in phrases like 'uncreated light'? On the other hand, if Samantha—or, I guess, Francine—is faking them in order to get attention, think how much more attention they would get if the text has weird and exciting deviations. On the third hand—if there's such a thing—why would Samantha want to make them less believable by throwing in 'uncreated light'?"

"Could they be doing this together?"

Lily thinks about what that means. "Yes. And then I would be the guinea pig."

"What do you mean?"

"Well, they're trying them out on me, in order to see if the whole thing could work. I'm their witness, in a way. I attest to the fact that they were stunned and surprised—just as surprised as I was."

"Yeah," says Tom. "That works, except for the Mediterranean guy—or guys."

"And I still don't even know if that's really happening. I mean, when I saw that guy across the street today, I felt sure it was the same guy I saw at Rick's Kitchen with you and Charlie the other night. But when I think back on it, I can't even remember what he looked like."

"So where does that leave us?"

Lily stands and leans over the photographs.

"I don't buy the someone-sending-these-in-order-to-disrupt-Samantha's-world theory. It's too ego-centered."

"Then what's left?"

Lily picks up the third photograph and holds it close, in order to look at the texture of the scroll. "It really looks like leather," she says. "And it also really looks as if it had faded down here." She points to the bottom of the page. She puts it back down on the table and sits next to Tom again, keeping her eyes on the photos. "Two possibilities, or sort of two and a half. First, that Samantha or Francine is responsible. That one of them wants or needs the attention so much that she has gone to an unbelievable amount of trouble to create these photographs. The half part is that they're doing it together."

"What about the postmarks?" asks Tom. "Can you tell where they're being mailed?"

"Oh, yeah," says Lily. "I forgot. They were sent from three different places—D.C., Seattle, and Vancouver. So if one of them is doing this, she's not doing it alone. Because someone else is traveling from D.C. to Washington to Canada."

"Could be Samantha flew to these places and mailed them herself. Or Francine. Or the two of them taking turns."

"I guess. They'd have to be working together, though. They're so—bonded. I don't think one of them could fly to Seattle and back without the other one knowing."

"What about the husband?"

"But that's the theory I already dismissed," says Lily. "That he's done all this in order to maybe, on a long shot, get Samantha—"

"No," says Tom. "That the two of them are working together. That they're not estranged anymore. That they both want to—what?—boost their dying careers?"

"According to Samantha," says Lily. "And he is traveling in the States."

"Well, then?" Tom looks at her and shrugs. "Could be, couldn't it?"

"I guess. But then why would she tell me he's here, if she's using him to mail the photos? Wouldn't she want that to be a secret?"

"Probably. So what's the other proposition?"

"That someone, and I vote for Nickolas, their friend on Athos, is smuggling these out by way of unsuspecting visitors. That's why they're arriving from all over the States."

"So he only gives them to U.S. and Canadian citizens?"

Lily stares down at the photographs, as if willing them to tell their story. "Christ," she says. "I don't know."

Tom pulls one of the photos toward him. "So that would mean—" He picks it up and studies it carefully.

"That these are photographs of a two-thousand-year-old manuscript recording Jesus' words."

Tom places the photograph back on the table. "Is that what you think they are?"

Lily shakes her head. "Maybe."

"Do you think someone is following you and Francine?"

"Maybe. I don't believe it, but I think it might be true."

"Yeah. It's too weird to be true, but its weirdness is one of the things that makes it true."

"Something like that."

Tom stands and pushes the chair under the table. "We need to find a safe place to put these things—a good hiding place, but a place you can get them easily, if you need to. Or can tell someone else how to get them."

"Why? What do you mean?"

"I'm thinking—if someone should show up, wanting these things, you need to be able to hand them over."

"Oh, right," says Lily. "You mean a kind of your-photos-or-your-life situation?"

"More or less. And then we should decide what we're going to do to try to find out what's really happening. Meanwhile, maybe we should get someone to follow you around for a few days."

"I suggested that. Francine doesn't want anyone else involved. She thinks it's too dangerous."

"That's why you need some help," says Tom. "That's

your instinct, right? To get some backup. Go with your own instinct."

"I'm not going to the police at this point."

"God. Me neither," says Tom. "What would we say? We have these photographs of a manuscript that might be written by a friend of Jesus, but they might also have been written by this friend of ours—a crazy woman. So, I know you're currently searching for Whitey Bulger, but maybe you could spare a couple of officers to follow—"

"Okay, okay," says Lily. "What did you mean?"

"There's a woman, someone I knew at the academy. She was a great cop, but she got fed up with the harassment, so she got her license and set up her own firm. She could use the work; we could use the help."

Lily glances out the window. The lights are coming on in apartments along Commonwealth. She tries to imagine what it will be like to know there's someone following her around, someone safe. "What about Francine and Samantha?"

"Would you consider not telling them, just for a while? It's for their own safety. You say they're worried about putting someone else in danger, but that's what Marty does for a living. Look—at least meet her. We can tell her whatever part of the story you want—as long as it makes sense to her. Just tell her you have something that could be very valuable, and this is what you think is happening."

Lily hesitates. Tom's plan makes sense. She doesn't like the idea of lying to Samantha and Francine, but she also doesn't like the idea of risking their safety—or risking the manuscript.

"Okay," she says. "I'll talk to her. But I'll have to tell them eventually."

"Let's wait," says Tom. "Let's see what Marty comes up with." Lily starts to object, but he beats her to it. "Yeah, yeah, it's a little sneaky. But we don't know what we've got here. One week. Then, if she doesn't find anything—no big deal. They can know or not. If she does find something, we'll take it from there. You'll like her. And she's perfect for the job."

"How come?"

"Her name's Marty Angel."

"Ha ha," says Lily. Across the street a man moves away from one of the streetlights into the shadow of the building behind. Lily waits to see him go up the stairs and open the front door, but he never does. "Let's call her now," she says.

20

MARTY ANGEL IS NOT AT ALL WHAT LILY EXPECTED—
or hoped for. She had in mind someone large and substantial, tough and intimidating. Marty is pretty and thin, with
small bones, dark hair, and bright red lipstick. She's wearing a black turtleneck, a tiny suede skirt, black tights, high
boots and looks about sixteen. But when she opens her
mouth, she sounds like a mob boss. Her voice is thick, and
she has an accent Lily can't place—Brooklyn, Sicily? After she's been at a table with the woman for ten minutes,
Lily feels safer than she's felt in a week.

Lily and Tom asked her to meet them for lunch in the
trattoria around the corner from the Women's Center. It's a
wintry Saturday afternoon, with gunmetal clouds threaten-
ing outside and a wind that rattles the plate glass window
at the front of the restaurant. Two men sit at the bar, and a
large group takes up two tables in the back room. A man

holds the front door open for a woman, who has paused to read something on the menu posted outside. Lily notices he's not wearing socks with his loafers; his bare ankles look vulnerable and pathetic. The wind blasts into the room through the open door.

"Do you mind?" Marty calls out to him.

"What?" says the man.

"Can she peruse the menu inside? We're freezing here."

"Oh," he says. "Sorry." He reaches out and pulls the woman by the elbow. She says, "Don't," in a loud petulant voice. He hisses something at her, and she comes in. She has chin-length hair, with natural-looking two-hundred-dollar highlights. Neither of them looks at Marty as they walk past into the back of the restaurant.

Marty rolls her eyes and shakes her head. "Where were we? Oh, yeah. Tom told me a little, but I want you to start again, from the beginning. Also, I know this sounds a little cheesy, but it would probably be a good idea to laugh a little, like we're telling jokes."

"Do you think someone's watching us?" asks Lily.

"You're the one hiring me. I don't think anything yet."

"But if they're watching now," says Lily, "won't it make it easier for them to recognize you later on?"

"I don't look like this when I tail people. You probably won't know it's me, even if you do see me—which is unlikely. We won't meet again for a while. I'll call Tom at work if I have something to report. You get information to me the same way."

"Why?" asks Lily. "Do you think my phone is tapped? How could someone tap my phone?"

"Look," says Marty, but as she leans forward to explain, the waiter arrives with their food—a huge dish of crab claws and a plate of roasted vegetables.

The waiter asks if they've decided what they want to drink. Marty orders a Coke, Tom orders a St. Pauli Girl, and Lily stares up at the waiter for a moment, then says, "Yeah. I'll have a beer, too. Same kind."

The waiter leaves.

"You're not drinking these days?" Tom asks Marty.

"Three years this January. New Year's Day. I figured it would be an easy anniversary to remember. Okay. What I was going to say was this: There are certain precautions one takes in this kind of situation. It doesn't mean anything is or isn't happening. It means a number of things could be happening, and we arrange our contact around those eventualities. I would like to sweep your place at some point, though. That way we'll know for sure. Does Tom have a key?"

Lily nods.

"Do I have your permission to go in when you're not there and check it out?"

She nods again, but then hesitates. "How come—"

"It's easier if I go in when you're not around. If you're not there, probably won't be anyone around waiting for you to come out, right? But we communicate through Tom, regardless. Okay?"

"You mean sweep it for microphones, to see if it's bugged?" asks Lily.

"Yeah," says Marty. "Also, I like to see where people live. It gives me a better idea of what I'm doing."

"Okay," says Lily. "But I shouldn't worry until we know something concrete, right?"

"Right," says Marty. "Conversely, stay alert. Like I said, if I'm doing my job, you won't see me. If I have to make my presence known, I will, but only if I'm sure it's necessary. Once I've done that, I'm not much good to you. It's better if you don't look around for me—you know what I mean? What's best is if you forget you've got a trail of people behind you. I'm gonna do the nine-to-five, and he's gonna do the five-to-nine. And weekends." She nods in Tom's direction. "That work for you?"

"Sure," says Lily. Then she realizes she's just hired Marty. That's not what she had planned to do. She'd planned to meet her and decide later. But the relief Lily feels in Marty's presence made the decision for her.

The waiter arrives with the drinks. He pours Lily's beer, and she watches it foam to the top of the mug. She waits until Tom has a sip of his before she tastes it.

"By the way," says Marty. "I like the boots."

Lily can't figure out what she means until Marty points to Lily's feet. "Oh, thanks. I grew up in Texas. They're not—you know—pretend."

"I figured," says Marty. "Okay. Tell me what I need to know here."

So Lily tells the story for the second time in twenty-four hours. Marty smiles and chuckles as she listens. She asks a couple of questions about Q and the manuscript. When Lily gets to the part about the man across the street from the Starbucks, Marty tips her head back and belts out a laugh that stops conversation up front for a few seconds.

"That was really convincing," says Lily.

Marty nods and smiles. "So that's the last time you saw this guy?"

"I guess. I mean, I'm not even positive it's the same man I saw at Rick's Kitchen. At the time, I thought it was, but I'm not so sure now."

"Does anyone want these last two crab claws?" asks Tom.

Lily notices she has more beer than Tom does, so she

takes a couple of sips. She imagines she feels the alcohol reach her brain and take the edge off her worries. She's not alone anymore; someone's watching her back, literally.

"I do," says Marty. "But I'm feeling generous, so I'll share. This place is great." She spears the claw with a fork and puts it on her plate, then turns to Lily. "Where did you put your photographs?" Her voice is a little lower, hard to hear over the noise of the chat and music around them.

Lily glances at Tom.

"We put them in my darkroom," he says. "The one in my apartment—in the files of photographs, under *p*, for photographs. They're probably two or three hundred prints in there."

"Good," says Marty. "Nice idea. Does it have a lock?"

"Yeah," said Tom. "Lily and I have the only two keys."

"Okay, good," she repeats. She turns to Lily again. "How well do you know Francine?"

"Not well," says Lily. "I just met her a couple of weeks ago, when we all went out to dinner together."

"Do you trust her?" asks Marty.

"I guess," says Lily, and then she thinks of overhearing Francine on the phone. She takes a few more swallows of beer.

"What?" asks Marty.

"A few days ago I went up to their offices to see the photos, and Francine didn't expect me. She was on the phone, and she was talking loud and slow, as if the person on the other end couldn't hear her, or understand her. When she saw me she looked caught—the deer in the headlights look. She said it was her mother, but I don't think it was."

"Who do you think it was?" asks Tom.

Lily notices her thoughts are a little fuzzy—she can't

tell one from the other, or she's not sure if she can. She's not sure what she's supposed to say, either, then she remembers the question. "I have no idea. It may have been her mother. I could ask Samantha if Francine's mother is hard of hearing."

"I'd wait," says Marty. She spears the last of the eggplant and a couple of potatoes.

"Why?"

"Let's see what I find out. Francine thinks someone is following her. You think someone is following you. That shouldn't be too hard to ascertain. If it's true, that makes it less likely that Francine, or Francine and Samantha, have set up this whole deal themselves. Once we know that, we'll know more about who to trust. You have pictures of either of them?"

Lily shakes her head and looks at Tom's beer mug. She's way ahead.

"If you're supposed to be following Lily, when are you going to follow Francine?" asks Tom.

"At night and on the weekends. When you're on duty, partner."

"But that's more than we asked for. And I'm not sure . . ."

"Don't worry about the money, okay? I just finished my best job so far—insurance company had somebody assessing boats, right? She was jacking up the value and then, when the boats mysteriously sunk, splitting the difference with the owners. I've got steady work with them whenever I want. You were one of the good guys when I was on the force. And I'll probably need a few favors along the way. Trust me, I'll collect. Besides, I'm interested. You know how boring this work is most of the time? So, okay," she says, turning to Lily. "Describe Francine and Samantha, and tell me where to look for them both."

"Aren't you going to write any of this down?" asks Lily.

"Nah," says Marty. "I make notes when I get home. But I don't like to keep a lot of stuff in writing. Besides, it looks weird if I record what we're saying at a friendly lunch."

"That's why she couldn't be a cop," says Tom. "She was smarter than all the guys and it drove them crazy."

"It doesn't drive them crazy that you're smart," says Marty. She drains her Coke and looks around as if she's wondering what to ingest next.

I know the feeling, thinks Lily, and drains her beer. Within a couple of seconds, she feels the low-grade panic begin—empty glass, empty glass.

"I'm not a cop anymore," says Tom. "I'm a photographer. And I'm not as smart as you. Plus, I'm a guy. I hide it better."

"Yeah," says Marty, nodding at him. "You do. You do all that jock talk. I couldn't get with the program, you know? All my life, I was supposed to let the guys be smarter. I don't mind if they *are* smarter. Don't get me wrong. But— never mind." She turns to Lily. "Describe them. Tell me where they live, what they drive, whatever you know about them. And describe this guy, too, the one you think is tailing you."

Lily starts to talk about Samantha, but Marty interrupts her.

"Sorry. Can we get some dessert?"

Tom laughs. "Where do you put it all?

"High metabolism," she says.

21

On Monday morning Lily takes her usual route to work—the Green Line to Park Street and the Red Line to Davis Square. She buys the *Boston Globe* at Park Street, because she figures that will keep her occupied. But she has a hard time reading. She tries to scan the crowds on the train nonchalantly, as if admiring the eclectic mix.

On the walk from the T-stop to the Tate campus, she stops once to put down her backpack and button her barn jacket. The wind that started on Saturday let up some, now and then, only to return. It seems trapped under a giant glass bowl over Boston. Ragged clouds are traveling across the sky at a dizzying speed.

She glances down the sidewalk as she hefts her pack. There's no one behind her—at least, no swarthy man and no petite woman in bright red lipstick—just a high-school co-ed in skin-tight flare jeans and an elderly black couple walking a Pekinese. Lily wonders if she'll be doing this nonstop for the next few weeks—checking over her shoulder. No, she thinks, people get used to almost anything. As Barbara says, "You could get used to hanging if it didn't kill you."

She previews her day as she walks—phone calls, e-mail, letters in the morning; a meeting with the Campus Life committee (she's been trying to beg off these since she started, given that she knows nothing about Campus Life); a meeting with the Catholic chaplain in the afternoon, to firm up plans (his phrase) for Advent services; office hours from three to five. She's going to avoid Samantha and Francine. She needs a break, and she's also interested to see if they let her stay away. That might tell her something about what's going on. If they've concocted this whole thing, they'll want to keep her hooked in—or that's her guess. Tonight she and Tom are meeting at the trattoria for dinner. Marty's supposed to call him before he leaves work to give him any information she's gotten from her first day on the job.

Until recently, Lily's need for the photographs to be authentic elbowed its way past the practical questions and made it hard to focus. But since lunch on Saturday, that's changed. Now she's just as interested in figuring out their source. She runs back through the options she'd listed with Tom—Francine and Samantha making it all up, Samantha and her husband making it up, Nickolas smuggling the manuscript off the island—and she comes up with a fourth one they hadn't included—someone no one has mentioned, from somewhere no one has thought of, for a reason nobody knows, yet. Interesting, she thinks, that she hasn't allowed for this before. Bishop Spencer always says God's imagination is better than ours. Could be true in this case.

She climbs the cement steps to the quad at the top of the hill. The wind whips a few loose strands of hair into her face and makes her eyes water. At the top, she turns and looks down at the crowd of students and professors on their way to nine o'clock classes. They're caught up in their lives, worried and happy, broke and in love, failing out of school, fueled by dreams of a gilded future that includes unlimited sex and money. And though none of them seems to be paying attention to her, someone is. She is being watched. She can feel it.

AT ELEVEN-THIRTY, SHE'S CALLED OUT OF THE CAM-pus Life meeting by the student assistant in the chaplain's office, a plain-faced sophomore with thick, luxurious black hair that she wears in elaborate braids and coils and nests on top of her head. She gets Lily's attention through the glass door of the conference room. Once they're in the hall together, she whispers in an urgent tone, "Professor Henderson called. She needs you to go with her somewhere. There's been an accident, I think—her assistant, I'm pretty sure. Anyway, she says could you please meet her in the parking lot behind Kerry Hall right away."

Lily excuses herself from the meeting, jogs over to her office, picks up her backpack, and walks to the parking lot. She is thinking, accident? In the car? No, or else Samantha wouldn't be meeting me in the parking lot. And not on campus, either.

Samantha is standing beside her car. When she sees Lily, she waves and gets in. Lily gets in beside her and looks over at Samantha's face, which is pale beneath two streaks of blusher.

"What happened?" Lily asks.

"I don't know exactly," says Samantha. She pulls out of the parking lot and turns right. "She was in the manuscript room at the Annenberg, and, from what I understand, the fire detection system was activated. At which point the vault doors on the manuscript room slam shut and gas is released into the air to prevent the fire from being able to spread."

"What kind of gas?"

"Halon," says Samantha. Her voice is high and nervous, but she's driving calmly. "I think it lowers the oxygen level."

"And what would that do—" Lily begins, and then is sorry she asked the question.

Samantha stops at a red light at the bottom of the campus and looks across at her. "I don't know," she says. "But she's alive. She gave them my cell phone number. Oh, for God's sake. I don't even know where I'm going." She pulls over to the side of the road and leans her head against her hand, at the top of the steering wheel.

"Where is she?" Lily asks.

"Mass General. Or they're taking her there now." Samantha sits up straight. "We're supposed to meet her in the emergency room. She didn't want to go, evidently."

"She must be okay, then," says Lily. "If she's that lucid. She's in no hurry to get help. That's a good sign, don't you think? And I know how to get there. We need to go out Broadway. Go to the rotary. I'll show you where to turn."

Samantha looks over her shoulder and pulls out into traffic. "I don't know what to think," says Samantha. Her voice cracks on the *think*. "Is this because of the manuscript?"

"I think we ought to wait and see what happened," says Lily, although she feels sure it *is* connected, somehow.

Samantha nods.

Once they're out of the rotary, they drive down Broadway in silence. They pass a Dunkin' Donuts and a twenty-four-hour car wash, a string of bars and liquor stores, a Store 24, a couple of sub shops. At the next red light, Samantha leans forward again, but she sits up before her head reaches the steering wheel. "What would I do without her?" she says.

And though Lily is struck again by the monumental selfishness of the woman, she's also touched by her. Samantha is shaken.

THEY MAKE GOOD TIME UNTIL THE BRIDGE. THERE'S A jam in front of the Museum of Science. Lily thinks Samantha might cry, but she starts talking to her, asking her to explain again what she knows, and it works. Samantha settles down and ten minutes later they pull into the parking lot by the emergency room entrance.

They luck out at the desk. A young woman with cornrows and beads knows who Francine is and takes them down a long hall of curtained cubicles—Lily can hear a child whimpering, the clipped and efficient voice of a man asking questions, a woman telling someone to shut up, somebody singing quietly under his breath—to one at the far end on the right. Francine lies on a gurney. Her hair is wet and plastered to her head. She looks pale, and her eyes are closed. She's hooked up to a heart monitor and another monitor—Lily can't tell what kind—and has a breathing tube in her nose. But there's no IV, and Lily takes that as a good sign. The doctors seem to be watching Francine, but not treating her for anything.

As soon as Samantha touches her hand, Francine's eyes

open and she holds on to Samantha's arm. "I'm okay," she says. Then she looks at Lily and adds, "Hi."

Lily walks to the other side of the bed and says, "Hi. Other than okay, how are you?"

"My head's killing me. I must have banged it on the light table when I grabbed for my stuff. And I'm cold. They had to scrub me down with something when I first got here. Halon gas, the stuff they use to extinguish fires in the vaults, has Freon in it, and Freon is—something—bad for the ozone layer. And, I deduce, not so good for humans, either, although I'm not supposed to worry. I don't know yet *why* I'm not supposed to worry."

"Shall we get you another blanket?" asks Samantha.

"No," says Francine. As she talks, she begins to shiver, then tugs the blanket up around her shoulders and takes a deep breath. "You've got to get my stuff. I had the photographs with me. It's all in the reference librarian's office— a Mrs. Fowler. She's supposed to be keeping everything until you get there."

Samantha is holding Francine's hand. She nods her head as she listens. When Francine finishes, Samantha says, "Don't worry about it. We'll get everything. Meanwhile, we need to get you warm."

"If they're not there, if the photographs are gone, check yours. Be sure yours are where you put them."

"Yes," says Samantha. Her voice is distant, as if she is distracted by what she's thinking.

Francine looks at Lily. "You, too. Make sure your photographs are where you put them."

Lily nods. "Okay," she says. "But are you all right?"

"Yes," says Francine. "I'm freezing. My head is killing me, and they can't give me anything because I have a concussion. And for some weird reason, I'm extremely hungry."

"Shall I get you something to eat?" asks Samantha.

"No," says Francine. "What you should do, both of you, is go pick up my things. If the photographs are gone, be sure yours are where you put them. And you should stay together."

Lily thinks Francine must be repeating herself because she's in shock. Then she understands. Francine is more frightened than ever.

22

MRS. FOWLER, THE REFERENCE LIBRARIAN, IS A THIN-faced blonde woman in her early thirties, wearing a blue shirtwaist dress and pearls. She does not look like someone whose place of work has, only a couple of hours earlier, been coated with an ozone-destroying chemical. Her desk is bare of everything but a desktop computer, a day planner, and a brown leather desk set, the pen holder full of identical blue ballpoints.

As Mrs. Fowler hands Samantha the black backpack filled with Francine's belongings, she says, "Can I ask you something?" She glances at Lily, leaning against the door frame. Lily notices Mrs. Fowler's eyes, which are an odd green color, almost golden.

"Yes," says Samantha, hand still resting on the pack. She nods as if to say it's fine to talk with Lily in the room.

"Is there any reason to imagine that someone is trying to hurt Ms. Loetterlee?"

"Why?" asks Samantha.

"Because there was no fire in the building today," says Mrs. Fowler. "No fire, no smoke, no cooking, no temperature fluctuations. The system employs two triggering mechanisms, to ensure against mistakes. This has never happened before, as long as I've been here, and that's almost ten years."

Lily thinks Mrs. Fowler must have stepped out of her black graduation robes and into the blue shirtwaist—or she is older than she looks.

"I also noticed," she continues, "that Ms. Loetterlee was extremely concerned about her materials. She told me perhaps five times that no one was to have them but you."

"She seemed to be in a state of shock when we saw her," says Samantha. "I don't think—"

"And one more thing," says Mrs. Fowler.

Samantha nods.

"I don't see how she could have fallen and hit the back of her head."

"Why not?" asks Samantha.

"Because she was presumably reading the manuscript transparencies on the light table. That means she was standing facing the light table." Mrs. Fowler turns sideways so she is facing her desk, to illustrate her point. "When we found her, she was on her back, as if she had fallen away from the table." She turns and points to the floor behind her. "But there would be nothing on which she could hit the back of her head if she fell backward, away from the table. She wasn't using a stool. She was standing. Do you see?"

"I do," says Samantha slowly. "And yet I don't see how

anyone could possibly know what happened. Wasn't she alone in the room?"

"Did she tell you she was?"

"She didn't say one way or the other," says Samantha.

"Oh," says Mrs. Fowler. She walks around behind her desk and stands facing Samantha and Lily, who is still watching from the doorway. "You might ask her." She seems to be done, but as Samantha turns to leave, Mrs. Fowler says, "The fireman with whom I spoke believed it was due to the age of the system—a faulty alarm. I don't think that's the case." She hesitates. "I have to think of the library first."

"Of course you do," says Samantha. "Thank you for your time."

Lily's impressed with Samantha's cool.

"GOD," SAYS LILY AS THEY WALK DOWN THE BROAD marble steps into the Harvard Quad. "Do you think she's CIA?"

"No, just Harvard," says Samantha. She stops at the foot of the stairs and begins to unzip the pack.

"What are you doing?" asks Lily.

"I'm looking to see if the photographs are here."

"Let's wait until we get to the car," says Lily.

"Why?" asks Samantha. Then she adds, "Oh."

Once they're in the car, Samantha begins to unzip the pack again, but this time Lily lays a hand on her arm and says, "Not here, either. I wasn't thinking. We need to be inside."

"Yes," says Samantha. "All right. Let's go to my place first."

Lily hesitates. "What about your afternoon class?"

"I canceled it when I got the call."

"I'm supposed to have office hours today—and I've still got—" Lily thinks about Francine in the hospital, about her urgency. "Never mind. I'll call from your apartment."

Samantha pulls out of the parking spot and heads toward Mass Ave. Lily watches out the window, registering the cold, brittle sunlight, a woman holding her coat collar up around her chin, a stream of small children crossing the street on their way toward the Common, their bright parkas flapping in the wind. After a few minutes of silence, she says, "What do you think happened?"

Samantha doesn't answer right away. She stops at a red light and stares out the window beside her. "I'm not certain. What's your impression?"

"I'm not sure," says Lily. "But I believe she knows something about what's going on, something she hasn't told us—or, at least, hasn't told me, although that's not so surprising, since I hardly know her. It is surprising she hasn't told you, though, isn't it?"

Again, Samantha waits a few seconds. "Yes," she says, stretching out the one word. "If it's true, it's very surprising." The light changes and they turn left onto Linnaean.

"But you don't think it's true?" asks Lily.

"It hadn't occurred to me until this moment—or, I should say, I haven't allowed myself to articulate the thought. But hearing you say it—yes, I think it's true."

"Do you know what it is, what she's hiding?" asks Lily. "I mean, do you have a guess?"

"I need some time to consider it."

"Don't consider it. Just make a guess, first thing that comes to your mind. If you had to name one thing right now, what would it be?"

"Nickolas."

As soon as she hears the name, Lily understands. "Do you think she's been in touch with him?"

"Why?"

"I walked in one day when she was on the phone, and I knew something was up, but I didn't know what it was. Now I think she may have been talking to Nickolas—or, I guess, someone in touch with Nickolas."

"Nickolas would never—" begins Samantha. "Admittedly, I didn't know the boy well. Neither did she. Still, I don't believe he would do anything to harm her, or anyone, for that matter."

"Maybe not," says Lily. "But someone would."

23

Off Mass Ave, just south of Porter Square, Samantha turns right into a narrow alley with a chain-link fence along one side, keeping a couple of trash cans from running amok.

"Where are we?" asks Lily.

"This is the back entrance to my building, to the covered garage."

"We didn't come this way last time I was here," says Lily.

"No, if I'm going back out again, I leave the car on the street. The place looks a bit sinister, doesn't it?"

Lily doesn't answer. Samantha maneuvers the narrow space and heads the car up a steeply graded ramp. She flips down the sun visor and touches a button on a keypad, and a garage door in front of them slides up. Once they're inside, the door closes with a series of loud clanks and whines.

"So this is what rich people do with their cars," says Lily.

"Rich, or obsessive, or both. In my case, only obsessive."

The garage is well-lit and about half-full. Five or six cars—including an old Porsche and a Mustang convertible—are parked in numbered spaces along the left-hand wall. Samantha pulls into the next to the last space; the number 7 is painted on the wall in bright red paint. It looks new. Samantha picks up the pack from near Lily's feet and asks, "Now can I open it?"

"Why don't we go inside?" asks Lily.

"You'll see," says Samantha. She unzips the pack, takes out the materials inside, and lays them on her lap. There is a thick spiral notebook, two hardcover library books, and three manila envelopes. She opens the envelopes one by one, peers in, and holds them so Lily can see inside—each of them is empty.

Lily takes the envelopes off Samantha's lap and checks for herself. It's not that she doesn't trust Samantha—she has no idea whom she trusts at this point—but she wants badly for this to be a mistake. She wants to find the photographs in their proper places. Lily puts the empty envelopes back in the pack and picks up the first book and thumbs through it. She knows the photographs couldn't be folded into the book without sticking out, but she needs to be thorough. She returns that text to the pack and picks up the second book. As she leafs through, she sees black-and-white photographs of Eastern Orthodox churches—or monasteries, judging from the size of the buildings—and fragile-looking shacks.

She stops at one of the photos of a shack—walls of sticks and branches with a roof of straw, surrounded by underbrush. Beside the hut, on the right edge of the photograph, stands a small man in black robes, with a long, thick beard, almost to his waist. It's hard to make out the details of his face, but Lily feels as if he is looking directly at her—his eyes stare out of the surface of the photograph, dark and alive and piercing.

After a moment, she closes the book and checks the spine for the title—*Let Your Light So Shine: The Secrets of Mount Athos*. She holds the spine of the book toward Samantha.

"Nickolas," says Samantha again. She gets out of the car and walks around to the trunk. Lily watches her through the rear window until the trunk opens. Then she gets out and joins Samantha.

"What are you doing?" asks Lily.

Samantha looks around the garage, listens for a moment, then says, "Do me a favor." She points to a pair of large double doors, with a window in each door, at the end of the row of parked cars. "Go stand by those doors, if you don't mind, and tell me if anyone's coming. And perhaps it would be best if you keep your back to me."

Lily does what she's asked. Clearly this has to do with the manuscript. And it makes perfect sense that Samantha would hide her photos in her car, her most treasured possession.

The windows look out onto another small alley, but this one is sunny and lined on the right side by dwarf pines in large terra-cotta pots. On the left is the brick wall of Samantha's apartment building, with a set of matching double doors about halfway down the alley. Lily keeps her eyes on the doors into the building and listens to Samantha. She hears her groan once or twice, as if lifting something heavy, and she hears the sounds of metal on metal. But most of Lily's mind is busy with Francine and the manuscript and Nickolas and Mount Athos.

Lily is so preoccupied that she sees but doesn't register

a tall woman with black hair, who has come out of the apartment building and is walking toward the garage. At the moment their eyes meet through the small window in the garage door, the woman looks startled, almost angry, and Lily reenters the present. "Someone's coming," she says. She turns to see Samantha bent over the trunk, holding a manila envelope, the spare tire at her feet, the contents of the trunk scattered near her—a small black case, a large emergency flashlight, a gallon of water, a blanket.

"You mustn't—" begins Samantha. But the woman is pushing open the door next to Lily. Samantha drops the envelope into the trunk and ducks her head. Lily holds the door for the black-haired woman and starts to smile at her, to say something about doormen and service and tipping, but the woman's face, the hard lines of fear and suspicion, which don't alter even when she looks Lily in the eye, stops Lily from saying anything.

The woman, who is dressed in a black cape and black jeans and looks as if she might be impersonating a matador, passes Samantha without speaking and walks down the row of cars, the sound of her high-heeled boots on the garage floor echoing in the cavernous space. In a minute or two, a small, black sports car backs out, the garage door opens, and the car disappears down the ramp.

Lily has turned her head again and is staring out the window into the alley. "Who was that?" she asks Samantha.

"The woman who lives above me," says Samantha. "Impossible person. But then she seems to feel the same way about me." Again, Lily can hear Samantha groan as she lifts something, hear the metallic scraping, and, finally, the sound of the trunk clicking shut. "You can turn around."

Lily turns to see wiping her hands on a red bandana. "So, are they there?"

"They're here," says Samantha. She pats the roof, as if the car were an obedient animal who had guarded the photos. "What do we do now?"

UPSTAIRS IN SAMANTHA'S APARTMENT, LILY LEANS back in a leather armchair and puts her feet up on the hassock. She can hear Samantha in the kitchen—the rattle of ice, the click and slam of the refrigerator door, the whoosh of running water. Lily stares at the pointed toes of her boots and the handworked stitching on the leather. She's had them resoled twice over the last ten years. Her father mailed them to her for Christmas, since she couldn't get back to Texas for the holidays back then, when she was working in a parish. She remembers opening the box and crying. They smelled like home, like him and her childhood and the ranch.

She's changed a lot, she thinks—not just the move from Texas and her slow, grudging transformation into a New Englander, but also her ideas of who she is and what she wants and what she believes is possible. Back then, as a young priest, she believed the church should and could and would, eventually, clothe the poor, feed the hungry, house the homeless, care for the orphans and widows. Not anymore. Her work at the Women's Center grows out of her need for change, and her work in parishes grows out of her need for faith—but she has long since given up on bringing the two together in one place.

Or she had given up, until she saw the photographs of the scroll. Staring at her boots, considering her past, she admits to herself that the words she's read with Samantha have made her feel something she hasn't felt in a while—hope and restlessness, as if the power to change the world were harnessed in those paragraphs.

Samantha appears with a tray and the pitcher and martini glasses Lily remembers from their first visit. She sets it all down on the glass coffee table, and Lily sees there's a plate of cheese—square, with a white rind—and crackers. Something about the whole presentation feels out of place. They're not exactly celebrating anything. But Samantha seems almost happy as she pours the drinks and sets the 'cheese plate out on the table.

Lily doesn't drink martinis. I don't drink martinis, she says to herself as she watches the clear, thick liquid coat the sides of the glass. But she doesn't say it out loud. Instead she says, "I need to call Tom."

"To let him know where you are?"

"Yes," says Lily. "And—I told him the story, about the manuscript. He found me with the photographs. I had to tell him the truth. Also—" She hadn't planned to mention Marty, but given how things are going, maybe it would be best.

"Also?" asks Samantha.

"Tom and I hired someone to help us find out what's happening."

Samantha sets down the pitcher and stares at Lily. "What do you mean?" she asks. "Who?"

"A woman, a friend of his. She used to be a policeman, but she quit the force and has her own detective agency now. It's not like she—or Tom—is interested in the manuscript. They couldn't care less."

Samantha sits down on the matching leather sofa, facing

Lily. She doesn't look happy anymore. Her small body sinks into the cushions, as if she has shrunk from the weight of the news The glasses stand untouched on the tray.

"It's really okay," says Lily. "Tom was worried about my—our safety. He thought if this woman, Marty, could determine whether or not I was being followed, then we'd know more about what we're dealing with. I'm sorry I didn't tell you sooner. This just happened over the weekend."

Samantha doesn't speak. She is looking down at her hands, resting in her lap. Finally she says, "I understand. And I don't think it's such a bad idea. But Francine feels very strongly—"

"I know," says Lily. "I heard her. And I understand not wanting to put anyone else at risk. But this woman does this work for a living. She's used to being at risk. And it's not as if her knowing, or Tom's knowing, jeopardizes the safety of the photographs. They don't know any Biblical historians."

"Francine won't like it," says Samantha.

"Francine was attacked in the library today. It seems like she's going to be fine, and that's great. But it could have been worse. You asked me to help you figure this out, but I don't have all the skills we need. I don't carry a gun, I don't have time to keep an eye on you and Francine, and, besides, it looks as if I'm being followed, too." Lily takes a breath. "Besides, there's too much here that doesn't make sense. Why would anyone want these photographs so much? I could understand if we had the real thing, the manuscript itself. But it doesn't seem to me the photos are of much use. And why is Francine lying?"

"We don't know that she is," says Samantha.

"You may not," says Lily. "But I feel pretty sure."

Samantha looks at Lily. "I'm not certain what to do at this point."

"What do you mean?"

"I'm just— Having other people know, that alters the situation. I should tell Francine. And I have to get used to this myself, first." Samantha shakes herself, almost imperceptibly, as if to get rid of a thought. "I should be grateful. I suspect we're all safer now that there are professionals protecting us."

Lily feels mocked, but she's not sure if it's real or if she's imagining it. "I still need to call Tom."

"Yes," says Samantha. "Use the phone in the kitchen, if you wish. Perhaps—it would be best if we all met together, you and Tom and his friend, the detective. Perhaps it would be best if we shared a strategy."

"That's fine," says Lily. "But I don't think she'll come. She's pretty wary about showing up around my apartment, and my guess is she'll feel the same way about showing up around your apartment. I'll see what Tom thinks. Maybe he can talk to her, and then meet us here."

"Yes," says Samantha. "Excellent plan."

Lily stands and walks into the kitchen. The phone is on the wall, next to the door leading into the dining room and living room. As she dials, she glances at Samantha on the couch. Lily watches as she raises a martini glass to her lips. I don't drink martinis, Lily says to herself.

24

THE MARTINI KNOCKS HER OUT—NOT LITERALLY, BUT almost. She hasn't eaten since breakfast, and something about the strain of the day, of the last few days, has left her hollow. It's like drinking gin and vermouth first thing in the morning. She can't finish it. She gets a little more than halfway through, excuses herself, goes into the bathroom, flips on the light, and can't, for a moment, figure out who that woman is in the mirror, with her heartshape face and sad, unfocused gaze.

It's a small, old-fashioned room, with a pedestal sink, a large tub, and black and white tiles on the floor. Lily runs cold water over her hands and wrists, then washes her face and dries it with a small white guest towel. She looks in the medicine cabinet and finds some Listerine, which she uses, and then finds a bottle of Advil, which is, for whatever reason, comforting. She takes two. She isn't sure exactly what she thinks they'll do, but she has a vague idea that she'll have a headache later, and it would be better to prevent it.

Finally, she turns out the light and lies down on the floor. She has to lie with her head in the corner, between the wall and the tub, her feet in the opposite corner, next to the door, and her knees bent. She imagines herself getting wedged in that position, not able to stand, so that Tom will find her like this when he shows up. At the thought of his face, the disappointment and disgust he'll feel, she's so sorry for herself she wants to cry.

But she doesn't cry. She's not sure how long she's been in there, and she doesn't want Samantha to come look for her. Tom said he wouldn't be able to get there for at least an hour, and that was about a half hour ago, so she has some time to pull herself together. He said he would call Marty.

The tile is hard and cold under her back. The darkness is comforting. Tom had talked to Marty once, though, already. She had called from Tate, after Lily and Samantha left for the hospital. She hadn't been able to follow them, because she didn't have a car, but she wanted Tom to know that Lily had gone somewhere with Samantha. She didn't know where they'd gone or why they'd left, and she was angry at herself for not having stashed her car on the campus just in case. But she did know one thing: Lily was being followed. She said she would give them the details later.

After a few minutes, Lily's not sure exactly how much longer it is, she stands and turns on the light, which seems blinding. She washes her face a second time, dries it, washes her hands, gargles, and looks at herself in the mirror. She's more recognizable. She feels as if she's looking at someone she knows or, at least, someone she's seen before.

• • •

BY THE TIME TOM ARRIVES, LILY HAS HAD TWO CUPS of tea and feels awake, though still disoriented. He's wearing a corduroy sports jacket and his tie with the balloons on it, which is loosened, the top button of his shirt unbuttoned. She's so glad to see him that she stops worrying about what he might notice and hugs him at the door. She can hear Samantha in the kitchen again, probably replenishing the tray of inedible cheese.

"You okay?" he asks.

"Yeah," she says. "It's been a weird day."

"I bet. Is Francine okay?"

"Evidently. The gas didn't hurt her, but they're going to keep her overnight because of the concussion."

"Concussion?"

"She says she fell backward and hit her head. But the woman at the library says that wouldn't have been possible. That there wasn't anything to hit it on."

"The woman at the library—one of the librarians, you mean?"

Lily nods. "The queen of librarians. The person from whom all librarians are cloned. Did you check to see if our photographs are there?"

"I did. And they are." He looks tired and worried.

"I'm sorry I got you into this," says Lily.

Tom smiles and puts his arm around her shoulders. "As far as I can tell, it goes with the territory." As they turn to walk into the living room, the buzzer by the door sounds again.

"Do you want me to get that?" Lily calls out to Samantha.

But Samantha appears, looking anxious, and answers the buzz. "Who's there?" she calls into the intercom.

"Pizza."

"You've got the wrong apartment," says Samantha.

"Is this Henderson? Number 32?"

"Yes."

"It's for you."

"No—" Samantha begins, but Lily interrupts her.

"Wait," she says. She has recognized the Brooklynesque vowels of the delivery person. "Let her in. It's Marty—I think."

Samantha presses the buzzer and opens the door. The three of them stand in the hallway, waiting. They hear footsteps on the stairs, fast and light. A couple of minutes later a delivery boy appears at the end of the hall, a young guy in baggy jeans, a Red Sox sweatshirt, and a backward baseball cap, carrying a large pizza box in one hand, shoulder level, like a pro.

"Henderson?" the kid asks.

Samantha nods.

"Come on in," says Tom. "I left my wallet inside."

"Okay," says the kid, who Lily can see, now, is Marty, without makeup and boots and suede skirt.

INSIDE THE APARTMENT, MARTY HANDS TOM THE pizza box and holds up her hand, to stop anyone from speaking. She looks around the apartment, then walks down the hall, peering into the rooms to the left, across from the kitchen and living room. Finally, she walks into the bedroom. Lily can hear her pull down the blinds and turn on the radio, fiddling with the dial until she finds music—a soft-rock station playing

"Killing Me Softly." She appears at the door and waves them all inside the room.

A small lamp by the bed is on, and the music is loud. Marty takes off the cap and her thick brown hair falls almost to her shoulders. She scratches her head. "I gotta get a haircut. I got too much to fit in there. You must be Samantha." She sticks out her hand.

Samantha shakes hands and asks, "Would you like to join us for pizza?"

"I would, but I better not. The guy out front is gonna wonder what happened to the delivery boy." Samantha starts to say something, but Marty keeps talking. "I'll tell you more about that in a minute. I thought you should have a chance to meet me, though. Here's the deal—"

They're crowded together at the foot of the four-poster bed, Tom with the pizza still in his hands.

Marty looks at Lily. "Like I told Tom earlier, you're being followed." She turns to Samantha. "So are you, I'm pretty sure. They're not professionals. If they were, you wouldn't have seen them."

"They?" asks Samantha. "How many are there?"

"I'm not sure. There's one guy on Lily—stocky, with a mustache, thick eyebrows. And another guy on you—bigger, beefier, no mustache. He's outside in a car—blue Ford Taurus—by that walkway that leads to the garage. Do you keep your car in there?"

Samantha nods.

"Is there any way in, except through the walkway?"

"I suppose I could—I can get to the far end of the building through the basement, then out onto Mass Ave, and up the alley. It's pretty roundabout."

Marty nods. "So see what you want to do. When you go to work, follow your usual routine, take the regular entrance. But if you're going somewhere you want to go alone, try the Mass Ave plan. It might work."

"Should we be afraid of these people?" asks Samantha.

"Well, I don't know them personally," says Marty. "But if anyone was sitting outside my apartment and following me around every day, it would concern me."

"What else should we do?" asks Lily. She likes the idea that there are plans to be made in the middle of the chaos—and that someone else is making them.

Marty shrugs. "You could go to the police. But I don't think these guys have done anything, yet. Is that right?"

"Not exactly," says Tom, and he tells her a short version of the story of Francine and the library.

"Yeah," says Marty. "You could go to them with that. Francine would have to admit she got hit from behind."

"For our purposes," says Samantha, "going to the police is premature."

"Why?" asks Tom.

"Because we would have to go public with the manuscript, and I'm not prepared to do that yet."

"You may not have any choice," says Tom. "If someone else gets hurt—"

"If that happens, we'll deal with it then," says Samantha. "But I'm not—"

"You're protecting the manuscript," says Tom. "I'm protecting the people. I don't give a damn about the manuscript."

"Folks," says Marty, raising one hand, palm out. "I gotta go. Hash this out and let me know what you decide. If you take it to the police, you won't need me."

"We're not going to the police," says Lily. "Not yet. I definitely want you to keep following me. Will you do that?"

"Sure," says Marty. Then she turns to Samantha. "Right now I'm working for Tom and Lily. But if you want to hire me, I can combine the efforts, check out your apartment, keep an eye on the two of you, at least when you're at work. If you want to talk business, Tom has all the details. Call him at work. Use a pay phone." She turns to Tom and asks, "So, you going to pay me for the pizza?"

"Oh, yeah, sorry," he says. He hands the box to Lily and digs his wallet out of his back pocket. "How much?"

"Eighteen bucks."

"Eighteen bucks? Where'd you get it, the Ritz?"

"It's a large vegetarian, with everything. They're expensive. But I figured it would be right for this crowd."

He hands her the money. "Am I supposed to tip you?"

She ignores him and turns to Lily. "Let Tom know if you need me. I'll be checking out your apartment sometime in the next few days. I'll let him know what day I'm going to do it. Meanwhile, I'll be around." Then she walks to the door of the room, waves, and says, "See ya."

Lily hears the front door close. The three of them are still standing in a small circle at the foot of the bed. The pizza smell fills the room, and Lily realizes she's hungry.

25

LILY WAKES UP TUESDAY MORNING EXHAUSTED AND disoriented. The sky is gray and heavy, an unbroken cloud cover as far as she can see. Tom is on his side, his back to her, snoring lightly. She feels hungover, but she can't think why. Then she remembers the martini—the half-martini— and the beer she drank with the pizza. They'd stayed late, talking, trying to persuade Samantha to sleep at Lily's until Francine could move in with her. Not that Lily wanted Samantha to stay with her, but Tom said it was sensible, and she knew he was right. Lily didn't have to worry. Samantha refused to sleep anywhere but her own bed, which was odd, since she knew she was being followed, and knew the people following them were capable of at least low-level violence.

Lily wants to go back to sleep. She tries—closes her eyes, turns on her side, so her back is against Tom's—but it's too late. The wheels have started turning. The only thing to do now is to get up and shower and eat—or lie here and go along for the ride.

Francine lied about what happened in the library, and she also seems truly frightened—much more frightened than Samantha. Is she more frightened than I am, Lily wonders, and then decides, yes, she is.

Tom rolls over and puts his arm around her, and she makes a sound to let him know she's awake. "What's up?" he asks.

"I think that's my line," says Lily.

"Okay," he says. "Ask me."

TWO HOURS LATER, LILY IS STILL IN HER PAJAMAS— plaid pajama bottoms and a green T-shirt with PRO-GOD, PRO-CHOICE printed on the back. Tom left for work an hour ago, after getting her to promise to take a day off and stay home. Two empty mugs, a plate smeared with crumbs and honey—the detritus of breakfast—sit on the table, near her right elbow.

She has read almost the whole paper, working backward from the sports pages, through business, and into metro—this method a holdover from baseball season. On page three of the local news, she sees a small piece in the lower left-hand corner of the right page, with a headline that reads, HARVARD LIBRARY FALSE ALARM. There's a brief outline of the events of the day before, a description of halon gas, a mention of a researcher trapped in the rare manuscript vault, and a quotation from an inspector for the fire department: "It's unclear what caused the mechanism to activate the fire suppression system. It does not appear to be a flaw in the mechanism itself. We are looking into the possibility of human tampering."

She tears out the small rectangle and lays it next to her on the table. Mrs. Fowler on the job, she thinks. Tom might recognize the name of the fire inspector who's quoted—although since the guy's from the Cambridge side of the river, this is less likely. She would like to find out what he learns. But she's not sure if that's possible. It's worth a try.

She calls Tom and finds him at his desk.

"Do you know a—hold on—Sergeant Ray Hillyer? He's an inspector for the fire department, in Cambridge?"

"Should I?"

"Don't all you guys drink together?"

"When would this happen, exactly? In my parallel life?"

"Do you know him?"

"No. Why?"

"Because his name's in the paper as the person investigating the thing at the library."

"Oh," says Tom. "But I still don't know him."

"Do you know someone who might know him?"

"I have no idea. But I bet I know someone who knows someone who knows someone who knows someone who knows someone who knows him. Is that six?"

"That would be true of all of us. I was hoping you might have a more direct connection."

"I might. Give me his name again."

"Ray Hillyer," she says, and then spells it for him.

"I'll find out what I can. I was about to call you. What are you going to do today?"

"Me? I don't know. Why?"

"Marty called. When I told her you weren't going to

work, she said she might watch Samantha's place for a while."

"I thought we weren't supposed to talk about this on the phone."

"Oh, yeah. I forgot. Everyone listening should ignore what I just said."

"Sometimes it's hard to believe you're a member of the police department."

"I think they find it hard to believe sometimes, too. Anyway, if it's okay with you, I'll tell her to go over to Samantha's, if she wants to."

"Sure, that's fine. I don't really need someone to follow me around my apartment. And it's a good excuse to stay put."

"I'll call her and let her know. And I'll see what I can find out about Mr. Hillyer."

"Sergeant Hillyer."

"Right. Love you. See you tonight."

She hangs up and stares into space for a few minutes. It's strange to be home on her own in the middle of the week. She's used to being busy, too busy, and this lull, in the middle of all the chaos of the last couple of weeks, makes her uneasy. Keeping track of Samantha and Francine and the photos and the manuscript, she's lost track of herself. She hasn't said morning or evening prayers in a few days, hasn't been to church since her visit to the cathedral.

She picks up her prayer book from the end table and opens it at the red marker. She knows the words by heart, but it still comforts her to read them. *O Lord, open my lips, and our mouth shall proclaim your praise.* As she reads through the lines, her mind clears, her shoulders relax. It's as if she's moving back into her own skin. But when she reaches the Lord's Prayer, an image of the words, in Hebrew, in the black-and-white photograph, distracts her.

That's what she'll do, she thinks, as soon as she's finished here. She'll go down to Tom's darkroom and get the photos. And she has all day alone to study them.

TOM'S APARTMENT IS SPARE AND CLEAN, AS IF HE HAS just tidied. It's always like this, no dishes in the sink, no socks on the floor, no towel thrown over the desk chair. The walls are white, the wood floors bare, except in the bedroom, where he took pity on the downstairs neighbor and found a thick green carpet at a discount store. The furniture is stuff his mother brought down from the attic—a faded green sofa, a painted rocking chair, a red Formica kitchen table with matching chairs. She's furnished four of her grown children's apartments out of her house. "It's like one of those clown cars," Tom says. "The furniture just keeps coming out the door, and you can't remember where it was in the first place."

What's surprising, thinks Lily, given the minimalist hodgepodge approach to decorating, is how much Tom's apartment feels like a home. It's the tidiness of someone who cares what his world looks like. The hall between the living room and the bedroom is lined with bookshelves, the books arranged by genre and alphabetized.

At the end of the hall on the right is the darkroom. Tom remodeled the walk-in closet in the bedroom, putting in shelves and cutting a skinny door between the closet and the bathroom. He keeps his files and supplies in the closet, and works in the two rooms, using a blackout shade on the bathroom window.

Lily goes to the closet and turns on the overhead light,

which glows red. She opens the file drawer marked O–Z and finds the divider marked P. Tom stores negatives and contact sheets together, each set titled, usually by place and date, and filed alphabetically. About a quarter of the way into the P section, she finds an envelope marked PHO-TOGRAPHS. As she pulls it out, she has a slight lurching sensation in her stomach; the envelope feels too light, as if it's empty. But she peers in and sees the three photographs, with the sheets of translated text and notes. She turns off the light, goes down the hall, and leaves, locking the door behind her.

As she's walking up the stairs to her floor, she hears someone above. Soon she can see the legs of a man in the blue uniform of the maintenance company hired to clean the building. He's polishing the metal bannister. She's about to say hi, but then realizes it's not the usual guy, who is middle-aged, Latino, and very friendly. This man is young and slender, with a strange scar down the right side of his face. The scar tissue stretches his right eye, so it seems to slant down at the corner. Lily tries to nod, but he never looks at her.

26

WHEN SHE GETS INSIDE HER OWN APARTMENT, SHE double-bolts the front door. She places the envelope on the dining room table and clears the dishes, setting them all in the sink. Her apartment seldom looks as if she has just tidied—even after she has just tidied. She puts water on for a fresh cup of tea, then stands at the table, where she takes the photos and translations from the envelope and lays the photographs out, in order. She gets a couple of copies of the Bible—the Revised Standard Version and the King James—and her copy of the Gospel Parallels, still on the night table in the bedroom, from the time, ten days ago, when she answered Tom's questions about Q. That day seems as if it were years ago.

The sky outside her windows is even darker than it was at dawn. She can feel the cold under her skin—it's going to snow before the day is out. She switches on the overhead light in the kitchen, then turns on a standing lamp by the couch and moves it nearer to the table. When the kettle boils, she makes tea and takes it with her to the table, but she doesn't set it down. Instead, she pulls the end table closer and puts the cup of tea there.

It's a ceremony, she thinks, getting ready to read these things—the lights, the tea, the rearranging the furniture. It's as if she's preparing a space for them. Is that because they're sacred or because she wants them to be? As she thinks this, she realizes that's the question: Are my desires for the manuscript clouding my judgment of what's real and what isn't? But it's a pointless question to ask herself, because if her judgment is clouded, how can she judge?

She begins to read the Hebrew words in the first photograph and the gate of the text swings open again, letting her enter. She can decipher the writing on her own, without using the translation. Of course, it's a familiar text, but it's more than that. She is not so much reading and translating each word as gathering the meaning of phrases—almost as if the text is speaking to her. *Love your enemies and do good to those who hate you.* She thinks, how can I explain this, and simultaneously thinks, don't try to explain this. The texts are what they are, they are letting themselves be read, and she knows in her bones they're sacred, the same way she knows it's going to snow.

After a few minutes, she realizes her hands are cold. She goes to get a sweatshirt and checks the radiator in the bedroom—the valve is open but there's no heat in the pipes. The radiator under the window in the living room is cold, too, but the valve is wide open. By the time she gets back to the manuscript, the gate has closed. It will open again, she tells herself. But for now, she makes do with matching the translation to the text provided by Francine's notes.

Bless those who curse you and do good to those who mistreat you. When someone hits you on the right cheek, offer them the other cheek, too.

Even when she uses the translation, the words still feel alive and real. They're three-dimensional. They require concentration. They are not as easy to understand as she's always thought they were.

And when someone takes your cloak from you, let them have your shirt. Give to anyone who asks. And if someone robs you, don't ask for your property to be returned.

Don't ask for your property to be returned? Then what are you supposed to do? Maybe the person who stole it needs it more than you do, she thinks. But what about—self-respect? What about justice? She can't read through these lines anymore without wondering, what did he mean? Because he meant them.

When she finally gets to the end of the page—*Don't judge and you won't be judged*—she stops. This is the one that pains her.

Lily feels as if her mind's being pulled in two directions—toward the text, away from the text. She wants to know what it says, but she doesn't want to hear the words. They're too hard. And her hands are still freezing. Her face and head are cold, too. She walks to the radiator. It never came on. She says, "Shit," and walks to the phone to call Ed Lanazetti, the superintendent, but she gets an answering machine. She leaves a message and makes herself another cup of tea, but even with the hot mug in her hands, she's too cold to concentrate. Finally, she gives up, grabs her keys off the kitchen counter, bolts the door behind her, and goes to find Ed.

No one is on the stairs. The halls are silent. She goes to the Lanazettis' apartment on the first floor and knocks. Ed's mother answers. When she sees Lily, she smiles and nods, then lets out a stream of Italian.

Lily nods and says, "Ed?"

An elaborate shrug, another four or five sentences, then she points to the basement, with a gesture that indicates he could be down there or in Calabria, who knows?

Lily goes through the metal door to the basement stairs, down a long concrete hallway lined with storage bins, and through a second door at the end of the hall. The basement is cavernous. Ed's office is to the left, at the end of another set of storage bins. To the right is a sunken area, which holds the boilers and the vast heating system. She hears a noise from that direction and walks closer, almost running into Ed.

"Sorry," she says.

"I know," he says. "The heat." He's a big man, blond with a blond beard and mustache. At the moment, his face is red and he's carrying a toolbox the size of a small refrigerator.

"Do you know what's wrong?" she asks.

"Yeah. The thermostat on the boiler's busted. But I can't figure out how it happened. It looks like it's broken, like somebody broke it. Beats me." He keeps walking toward his office, and Lily falls into step beside him.

"Can you fix it?" asks Lily.

"No way. I gotta call the oil company."

"Any idea how long that will take?"

"Nope. You might want to find someplace warm to go."

"Great," says Lily. Then she thinks of the man on the stairs, the one in the uniform of the maintenance company. "Where are the regular maintenance guys—Roger and Bruno?"

"I don't know. Vacation. Maybe they went back to Brazil. Why?"

"Nothing. I just didn't recognize the guy cleaning the stairs."

"The one with the scar. Yeah, I don't know him either."

"Did he come with someone else?"

"Yeah. Some guy."

"But you recognized the other one?"

"I think so," he says. "Why?"

"Nothing. I just wondered." Suddenly she wants to turn around and run back upstairs to her apartment. "Okay. So, do you mind if I check in with you later?"

"You can check in," he says. "But the heat'll either be on or not. You won't have to call me to find out."

"Good point," she says. "But maybe you'll have some information about how long it's going to be.'"

"Let's hope," he says.

They've reached his office. He sets down the toolbox and pulls out a set of keys that makes Tom's collection look meager. He opens the door and she stands outside as he picks up the toolbox and carries it in and sets it on a shelf by his desk. Above the desk, the wall is covered in pairs of keys hanging from small metal hooks.

"Thanks," she says and turns to go.

"By the way," he says. "Thanks for being so decent to my mother since she got here. She's a little confused. She was almost ninety when we brought her over. It's like she just didn't want to bother with making the adjustment. Sometimes I think she's still over there. Most people walk away, but you listen to her when she talks, and that makes her feel good, you know? I appreciate it, I really do. She's a good lady, she's been through a lot. She deserves respect."

Lily tells him it's no problem. She's happy to listen to his mother. They're taking her home to see everyone, he says, during the holidays. He hopes it doesn't get her more turned-around than ever.

The small worry that began when Lily saw the stranger in the stairwell becomes larger as they talk. She needs to get back. She thanks him and climbs the stairs, two at a time, to her apartment. She begins to unlock the door and discovers the deadbolt is off. She tells herself she must have forgotten to turn it when she left. But she knows that's not right.

She opens the front door. Outside the windows, snow is falling fast and hard. The dining room table is empty.

27

Lily sits at the table, in front of the space
where the photos used to be. The snow's stopped. She
doesn't know how long she's been like that, sitting at the
table, staring at nothing.

Her first impulse was to run back downstairs and tell Ed
what had happened. But what good would it do? He would
call the maintenance company and the guy would be gone.
And they'll never hear from him again, she thinks. That's
how this works.

Then begins the how-could-I-be-so-stupid parade of
thoughts. She never thought they could get into her apartment. It didn't occur to her. It should have occurred to her.
After what happened to Francine, they should all be on
their guard. She knows that. She knew that.

When the phone rings, she doesn't move. She hears her

own voice on the answering machine, then Samantha's voice.

"Hello, it's Samantha. Please call me at home when you return. There's been—we would like to speak with you as soon as possible." She leaves her number and hangs up.

Lily's mind tells her to get up and call back, but she doesn't do it. Too much is happening. She's too cold to think. And the empty space on the table feels like a hole that's growing wider and deeper and drawing them all into it.

FINALLY SHE PHONES TOM. HE'S NOT AT HIS DESK, SO she leaves a message. Then she calls the number Samantha left on the machine.

When she finds out who it is, Samantha says, "We shouldn't talk on the phone."

"I know," says Lily.

"Can you come over here right away?"

"Is it an emergency?" asks Lily.

"Yes," says Samantha. Then she asks, "Are you all right? Your voice sounds odd."

"Not exactly."

"Has something else happened?" asks Samantha.

People are not very good at this, thinks Lily. "Why don't I explain when I see you?"

She writes Tom a note, grabs her parka, and leaves, double bolting the door again. They must have gotten a key from Ed's office, she thinks. She decides to walk part of the way, to clear her head and figure out what just happened. The air is raw, and new dark clouds are moving in from the northwest. More snow. Snow makes her think about the photographs.

They got the key from Ed's office but they hadn't expected me to be home. So they broke the thermostat, assuming I would leave eventually if it got too cold. But they got lucky. I went down to find Ed, they walk in, and there are the photographs, in plain sight on the dining room table. Suddenly she has tears in her eyes. How could I be so stupid? she thinks for the fourteenth time. Now I don't have them.

These thoughts repeat in no particular pattern. She crosses the pedestrian bridge over Storrow Drive and takes the stairs down to the esplanade. The river is gunmetal—shiny and cold and caught by reflected light from the brighter patches of sky. Who are they? She's assuming it's a group—a group of men who care deeply about the manuscript. Who care deeply about no one knowing the manuscript exists. Why else would they go through all this to get the photographs back? They don't want any evidence of the manuscript to exist.

The wind has picked up. Lily takes a red wool watch cap out of her pocket and puts it on. The gloves aren't with it, so she draws her hands up into the sleeves of her beat-up black parka. The walk along the river is deserted. No one else is out in this weather.

In her dreams last night, the blonde woman sat at a dinner table outside in a fancy restaurant. Her face began to change, and each time Lily—or the Lily in the dream—noticed it, the woman seemed older and sicker. Finally, the man next to the blonde woman stood and took her out of the restaurant, and Lily—the Lily in the dream, who was young, a child—was suddenly alone. The restaurant was gone and the people were gone and she was standing by herself on a sidewalk, on the curb, of an empty street. Then the bearded man—the one from earlier dreams—

was with her and they crossed the street and stood by a river. The river looked a lot like the Charles at this moment—dark and shimmering with small points of light—then the light spread and took over the dream. Then he said a few things to her that she can't remember.

And now she knows the blonde woman is her mother. She knows that one of the things he said was, "Don't judge and you won't be judged." And then, something like, "You've got to let go to go on." Jesus as L. Ron Hubbard, she thinks.

BY THE TIME SHE DECIDES TO STOP WALKING AND TAKE public transportation, she's almost to Central Square. She walks down River Street and boards the Red Line to Porter Square, where she takes the long, eerie escalator up to ground level. The snow has started again, mixed with small hard pellets of ice.

She crosses Mass Ave and runs the rest of the way to the door of Samantha's building. But when she buzzes the apartment, no one answers. She presses the button two more times, then stands back and peers through the glass door into the small lobby. No one is around, and they probably wouldn't let her in even if they were. The more expensive the units, the more paranoid the tenants.

Lily remembers that Samantha hid her photographs in the trunk of her car, so she decides to check the garage. She runs out into the courtyard and around the corner, down the small alley lined with terra-cotta pots. Through the window at the top of the garage door, she sees Francine staring into the alley.

Francine opens the door and lets her in. They walk together toward Samantha and the car, which is draped with a fitted gray cover. When Samantha sees Lily, she lifts the cover. The entire body is streaked in blistered red paint. The metal shows through in swathes. Lily opens the passenger door and sees that the black leather seat has been slashed from the headrest to the bottom edge. White stuffing flows out, as if it had been pulled from the inside. The car looks like an animal, violently gutted and skinned.

"My God," says Lily. "When did this happen?"

"Sometime last night," says Francine.

"What about the engine?"

Francine shakes her head. "Looks like maple syrup, or honey, or something in the gas tank. The engine was warm, so they must have started it and let it run."

Lily walks close to Francine and asks, "What about the photographs?"

"The trunk was emptied completely. The spare, the jack, even the lining."

"So they're gone?"

"They're gone."

28

MARTY AND TOM ARRIVE AT SAMANTHA'S THAT evening about five minutes apart. This time, Tom has the pizza and Marty is carrying a paper bag that clanks when she sets it down. She wears navy overalls, like the ones worn by the maintenance crew of Lily's apartment building, a parka and a watch cap. She looks like a miniature janitor.

Lily introduces Marty to Francine, who seems more diffident than ever. She turns away immediately and leads them into the kitchen. After they put the bags in the kitchen, Marty takes off her cap and turns on the kitchen radio, tuning in to an oldies station. Then she pulls something that resembles a small metal detector from the pocket of her parka and whispers to Samantha, "Do you mind?"

"Mind what?" asks Samantha, her voice low.

"I want to check the place before we talk—just to be sure."

"Check it for—what, exactly?"

"Listening devices, bugs. Is that all right?"

"Of course," says Samantha. "But is the music absolutely necessary?"

"Just until I'm done."

Marty turns on the device—a small control box with a wand attached—and holds it near the light fixture, runs it along the base of the cabinets and under the small table, takes it into the pantry. When she comes out, she says, "This room looks okay. I'll just check out the rest, and then we can decide where to be." She heads for the living room, turning off the radio as she walks past.

"You want to eat?" Tom asks.

"Sure," says Lily. "Anyone else?" She turns to Francine and Samantha.

Samantha's face is blank, the way it's been since they came upstairs from the garage.

"What kind of pizza is it?" asks Francine.

"I think she got the same thing she got last time—the vegetarian deal. But you weren't here, were you?" says Tom. He turns to Samantha. "How about some plates and glasses? We'll think better if we've eaten."

Francine begins to get out plates and napkins and set them on the counter, next to the pizza.

"What are we going to think about?" Lily asks him.

"Marty and I want to know what happened today—to you and Samantha. And we need to hear Francine's version of the library thing, too. We'll see what all those pieces look like next to each other. Then, we'll start guessing."

"Good plan," says Lily. "I especially like the guessing part."

"I could call it something bigger—you know, strategizing—but we'd still be guessing."

"How can we know everyone's telling the truth?" asks Samantha.

"The truth about what?" asks Tom.

"About what's happened to them."

There's a brief, uncomfortable silence.

"We can't," says Tom. "Do you think somebody won't be telling the truth?"

Samantha doesn't answer. After another awkward moment, Francine asks what people want to drink, and then Marty returns. In her hand she has two small metal circles and a tiny black plastic box. She dumps them on the kitchen counter. "Two in the phones," she says. "One under the sidetable in the living room."

Lily picks up one of the metal circles. "This goes in the phone?"

"Yeah," says Marty. "Into the handset."

"So they know everything," says Samantha.

"They know a lot," says Marty. "Maybe not everything. I've gone over the living room a few times. Let's go in there, turn on music—in case I've missed something—and figure this out."

Samantha seems to have rallied. She goes to a large cabinet in the dining room and opens the doors, revealing an elegant-looking sound system—slender, weightless components made of silvery metal and black plastic. In a minute or two, Lily hears the opening strains of *La Traviata*. She knows it's going to drive her crazy eventually, but she doesn't say anything now. She's thinking about the paper bag that clanked when Marty set it down.

. . .

FRANCINE AND LILY AND MARTY ARE ON THE LIVING room couch, Tom in the matching armchair, Samantha in an antique leather and wood chair that looks as if it would break if anyone else sat in it. The pizza's gone and the music's been changed to the Mozart horn concertos. Lily would be able to concentrate if it weren't for the slender crystal wineglass, filled with white wine, in Samantha's right hand. The bag was full of Perrier and soda—Pepsi and ginger ale—so Lily decided to drink sparkling water with her pizza, not a great combination. The glass sits on the table in front of her, a crystal tumbler with ice cubes and water, the ice half-melted.

They decided to take turns. Marty's going first. She's explaining what she's found out so far.

"Lily, your place was bugged, too. I checked it out on the way over here. I think I got everything, but it's hard to know. And these guys might come back and replace them. Everyone is being tailed. Well, I'm not sure about Tom. Can you tell?"

"I haven't seen anyone," he says.

"You three," Marty says, indicating Lily, Francine, and Samantha, "each have a specific person on you. I described the guy outside here," she indicates the street along Samantha's building. "The big one with the beard. Your two look a lot alike, except one's got a mustache."

"Have you seen anyone with a scar down this side of his face?" asks Lily. "So his eye's pulled down toward the cheek."

"No," says Marty. "Where did you see him?"

"In my building today. He was working with the maintenance crew, but he's never been there before, and the super doesn't know him."

"Oh," says Marty. She sits quietly for a moment, as if

rearranging information in her mental records. "Okay. He's never been with any of the other guys. The three I followed are living at the Days Inn over in Brighton, across from the river, next to the IHOP. I didn't see them with anyone else. But if he's part of them, that makes at least four."

"So they're not local, right? If they're living at the Days Inn?" asks Lily.

"Maybe. Maybe not," says Marty. "Days Inn rents by the month, too. They could be living there full-time. Hard to say. I'm pretty sure they don't speak English when they're together, but I'm guessing from reading their lips. And then there's the question of numbers."

"Yeah," says Tom. "I've been wondering about that."

"What do you mean?" asks Lily.

"They've got resources," he says. "They can bug places and tail people and rent rooms. But so far we've only seen three of them, maybe four. Generally, you're going to put a decent tail on someone, you use two people. It's like they don't have anyone to spare."

"Which leads you to believe what, exactly?" asks Samantha.

"What Lily said—that they're maybe not local. This is a delegation. They've got an assignment. They finish it. Then go back to the mother ship."

"Here's what I'm wondering," says Lily. "We don't actually know that all this stuff has been the work of one group, right?"

"What do you mean?" asks Tom

"Aren't we getting into the general?" asks Francine.

"Yeah, but wait a minute," says Marty, and turns to Lily. "I'm pretty much done with what I know. Tell us what happened today. Then explain your point."

Lily tells the story of the heat going off and the photographs disappearing. At the end of which she says, "My sense is that they believe in efficiency, and as little uproar as possible. Nothing was broken. They didn't trash my place to make it look like something else. They just took the photographs and left."

"They didn't have much time," says Tom.

"True. But look at this thing with Samantha's car. They were in a public place, or semi-public. Anyone could have walked in. Why risk getting caught by spending an extra half-hour destroying the paint job? It feels different to me, more personal."

"What do you think?" Marty asks Samantha.

"I have no idea," says Samantha.

"Fill us in on what happened."

"I didn't sleep well last night. I was awake early— around five. I thought I would drive up to the beach to see the sunrise. I got dressed, went downstairs, and found the car destroyed."

"Did you hear anything unusual last night, anything in the building, in the hallway? Did anyone ring your buzzer?"

"No," says Samantha. "After you left, I read and went to sleep. Or tried to go to sleep."

"So, you woke up this morning and found the car. Then what?" asks Marty.

"I put the cover over it, so no one else would see it. I knew my paranoid upstairs neighbor would call the police if she saw what had happened to the car, and I wanted to avoid that. I came back to the apartment. I'm not sure what I did then." There's a pause, as if Samantha is leaving something out. "After a while, when I calmed down, I called the hospital. Francine said I could pick her up at noon. I told her about the car, and she suggested I check on the last set of photos—" Samantha's eyes get big. She and Francine exchange a look.

"So they know," says Francine.

"Yes," says Samantha. "They know. But we didn't say which bank. And I was extremely careful when I left. I went out through the basement, then crossed the street into that little mall and went out the back door, through their parking lot, and into the T-stop from there. I don't think anyone followed me. I did my best."

"Sounds like you did a great job," says Marty. "Which bank do you use?"

"First National, in the Square."

"And were the photos still there?"

"Yes," says Samantha. "It's quite secure. Francine and I opened the box together. You have to have two forms of ID and the key in order to get access."

"So, wait," says Marty. "Where were your set of photos, not the ones in the safe-deposit box, the other ones?"

"Under the lining in the trunk of the car. There's an open space around the spare, so I slipped them in from there."

"Was the lining ripped out?" asks Tom.

Samantha nods. "The trunk was emptied. The contents were piled neatly beside the car. The spare was slashed, along with all the other tires. I replaced the contents of the trunk before I covered the car."

"Can we go down and look before we leave?" asks Marty.

"Yes," says Samantha. "But we'll have to be careful. I don't want any of my neighbors to see it."

Marty looks across at Tom, then at Lily. "I think you're right," she says. "Your thing and Samantha's thing—they don't sound the same."

"What about Francine?" asks Samantha. "Where does her encounter fit?"

They all look at Francine, who blushes. Then she glances at Marty and shrugs. "I don't know," she says. "They tampered with a sophisticated alarm system, so I suppose it falls into the nonviolent category."

"I haven't heard the story," says Marty. "Tell me what happened."

"I was working at the light table, studying a set of transparencies—"

"And the light table is, where, against a wall?" asks Marty.

"Yes," says Francine. "I was standing, facing a wall."

"Did you hear anything?"

"I thought I heard someone come in, but I didn't turn around. There are stacks, for the manuscripts, so a lot of people are in and out. Then the alarm went off, I grabbed for my stuff, and I must have slipped. I woke up with a blonde woman kneeling next to me. The EMTs came. I went to the hospital. That's it."

"I don't get it," says Marty. "You think you hit your head, is that what you mean?"

"Yes," says Francine.

"And when the alarm goes off, and the gas goes on, doesn't the door to this room slam shut, to keep the gas in there?"

"Probably," says Francine. "I didn't see it happen."

"Because what confuses me is this—assuming the guy wanted the pictures, he would have had to grab them before the alarm went off, right? Or else he couldn't have gotten out."

Francine shrugs. "I was confused. And I may not remember everything perfectly, because of the concussion."

"So maybe someone hit you from behind before the alarm went off?" asks Lily.

"No," says Francine. "Or, I don't think so."

"Okay," says Marty. "We'll leave that for now."

Lily glances at Samantha and the older woman's face startles her; she's staring at Francine with a look of stone-cut rage.

Evidently, Marty sees it, too, because she says, "What?" to Samantha. Then again, "What?"

Samantha turns to Marty and her face relaxes into mild surprise. "I beg your pardon?" she says. She finishes the wine and sets the glass on the table.

Marty takes a long swig of Coke and leans back on the sofa.

"I agree with Lily. I got a sense that these guys—the ones I'm following, anyway—don't want trouble. They want the copies of the photographs. But they're not out to, like, punish anyone for having them." Samantha starts to speak, and Marty nods. "I know. In your case, that's different. In your case, they even risked letting other people see the car and report it. I still don't get that."

"So what do you think?" asks Tom.

"They're also organized and determined. These tails are amazing—they'll sit out there for eight, ten hours, on their own. They don't read the paper, they don't eat doughnuts. I don't know what they do to stay awake. I sure as hell can't keep up with them."

"And?" says Tom.

"They're willing to do whatever they have to do in order to get all the photos back. In other words, here's what I think: They'll do as little as they can for as long as they can, and then, they'll do whatever it takes. And it looks like they're getting impatient. Is that clear?"

Tom nods his head, then says to Marty, "You mean you think this stuff will escalate, eventually, if they can't get what they want through the cunning methods."

"Yeah," says Marty. "Exactly."

"Let's assume," says Samantha, "that they know there's one more set of photographs, and from listening to our conversations, they have a sense that no one else has seen them. That we've kept them to ourselves. What would be next?"

Marty shrugs. "They'd want to get hold of that last set."

"Then the question would be," says Lily, "can they find a way to get to the last set of photos without using one of us?"

"That would be the question," says Marty. "To my mind."

"What do you mean, 'using one of us'?" asks Francine.

"Let's say, finding a way to make you give them the pictures," says Marty.

"Oh," says Francine.

"Yeah," says Marty. "Oh."

29

"I APOLOGIZE FOR THIS," SAYS MARTY. "BUT IN ORDER
to figure out what we're dealing with here, I need a better
sense of what this manuscript is. Lily explained it when we
first talked, but I have a feeling I'm missing something.
Talk to me about it some more."

Lily suspects Marty is changing the subject on purpose.
She also suspects Marty will be asking Francine more
questions later on.

Samantha tells the story of Matthew and Luke and
Mark and Q. "The thought of Q existing at all is almost beyond imagining, but the concept of it's existing in Hebrew,
in an Aramaic script, a script whose idiosyncrasies indicate
a date during the Herodian period, which would be the
time of Jesus' life—you see what this could mean."

Marty half nods, half shrugs, and looks at Tom. "Do
you see what this could mean?"

"Big bucks," says Tom.

"Don't worry about them," Lily says to Samantha. "They're both Catholic. To say the Bible's not a big deal is a mild understatement."

"Go on," says Marty to Samantha.

"When we had just gotten used to this astonishing possibility, the third mailing arrived. It contained material unlike any I have ever seen—at least in what would be considered standard sources. In the familiar story of Jesus healing, or exorcising, the man possessed by demons, there were two significant deviations in the text. First, the text shows Jesus touching the man in the middle of the forehead. Second, Jesus uses the term 'the touch of uncreated light.'"

"So—what *does* it mean?" asks Tom.

"I don't want to say too much about what these lines could indicate—largely because I don't know. But some of the questions we might ask ourselves would be, starting at the beginning: If we have come to think of this manuscript as authentic—a manuscript written during the Herodian period, on parchment scrolls, in Hebrew, recording Jesus' words—is this the document of an early sect, for whom healing and mystical powers were central to their concept of Jesus, perhaps an aberration of an original text? Is the Q text itself the product of a sect, and did later versions expunge material which didn't agree with orthodox teachings? Or, if this is the long-lost Q text, might it have been recorded by someone close to him, even by one of the apostles, and thus be an accurate portrayal of Jesus and his words?"

Lily looks at Tom's face and says, "Here's the deal. We've never seen these lines before, so it's hard to know where they come from. But it might mean—just maybe—

that these are recorded sayings and actions of Jesus that are completely unknown—at least in the Western church."

"You're saying this might be new information about Jesus, after all this time?" asks Marty.

"Possibly," says Lily.

The light has settled outside the windows, gathering into a corner in the west, just to the right of the building across the street. Lily has an impulse to turn on all the lamps, to clear the room of something that's gathering.

"I get it," says Marty. "Do you?" she asks Tom.

"I'm beginning to," he says. "I'm not sure I understood it before. If this manuscript is the real thing, whoever owns it will go to a lot of trouble to keep it."

"And that raises some interesting questions," says Lily.

"What do you mean?" asks Tom.

"Okay," she says. "What are the possibilities here? One, someone has found the manuscript and is letting a few select people know it exists by sending them photos."

"So who are the Mediterranean goons?" Marty asks.

"Maybe one of those select people wants the manuscript—or has already gotten it—and doesn't want anyone else to go after it, or even to be able to prove it exists."

"Or maybe the person who sent the photos has changed his mind, has decided to keep it," says Tom.

"Yeah," says Lily. "Maybe. Or maybe the manuscript has been around for centuries, kept a secret, and someone has found out and is spreading the word."

"But why? What's in it for the guy spreading the word?" asks Marty.

"The truth?" asks Francine. "Maybe it's just someone interested in the truth."

"Okay," says Marty, but she sounds skeptical.

"I have a different take altogether," says Samantha.

"Someone is working on this manuscript, waiting to publish his findings until he's absolutely certain they are accurate. This person would not want anyone to have an inkling of the existence of this text beforehand."

"So who's blowing his cover?" asks Marty.

"Perhaps a competitor. An enemy. A saboteur in his camp."

"You guys take this research stuff seriously, huh?" asks Marty.

"You have no idea," says Samantha.

After a few seconds of silence, Tom says, "So much for sticking with the specific facts."

"Well, yeah," says Lily. "Think about it. You put a bunch of seminary graduates together in one room and tell them to stick to the facts."

"It's like herding cats," says Tom.

"Okay," says Marty. The force of her voice breaks the spell. "What's left? Who else has stories to tell?"

Again, Lily appreciates Marty's conducting. She's given them a break from the hard stuff, and now it's time to shift back to basics. She looks at the faces around the room. Everyone seems more relaxed, except for Francine, whose face is pale in the dim light. The skin around her eyes looks almost bruised. "Are you feeling okay?" Lily asks her.

Francine smiles at her. "I'm exhausted. And my head hurts."

"Do you want to call it a night?" asks Lily. "We can do the rest of this tomorrow."

"That might be better," says Francine.

There's a pause, in which no one moves for a moment. "How about this?" Marty says, finally. "What if we just wrap up now, without a break? It shouldn't take long. I'd like to have all the info I can get when I leave here."

"All I've got it is the fire inspector's report," says Tom. "Which doesn't tell us much."

"How did you find it?" asks Lily.

"Called in a few favors. You want to hear it now, or should we wait until tomorrow, or what?"

"Why don't you summarize it for us?" asks Samantha. "Then we'll be done. Will that be all right for you?" she asks Francine.

Francine nods, but Lily's not thrilled about the young woman's color.

"So, here goes," says Tom. "Basically, the report says the wiring might have been tampered with. But it's an old system, and it also might have gone off by mistake—although he doesn't seem to be able to explain how that would have happened."

"Does he explain how someone could have set it off?" asks Lily.

"More or less. The way the system works, you've got two separate alarm devices, and one works as an override on the other. So you'd have to disengage the override system. Also, just to make it more complicated, the halon gas is expensive, so each location has its own separate panel. You'd need to know which panels were linked to which rooms."

"Once you disengage the right override, though, then the thing works like a regular system. It reacts to anything that vaguely resembles a fire. So you hold a match to a heat detector and the alarm goes off."

"High tech," says Lily. "Can't they look at the wiring and see if it's been changed around?"

"Not necessarily. I don't understand everything I read, but it looks like it wouldn't be that hard to disengage the override for thirty seconds and then reconnect it."

"That would need three people, then," says Marty.

"Someone to fool with the system, someone to light the match—or whatever they did—and someone to steal the photos."

"Right," says Tom. "And I don't think the inspector buys that. As far as he's concerned, there's no reason for anyone to go to all that trouble."

"Understandably," says Samantha.

"So," says Lily. "They're not going to investigate."

"Doesn't look like it. Unless the library insists."

Lily glances at Samantha, and they exchange a look in honor of Mrs. Fowler, the librarian.

"I suspect the library will insist and will eventually get its way," says Samantha. "But the whole process buys us time before the authorities become involved."

Marty looks at Francine. "You feel well enough to go back over a few things that weren't clear?"

"I don't have anything helpful to add. I was working in the manuscript room. I heard someone come in, but I never saw them. The alarm went off. The doors started to shut. I panicked, and fell and, I guess, hit my head on the light table."

"Did you smell or hear anything like a match being struck?" asks Lily.

Francine shakes her head.

There's a few moments of silence. Finally, Marty says, "So, we know there were at least three of them there, right?"

No one answers.

"What?" says Marty. "Where is everyone?"

"You didn't hit your head," Samantha says to Francine. "Someone hit you. And you knew it."

Even Marty is stumped, at least for a few seconds. Finally, she asks Francine, "Is that true?"

Francine gazes at a spot about three feet in front of her, somewhere near the center of the coffee table. She nods again, once, and then leans her head back against the sofa. "I was standing at the table. I heard someone come in. Then I heard surprising noises, loud, as if someone were climbing on the shelves. I started to turn around, but I was grabbed from behind."

"What happened then?" asks Marty.

"He said something to me, in Greek. I didn't understand it perfectly, but it was something like, 'The book belongs to us. If you return the pages, no one will be hurt.'"

After a moment of silence, Marty says, "That's it?"

"No," says Francine.

"So?" asks Marty.

"He said if we didn't return them, he would kill us."

"But why didn't you tell us?" asks Lily.

"Because you would have wanted to give them the photographs, and I can't let you do that."

"We may have to," says Lily.

"You can't."

"Why not?" asks Lily.

"I can't say anything else right now," says Francine.

"I think maybe you better tell us the whole story," says Lily, as gently as she can. "We all need to know what's happening."

The silence and the darkness merge and become a presence. Everyone's waiting.

Tom shifts in his chair and clears his throat. "Can you give us a hint?" he asks.

"Bullshit," says Samantha. "I want to know exactly what's going on."

"You have to wait," says Francine. "At least until tomorrow. It's not my information to give."

"Whose is it?" asks Lily.

"Come to my apartment tomorrow night, around eight, you can know then."

"For Christ's sake," says Samantha.

"And now," says Francine. "I want to go home."

30

EARLY WEDNESDAY MORNING, LILY SITS AT THE
kitchen counter and stares down at her appointment book.
She's been skimping on work at the Women's Center;
Monday she skipped out on her appointments at Tate; and
her own life—laundry, food, kitchen sink—are showing
signs of severe neglect. Something is starting to smell; she
thinks it's in the produce drawer of the refrigerator. She
picks up a pen and moves a legal pad in front of her and begins to make a list of what she has to do to catch up.

Within moments she finds herself conjugating *cotev,
cotevet*—the extent of her Hebrew, except when she reads
the manuscript and the words reveal themselves. She feels
as if she's been reading the manuscript all night, because
her dreams were so vivid. The blonde woman was at the
restaurant again. Someone said the words, "Don't judge
and you won't be judged." The woman fell face first into

her plate, and Lily was alone and afraid. Judgment comes from fear, she thinks.

She hasn't seen her mother in almost twenty years. When Lily was a senior in high school, her mother showed up at the ranch. No one knew her mother was coming. Her father wasn't there—only Mrs. Grossman, the cook and housekeeper, and two of the hands. Lily was in the kitchen, at the table, drinking sweet iced tea with fresh mint and complaining to Mrs. Grossman about her part in the spring play—how she had once again been cast as a boy because of her height—when a taxi pulled up and Mrs. Grossman said something in German and Lily walked over and stood next to her at the window. She had never seen a taxi at the ranch, or anywhere in Benton, for that matter.

A woman got out and Lily knew right away it was her mother, but she pretended she didn't. "Who's that?" she said. She hadn't seen her mother, then, in three years, since she spent the summer with her in Scotland. Her mother had been remarried and the man had drunk too much and thrown her mother's dog off the landing on the top story of a huge old house, a castle. That was the end of her spending summers with her mother. Lily had remembered her mother as large and blonde, but that day at the ranch she looked frail, with washed-out light brown hair.

"You don't know?" asked Mrs. Grossman.

Lily shook her head.

"It's your mother," said Mrs. Grossman. "I wish Mr. Connor were here. Well, he's not. So let's do our best."

Lily followed Mrs. Grossman out into the front room. The woman, her mother, stood at the screen door and knocked on the frame. It was bright and hot outside, and the woman was silhouetted against the screen. She peered into the room and saw Lily and Mrs. Grossman, and she

started to speak but her voice broke. Lily wanted to disappear, to go through the floor into the cool root cellar under
the house. There was no place to hide.

The woman, her mother, finally said, "I'm sorry to
bother you. I should have called. But I was afraid he would
tell me not to come."

"My father's not here," Lily said.

The woman nodded. It was hard to see her face through
the screen. "Can I come in?" she asked.

Lily walked forward and opened the screen door. Mrs.
Grossman made a sound, maybe to stop Lily, maybe to
welcome the woman, Lily wasn't sure. Then they all stood
in the room together.

AT NOON, LILY SITS IN THE CHAPEL OF THE MONASTERY
where Charlie lives. The noon service on Wednesday is a
Eucharist. The colors of the stained glass deepen and
change as clouds move overhead. She hasn't been to
church since the evening prayer service at the cathedral.
And she can't remember the last time she took communion. Yes, she remembers, the Sunday she celebrated at
Tate—was it only ten days ago?

But she's not sure she can take communion today anyway. The Catholicism of her childhood still has a visceral
hold on her faith and her imagination. Today, she needs to
go to confession before she takes communion. But she
doesn't know where to go, so she has come here, to Charlie's monastery.

The brothers fill the pews at the end of the enclosed
space, facing the altar, and Lily catches Charlie's eye as he
passes her. He stops and whispers, "Hi. What's up?" And

she shrugs, as if to say she doesn't know. "Can I talk to you afterward?" she asks. He nods and goes to his place.

Recently, Lily has been growing tired of the monastery chants and voices—so precise and precious and a little feeble. So male, she thinks, although not bass male, tenor male. Today the whole service feels especially closed down, and she wonders why she bothered to come.

The gospel reading is from Matthew, chapter seven. When Lily hears that, she can feel a tingling sensation at the base of her neck, along her hairline. "Judge not, that you be not judged," reads Brother Franklin. "For with the judgment you pronounce you will be judged, and the measure you give will be the measure you get. Why do you see the speck that is in your brother's eye, but do not notice the log that is in your own eye? Or how can you say to your brother, 'Let me take the speck out of your eye,' when there is the log in your own eye? You hypocrite—" At this, Lily looks up, as if being directly addressed. But of course it's part of the text. "—first take the log out of your own eye, and then you will see clearly to take the speck out of your mother's eye."

Surely he didn't say, "mother's eye." He said, "brother's eye." She doesn't hear much else—she misses the sermon completely, which is too bad, she thinks, because she could use some guidance. All morning she has replayed the scene at the ranch between her mother and her. Lily let her mother in, that day, and they all stood in the living room for a few minutes. Her mother had to ask if she could sit down. Then she asked for a glass of water.

When Mrs. Grossman left to go to the kitchen, the woman turned to Lily and started to talk in a hurried, quiet voice. There was perspiration on her upper lip and forehead. "I've come to apologize to you. I don't think it could possibly be enough. I don't think I can make it up to you, not having a mother all these years. But I want to say I'm sorry, at least. And I thought that maybe, if you someday forgive me, we could try again." Her accent was different from the people Lily had grown up with; it sounded softer, as if people who spoke that way must live among rolling green hills, someplace it rains a lot.

Her mother said a few more things, but Lily can't remember them very well. She said something about not drinking anymore, about trying to turn her life around. At the time, Lily was listening for Mrs. Grossman in the kitchen. She never answered her mother. She doesn't think she even nodded or acknowledged that she had heard. What she knew, without being conscious of knowing, was that to answer her mother was to admit that all these years she had longed for the woman to show up and say these very words. To answer her mother was to betray herself, and her father. So when Mrs. Grossman appeared with the water, Lily stood and said, "I've got homework," and left the room.

The woman didn't stay much longer. Lily heard the screen door slam and heard the door of the waiting taxi open and close. When she dared to look out the window, all she could see was the back of her mother's head through the rear window of the cab.

Lily doesn't tune into the service until they've already started the Lord's Prayer. "Forgive us our debts, as we forgive our debtors." She remembers what these lines look like in the Hebrew text. And she thinks how judgment and forgiveness weave together, how the moment you stop judging people, you've already forgiven them. That forgiveness isn't a separate act of magnanimity, a moment marked in time. It's the period of time over which judgment languishes and ceases. It's a spectrum, at the end of which, the other person, or people, or idea stands clear on its own, without the distortions of judgment.

She mouths the word to the last hymn—"The light of the world is Jesus"—and then waits while the brothers leave and one of them returns to put out the altar candles. She watches as he carefully raises the long stem with the cup on the end and snuffs each flame, until the air is filled with thin trails of smoke and the smells of lingering incense and melting wax.

IT's TOO COLD TO SIT OUTSIDE IN THE GARDEN, SO Lily and Charlie go to one of the small offices on the first floor. Lily sits in a blue armchair and stares out the window into the guesthouse courtyard, a walled garden with a stone bench and a statue of Saint Francis at the other end. The sky is still dark, but now the heavy clouds appear to be locked into place, like a thick ceiling.

"So," says Charlie, as he sits in the matching chair across from her. "How are you? I haven't heard from you in a while."

"I'm thinking it's time for me to stop judging my mother."

"Right," says Charlie, and nods a couple of times. "Let me just catch up. You think it's time for you to stop judging your mother. What got you here after thirty years of intractable resentment?"

"Something...I've been thinking about judgment, and then when I heard the gospel today, I realized it was time to move on, basically. To give it up. Enough already."

They look at each other for a moment, and then Charlie asks, "What do you want to do?"

"I don't know. What should I do?"

"Is that why you didn't take communion?" he asks.

Lily nods.

"Do you want to make an individual confession?"

"Yes," she says.

"Is there anything else going on you want to tell me about first?"

She looks out into the garden and frowns, then turns back to him. "I do want to tell you, but I don't think I can, yet. Let's just say...Let's say I'm beginning to see the gospels in a new light."

"What light would that be?" he asks.

"I don't know," she says. "Maybe I'm beginning to believe they're true."

31

WHEN SHE GETS TO HER OFFICE AT TATE THAT AFTER-noon, there's a message on her answering machine from Jim—whom Lily still thinks of as the *real* chaplain—in Virginia. Things are going great there. His mother's settled in, and he hopes to be back at Tate sooner than he expected—before the holidays. He includes his number, which Lily calls, but she ends up leaving him a message in return—something to the effect that it's great news and he should just give her a date as soon as he knows his plans.

As she reads through memos and answers other mes-sages, she keeps glancing toward the doorway. At first, she assumes it's because she's waiting for Samantha or Francine to show up and tell her something else has erupted. But then, after the third or fourth glance, she real-izes she's thinking about Annie Kim, the homesick freshman she hasn't heard from in almost two weeks, since the young woman came to the chaplain's office for help. Lily wishes she had been able to say something more useful, but she's not sure what it would have been. In fact, Lily feels that way about her whole stint at Tate—she wishes she could have done something more useful, but she's not sure what it would have been.

AT SEVEN-THIRTY SHE TRUDGES THROUGH PORTER Square, leaning into a brutal wind. The clouds haven't budged, and the reflected city lights throw a green tinge over the parking lot and shops and cars and people. She takes out the directions Francine gave her last night—it's at least a fifteen-minute walk from here, and she dreads it. She still hasn't remembered to put her gloves in the pocket of her parka. She's wearing khakis and a long-sleeve T-shirt, as if winter hasn't arrived. The wind rushes up from the pavement, into her clothes, through to her skin.

When she crosses Summer Avenue, a driver honks at her. She peers out from beneath the hood of her parka, wondering what gesture to make. But it's Tom's pickup truck she sees, his face smiling at her through the windshield.

She climbs into the warm cab and kisses him. "You're early."

"So are you," he says. "Did you eat yet?"

"No," she says. "But we may not have time—"

"We can stop in Davis Square and get roast beef sandwiches, and some drinks and fries. Marty's always hungry. Something tells me Francine isn't going to be serving wine spritzers and hors d'oeuvres."

"It's kind of hard to imagine her living anywhere, you

know? It's as if she exists only in Samantha's presence, then disappears until she's needed again."

"Yeah—I thought that, too, until last night."

"She seemed different, didn't she?" asks Lily.

"Definitely." He pulls into an illegal spot, next to a hydrant, in front of Hacker's Famous Roast Beef Sandwiches. "Stay here," he says. He leaves the engine running, the heater on, and opens the door. "If anyone hassles you, tell them your boyfriend's a police photographer."

She watches him go into the shop and order. They know him there, and the young man behind the counter shakes his hand, then tells him something that makes them both laugh. I know good people, she thinks. There is goodness in the world. This place makes great sandwiches and coleslaw and fries. And Tom always remembers to eat, even when I don't. For some reason, that last thought makes her feel like crying.

She hears a sound like small stones hitting the roof of the truck, and then she sees it's hailing—tiny pellets that bounce off the sidewalk and tick against the windshield. The wind drives the hail sideways, into the faces of people walking past. It hits against her window, fierce and persistent, as if it wants in.

FRANCINE LIVES ON THE TOP FLOOR OF A NARROW Victorian, the last house on a dead-end street. Lily and Tom walk through a deep front yard and up a set of concrete steps, already slippery from the ice. Lily begins to look for Francine's name on the list beside a row of buzzers, but before she's done, she sees Francine's face framed by the glass of the inner door. Lily waves, and Francine opens the outer door and leads them inside.

"Are you on your way out?" asks Lily.

"No," says Francine. "I decided to wait for everyone here. I thought it would be easier than trekking down and back every time someone rang."

"You have to come all the way down here each time you have a visitor?" asks Tom.

"Only tonight," says Francine. "Usually I can just buzz people in, but we didn't want to take any chances. I wanted to be sure I knew who was at the door."

"Who's we?" asks Lily.

Francine hesitates, then says, "Marty's already here. I asked her to come early to do her inspection, to be sure it's as thorough as possible."

"So we're just waiting for Samantha?" asks Lily.

"More or less," says Francine.

"What do you mean?" asks Tom.

"We talked earlier today. She insisted on knowing everything then, immediately, and I wouldn't tell her. We didn't part on good terms."

"But would that keep her from coming?"

"It might," says Francine. "If it ensures that she remains the center of attention."

This sounds *almost* true to Lily; she doesn't take the time to think about the less true aspects.

LILY KNOCKS ON A BLUE DOOR AT THE TOP OF THE stairs, and someone opens it—a young kid in tight flare jeans, a Red Sox cap, and a hooded sweatshirt. "Oh," says Lily.

"Relax," says Marty, "It's me."

"Oh, yeah," says Lily. "You were dressed like that one time when you followed me to work, weren't you?"

"Yep. I smell roast beef."

"That's the bloodhound in you," says Tom.

"Ha ha," she says. "Where is it?"

The apartment is dark, with a single light in the front room—which serves as a dining room, living room, and study, judging from the furniture—and another light over the stove in the kitchen. The dimness, the sound of the wind, and occasional clicks of hail on the windows make Lily uneasy. Marty and Tom have already gone into the kitchen to start on the sandwiches.

Lily follows them. "Is someone else here?"

Marty turns around. "Francine's downstairs. But you saw her, right?"

Lily nods.

"I think that's it, then. I checked the place pretty thoroughly. I found these." She holds out a single metal disk and two of the small boxes. "One in the phone, one in the front room, one in the kitchen. Why? Did you hear something?"

"No," says Lily. She notices the clock on the oven panel. "It's eight-fifteen."

"And?" asks Marty.

"I'm surprised Samantha's not here."

"Maybe she's just late," says Tom. "She may be having a hard time getting around without her car."

"She doesn't strike me as the public transportation type," says Marty. Her mouth is full. She's already unwrapped one sandwich, dug out a dish of coleslaw, and dumped half of it on the bun, then closed the sandwich and taken a bite. "Plus, Francine said they had a fight, that she might not show up at all."

"I know," says Lily. "She told us. But I don't believe it—I don't believe she'd miss this."

"Face it," says Marty. "She's weird."

• • •

AT EIGHT·FORTY·FIVE FRANCINE COMES IN THE FRONT
DOOR OF the apartment. Lily and Tom and Marty are at the
small table in the front room, finishing their sandwiches.
The hail has stopped, but the wind pushes through the old
casements. "So?" asks Marty.

"Samantha's not here," says Francine. "And we need to
get started."

"We should call her," says Lily.

"I already did," says Francine, and takes her cell phone
out of her back pocket. "Twice at home, once on her cell
phone, and once at the office."

"And nothing?" asks Lily.

Francine shakes her head.

"What do you think?" Marty asks, addressing everyone.
"What should we do?"

Tom shrugs. Lily looks at Francine, who glances at the
door to the bedroom, and says, "We should start. I'll try her
again later."

"Okay," says Marty. "That's good by me."

"I'll be right back," says Francine. She opens the door
to the bedroom and goes in, closing it behind her.

Lily sees Tom and Marty exchange a glance, something
like, Now what? In a few minutes, Francine comes out and,
again, closes the door behind her. She sits down at the table
with them.

"You want a sandwich?" asks Marty.

"No thanks," says Francine. "I have something I have to
explain. We need to sit in the bedroom, because I don't
have any curtains or shades out here."

"Frankly," says Marty, "at this point I'm not sure how

much it matters. They've seen all of us. They might not recognize me in street clothes, but I'm sure they've overheard enough to know who I am."

"This is different," says Francine. "Come in when you're through eating and close the door behind you." Then she gets up and returns to the bedroom.

"Is someone else in there?" asks Lily.

Marty shakes her head. "Can't be. I checked it out when I got here. It was empty. The closet, too."

"Let's go," says Tom. "I want to see what's going on."

Lily collects the bags and wrappers and leftover french fries and starts to throw them all away.

"Where are you going with those fries?" asks Marty.

Lily hands her the fries and takes the garbage into the kitchen. Then she returns and stands behind Tom, putting her hand on his shoulder. "This is weird," she says. "I feel like we're walking into another dimension."

"I know," he says. "Don't worry, though. I'm a police photographer."

THE BEDROOM HAS ONE LIGHT, IN THE FAR CORNER, a lamp on the bedside table by the closet door. The shades are pulled—they look as if they have some sort of thick backing. There's a double bed with a red Indian print bedspread, two sets of bookshelves, and three chairs. Francine sits on the bed, leaning against the wall, and in the corner to her right sits someone else, a young man. As Lily's eyes adjust to the dimness, she sees he's stocky, with a large head, dark eyes, and a wide mouth. His hair's short, almost a buzz cut, and he wears black sweatpants and a matching hooded sweatshirt. His hands rest on his knees, and he watches the new arrivals with a calm smile.

"This is Lily, Marty, and Tom," Francine says to him, then she turns to Lily. "And this is Nickolas."

32

"How did he get in here?" asks Marty.

"Sit down," says Francine. "I'll explain."

Lily sits nearest Nickolas, in a high-backed wooden chair. Tom sits next to her, and Marty perches on a stool near the foot of the bed. Now that she can see Nickolas clearly, Lily notices the deep hollows under his eyes and cheekbones. His hands are thick and strong-looking. When she glances at his face, he looks directly into her eyes.

"He's been staying with me since last night. There's a crawl space from my closet into the attic."

"He's living in the attic?" asks Marty. "So, he's hiding from—what?"

"Please." His voice is soft. "You can speak to me directly. My English isn't perfect, but I can understand your questions." He speaks English with a noticeable accent, part British, part Greek.

"Okay," says Marty. "So, you're hiding from—what?"

"Is it possible for me to tell you the whole story, from the beginning?"

"The whole story would be great," says Marty.

"Then I'll tell you the whole story," he says. "And Francine will help me."

She nods at him.

"Francine has been my closest friend for the past few years," he says. "If it were not for her, I would now be alone."

"I thought you met this summer, in Greece," says Lily.

"We met in England, four years ago," says Francine. "I had a Rhodes, and he was at Oxford."

"But I thought Samantha said—"

"We didn't tell Samantha," says Francine. "We pretended we had just met."

"Why?" asks Tom.

"We needed her to help us, without knowing it," says Francine. "Or without knowing everything. We needed her name, but we were afraid if we told her—"

"I think we should do as we said," says Nickolas, "and start from the beginning."

Francine leans back against the pillows on the bed, and Nickolas turns to the other three. "This is a long story, with many parts. I'll try to tell it as efficiently as possible, but the nature of the material makes efficiency difficult." He takes a breath. "For seven generations, my family has had a member who has become a monk on Athos."

"And Athos is?" asks Marty.

"A peninsula in Greece, at the southern tip of which rises the Holy Mount of Athos. It is the center of Orthodox monasticism. There are twenty ruling monasteries, and many smaller settlements, plus a number of hermit huts."

"Did you go there?" Marty asks Francine.

"No women—well, no females of any kind are allowed. Samantha and I sailed the perimeter, so we got to see some of the monasteries, from a distance."

"What do you mean, no females of any kind?" asks Marty.

"Goats, sheep, cows—you name it," says Francine.

"Although there rages a debate concerning hens," says Nickolas.

Lily looks at him. He isn't smiling, but he's making a joke.

"You're kidding, right?" asks Marty.

"Would you like to hear the myth of how this came about?" asks Nickolas.

"I would," says Marty. "But maybe we shouldn't waste time—"

"It isn't wasting time," says Nickolas. "The more you know about Athos, the more you will understand of my story. The myth is this: When the Virgin Mary was an old woman, she got a message from her close friend Lazarus, who was then a bishop of the church in Crete. He wanted to see her again before he died—the second time."

"Oh," says Marty. "That Lazarus."

"She agreed to make the trip from Palestine, but instead of reaching Cyprus, she landed on Athos. Some say it was because of a storm, others say it was a mistake on the part of the captain. When she set foot on the shore, all the pagan statues crashed to the ground, wailing and calling out to the inhabitants that they must hurry to the harbor to see the *Panaghia*, the Holy Mother, who was, in her own turn, awestruck by the natural beauty of the mountain. So she made the peninsula holy ground, baptized all the inhabitants, and never left. But she decreed that no other woman should ever set foot on Athos."

"Sort of a weird thing to decree, if you think about it, since she's a woman," says Marty. "I guess she never got to Cyprus. Was Lazarus disappointed?"

"They say so," says Nickolas, smiling for the first time. "That is one of the many myths concerning Athos. When you have seen it, and lived there, it becomes less hard to believe these stories. In fact, they begin to seem true, but true in a way that is different from how we might understand the truth here, in this room."

"I don't know," says Marty. "I'm already beginning to feel a shift in that area."

"Good," says Nickolas. He is not smiling this time. "That will make the rest easier."

"How long were you there?" asks Tom.

"A short time. Five months. I went the day after Francine returned to America, and I myself left the peninsula—and the country—last month. But what I need to explain to you begins before I reached Athos, when I was a young boy.

"As I said at the beginning, my family has always sent one member from each generation to Athos. My father's brother became the monk in my father's generation. For the first few years he lived on Athos, my father took me for annual visits. My uncle's monastery was Vatopedi—one of the most beautiful and most comfortable—and one of the oldest."

As Nickolas speaks, Lily grows aware of a tapping sound against the windowpanes. The hail has started again. And there's still no word from Samantha.

"The first few years, we visited him at Vatopedi. One

year, we went to the monastery, but my uncle had to be called from a different settlement, one of the *sketes*."

Marty opens her mouth, but before she can speak, he says, "A *skete* is a small community of huts, sponsored by one of the monasteries. Often the monks who live there are artisans, painters of icons, carvers of prayer beads, or, sometimes, copiers of manuscripts.

"My uncle had gone to college. He was a learned man. This is relatively rare among the monks, although becoming less so. In the *skete,* he studied the art of copying manuscripts. He had been chosen for this task because of his education."

"Wait," says Marty. "Why would they copy manuscripts they already owned? I mean, what's the point of making another copy?"

"Many of the manuscripts are old, some of them very old, and some are becoming illegible. Many came to the peninsula centuries earlier, for safekeeping. During the fall of Constantinople, and during times of upheaval since, Athos has become a repository for the valuables of our church."

Marty nods. "Okay. So go on about your uncle."

"Our next two visits were the same. They sent for him, and we met him at the monastery. But he became more distant each time, and less willing to speak about his life. My father believed he was becoming holy. But for me, as a boy, my favorite uncle..." He shrugs his shoulders. "You can imagine. He seemed to me to be dying. On our last visit, we were not allowed to see my uncle. They said they had sent word to us at our home, telling us not to come, but we never received the message. He had moved to a *kellia,* a smaller community, to which visitors were not allowed.

And from which the monks were not allowed to travel, even to their sponsoring monastery."

"Was he alive?" asks Marty.

"Yes," says Nickolas. "He was alive. They assured us he was fine. My father would never . . . it would never occur to my father to doubt a monk. We made our pilgrimage and went home. My father never saw or heard from my uncle again."

"That's it?" asks Marty. "That's the end of the story?"

"No," says Nickolas. "That's the beginning of the story. But I need some water and something to eat before I continue."

33

NICKOLAS NEVER MOVES, SITTING QUIETLY IN HIS chair while Francine calls Samantha again and Tom stretches and Marty brings the food. Lily sits with him in the bedroom. He says a silent prayer and crosses himself before he eats. His movements are slow and methodical, like his speech. When everyone's settled again, Lily asks him, "Where have you been since you left Greece?"

He takes the last bite of his sandwich, then wipes his mouth with the napkin. He puts down the napkin and finishes the glass of water. Then he turns to Lily. "To answer that would be to jump ahead of myself, and I would prefer to tell the story in sequence."

Lily nods.

"This food was very good," he says to Marty. "Thank you."

"He bought it," says Marty, pointing to Tom.

"Thank you, too. To get ready for life on Athos, I gave up eating meat. But since I have been traveling, I eat what's available. And, I have to admit, I prefer eating meat to not eating meat. Especially sandwiches. And cheeseburgers."

"The cheeseburger is the staple food of our country," says Tom.

Nickolas smiles at him. He folds the paper napkin and tucks it under the plate. Then he sits back in his chair. "Now I'll continue. My father died when I was sixteen. After the funeral, I received a letter from my uncle. He wrote to say he hoped I had not given up my aspirations to become a monk on Athos. I wrote him back and told him I could not say what I planned to do. I was the only boy in my family. I have three sisters. And though I am the youngest, I did not think I could leave them on their own. But my oldest sister married a wealthy man in our town, and he became the head of our family. He's a good man, and he saw to it that I went to university.

"While studying in Athens, I wrote my uncle again. I told him I would like to...I think I said I would like to consider joining him on Athos. In truth, I had always wanted to go. I have a vocation to monastic life, fed, no doubt, by my boyhood visits to Athos, which created a world in my mind.

"Once, while riding a donkey up a steep path, I saw a young bearded monk, drawing honey from a hive. The bees flew into and out of the hive, but none of them bothered him. He was surrounded by wild lilies—or that is how I remember him. And the bees flew all around him."

His voice is beautiful, Lily realizes, almost melodious. And the image of the monk on the hillside stays in her mind, calming her.

"In his next note, my uncle urged me to visit him as

soon as possible. I went in the spring, during Holy Week. Of course, the monasteries are filled with pilgrims then." He takes a sip of water and closes his eyes. When he opens them, he looks at Francine. "What did I just say?"

"You visited your uncle during Holy Week."

"Yes," he says. "Because the monastery guesthouse was full, I was to be allowed to visit him at the *kellia*—or I thought that's why I was allowed to go there. We walked from Vatopedi for a day and a half, staying the night in the *skete* where he had first lived. The second day, the monk accompanying me led me only so far, then told me the directions. I went on to the *kellia*. I was to meet my uncle in a hut on the path—just outside the community.

"The *kellia* was near the Holy Mountain, so that all one's attention was turned, always, toward that presence. The land is rough, high up, so one can see, also, the ocean on the west coast, the more beautiful side of the cape. There, it is a thick forest of cypress, fir, chestnut, pines— then clearings filled with yellow broom, wild orchids and iris, and the lilies—and all rising toward the Holy Mountain, with white cliffs dropping to the sea."

As she listens, Lily forgets the hail and Samantha and the fear of the last few days.

"I expected to see only my uncle, by then a man of eighty, but outside the hut sat a monk with a thick, black beard and a steady gaze. He watched me as I walked toward him. And when I got closer, I saw it was, indeed, my uncle. He said..." Nickolas pauses, as if to translate, then continues. "'I cannot rise to greet you, because my legs are not working well today.' I kneeled and embraced him. His face and torso were that of a man twenty years younger."

"What happened to his legs?" asks Marty.

"He never said. He explained that his *kellia* was devoted

to the protection, study, and worship of one single manuscript. That he would like me to join this *kellia* after my
novice year. That he could tell me nothing of this manuscript before then—nothing, other than that it was sacred,
and ancient, and a document at the heart of Orthodox faith.
He advised me to study Biblical Hebrew, Biblical history,
including recent discoveries, such as the finds of Qumram
and Nag Hammadi."

"How would he know about those finds?" asks Lily.
"Especially Nag Hammadi?"

"The monks are not cut off from the world altogether. A
man as knowledgeable as my uncle had correspondents."

"Why do you say, 'had'?" asks Lily.

"I doubt . . . I can't know where he is now, or how he is,
or if he is in touch with the world outside any longer."

"Since you left, you mean?" asks Lily.

"Yes," says Nickolas. "Since I left."

"With the manuscript," says Lily.

"For that information you will have to wait," says
Nickolas.

Lily nods.

"At the end, he told me I should receive my—what you
would call my graduate degree at Oxford, studying there.
He gave me the name of a man, a professor at Oxford,
who would ensure my admission and make it possible for
me to go. He gave me a letter to carry to this man and told
me to hide it, not to show it to anyone, not even to talk
about it before I reached Oxford. I returned to the boat,
and to my life.

"One year later I arrived in England and found my uncle's friend. He did not read the letter in front of me, but a
few days after I gave it to him, he called me and invited me

to his house. I studied with him throughout my time in Oxford. He was a great Biblical scholar, as well as a man of faith. Slowly, through our studies, he revealed to me the identity of the manuscript. He believed it to be the original version of what Western scholars call Q, the second source for Luke and Matthew. But to us, this manuscript is known as something different. Though recognized as a source for the gospels, that is its second identity."

"And what's its first?" asks Lily.

Nickolas says a Greek phrase, and pauses. "I have never translated the title," he says. "In English it would be something like *The Book of Light*."

Lily feels a wave of recognition flow through her. This is the text she has lived with these past two weeks.

"I'm confused," says Marty. "So, are they the same thing—the Q book and *The Book of Light?*"

"My friend believed there exist, or existed, later copies of the original book with deletions made by the early church, possibly by Paul. Even then, the Western church did not like this portrait of Jesus as a mystic. Those revised versions, now known as Q, became the source material for Matthew and Luke. So, in a sense, yes, they are the same, with a few crucial differences."

"And why did your uncle send you to this man—what's his name?" asks Lily.

"Edgar Proctor."

"Why did he send you to study with Proctor?"

"Because my uncle had a plan. I believe he revealed the plan to Proctor in the letter I delivered. From then on, I became part of the plan, though I didn't understand all this for the first two years I was in Oxford."

"And the plan was?" asks Marty.

"To share this book with the world."

"So why not send it to the *New York Times?* What's the big secret?" asks Marty.

Nickolas looks at Francine and nods, but she shakes her head. Finally, Nickolas says, "Because of the value of the manuscript, it is closely guarded."

"By the church?" asks Lily.

"The church, and others—members of the church..." Nickolas begins.

"You need to let us tell the story first," says Francine. "Otherwise, we'll all get lost."

Nickolas shrugs once and leans back in his chair.

"Is that when you two met?" Lily asks Francine. "When you were both at Oxford?"

Francine nods. "I was only there for a year, but we became close." She blushes and glances toward the window. "I didn't know or understand everything that was happening, but I knew about the studies, and, eventually, I knew about the manuscript."

"I told no one else," says Nickolas. "Only Francine, and even then she knew a small part of the truth."

"Okay," says Marty. "So what happened next?"

"Eventually," says Nickolas, "Proctor explained to me my uncle's proposal—that I return to Athos as a novice, that I become a part of my uncle's *kellia,* gaining the trust of the monks. Then, after a few years, I give up my vows, making it known to all that I am not called to be a monk. But this time when I leave, I bring not a letter but the manuscript itself to him in England. He had agreed to present it to the world for no personal gain, and to keep the source a secret. That was the most important part—that no one should know where it came from."

"But wouldn't they figure out it was you, once it disappeared?" asks Tom.

"Perhaps. Eventually. But my uncle was preparing a copy to replace the original, so that its absence would not be known for many months—or even years. There was always thought to be more than one copy in the world. Why wouldn't one of the others turn up eventually? And, besides, by then, I would have disappeared—become a man with a different name in a different country."

"Why not send the copy?" asks Marty. "That way, no one would ever know."

"The copy would convince no one. After a single carbon test, the materials would be proven to be modern. The whole thing would become another prank in the world of Biblical history. And, besides, it isn't just the contents of the manuscript that have healing powers—it is the object itself. My uncle and many others, including Proctor, believe that such a message and a power belong to the world, not just to a handful of people."

In the silence that follows, Lily notices that the hail has stopped, but a fierce wind still rattles the windows. She remembers Samantha and now feels sure that the woman's absence is linked to what they're hearing in this room.

"What happened to the plan?" Marty finally asks.

"A month before I was to leave England, to return to Greece, my friend and teacher died."

"Whoa," says Marty. "That's a wrench in the works. What did you do?"

Nickolas doesn't respond, so Francine takes over. "He wrote me and told me the whole story. He asked me for my help. And I offered him Samantha. She's a famous, respected Biblical scholar, not unlike Edgar Proctor. In fact, they knew each other years ago in England. After preparation, she would have been able to do the same thing he was going to do, present the book to the world, so that people would understand it and believe in it."

"But at that point she didn't know anything about this, right?" asks Lily.

"Yes," says Francine. "And Nickolas wouldn't agree to anything before he met her. I arranged the trip to Greece. They met. And he agreed. When we returned, he took his novice vows and set our plan in motion."

"I took my vows," says Nickolas, "but was not allowed to visit the *kellia* right away. By the time I saw my uncle next, he was an old man, weak and ill. And the copy wasn't finished. After Proctor's death, he had given up hope. But I told him of Samantha and Francine. He was reluctant—" Nickolas glances at Lily and then looks at his hands, lying quietly in his lap.

"He didn't want women involved," says Lily. "But he relented, eventually, right?"

"Almost," says Nickolas. "He did not know Francine and Samantha, and he had no way of trusting them. He was not ready to deliver the manuscript into their hands. Proctor had spent years preparing to introduce the book into the world, whereas Samantha knew nothing. Also, if I simply delivered it to them and they revealed the existence of the book immediately, the monks might well check the incomplete copy and know the source. He insisted we draw the plan out, test their integrity, see how they treated the information we gave them. Then, if everything went well, we would, eventually, give them the real thing."

"So that's what was behind the travel and the photos and the secrecy?"

"In part," says Nickolas. "Now I will tell you the other

part, what I know about the ones who guard the book, and the ones who practice its healing powers."

"What's that supposed to mean?" asks Marty.

"There are two groups, two Orders, both devoted to the book. The men who have been following you are members of one Order, who call themselves, with some irony, I feel, what would translate as the The Order of Light. Yet these men—because this group is entirely male—believe the book is the sole property of our faith and, specifically, of the monks of Athos. They may even believe that our entire faith rests on the existence of this book, and without it our church will crumble."

"Why do you say 'may believe'?" asks Tom. "You don't know for sure?"

"No one knows their vows. They ally themselves with the powers of the church, yet keep themselves separate and apart. Most of them have lives in the outside world, some are wealthy and prominent—at least, that's what is believed. My uncle considered them ignorant thugs, people looking for an identity. But Proctor presented them to me quite differently. He believed they are serious and dedicated, however misinformed. He assured me that my uncle, and he, and I were all risking our lives."

"So, what about the other group?" asks Lily.

"Allies of Edgar Proctor and my uncle, learned men and women whose families and teachers have, over centuries, pieced together the text of the book and passed on its contents and practices, who believe the book has the power to heal not only illness but hunger, anger, strife. It is to a member of this group—a priest—I brought the manuscript, and it is from other members I once received money and instructions and photographs of the manuscript pages."

"*Once* received?" Lily repeats.

"Yes. After I met with the priest, he sent me on to Athens. There I moved from house to house, until plans were made. Finally, I was given a ticket to America. I would go to a specific post office in this country and receive a packet with a photograph, American money, travel arrangements, and instructions for the next packet. I would mail the photograph to Francine, and proceed to the next destination. But four days ago, the packet was not at the proper post office. I waited a day and then came here."

"What do you think that means?" asks Tom.

"Exactly what it appears to mean," says Nickolas.

34

"OKAY," SAYS MARTY. "I KNOW I'M BEING THICK, BUT I still need this spelled out. How did Proctor die?"

"An accident," says Nickolas "A truck collided with his car, head on. Both drivers were killed. The truck driver was Greek. He had no family. His past could not be traced. It was as if he existed only for the period he worked for the trucking company."

"So you think the driver was part of the first group—the bad guys?" asks Marty.

"I don't know," says Nickolas. He looks at her as if to say, of course he was.

Lily watches the shade on the window. The wind gets through the cracks enough to cause the fabric to move back and forth, slightly. She feels at once disconnected and clear-headed. "I'm worried about Samantha," she says.

Everyone turns to look at her.

"I'll call her when we're through here," says Francine. "It won't be long."

Lily nods, but not because she feels reassured. She feels resigned.

Marty continues. "So, these guys who have been following Lily and Samantha and Francine are all part of this group—the so-called Order of Light. What else can you tell us about them? Is there a leader? Where are they from? How's the group organized?"

"I have told what I know. I believe they are a mix of true believers, fanatics, and lost souls. I'm sure there is a strict hierarchy—the wealthier men in power, surrounded by lesser men willing to do what they're told. A group like this attracts the ones looking for a cause and a structure. When they find it, they become single-minded. That is, their dedication to the protection of the manuscript—which extends to preventing all outsiders from knowing of its existence— appears to be absolute."

"Meaning?" asks Marty.

"Look for yourself," says Nickolas. "They are not above damaging property. They are not above damaging human beings. As with all earthly absolutes, their belief in their own rightness—is that a word?—renders them beyond limit and judgment."

"Yeah," says Marty. "That's what I thought you meant. So these other guys—the members of your uncle's group, the good guys—they've been sending you single photographs—on a certain schedule to a certain prearranged address—which you then send on to Francine."

"Precisely," says Nickolas.

"And then they stopped, right? But you don't know for sure what's happened?" Marty says.

Nickolas shakes his head, slowly, and shrugs.

"Do you think—" Lily begins, and then stops. "Have you been able to contact the priest, the one with the manuscript?"

"I'm not supposed to be in touch with him again. Or with my uncle. But I suspect I would not find him at home."

Lily nods. "So you don't have any idea where the manuscript is now?"

"No," says Nickolas. "But I am afraid we no longer have it."

"You think they've discovered everything—all of the contacts?"

"How else can I explain the silence?"

"But how did they find out so fast?" asks Marty. "And if they're really responsible for Proctor's death, it looks like they knew the plan before you ever got back to Athos, right?"

"Yes," says Nickolas. "I believe that's true."

"So, how—" Marty begins.

"Someone told them," says Nickolas. "I don't know who, or why, or when, but somehow the information reached them. That is clear."

"How much danger are you in?" asks Tom.

Nickolas smiles at him. "Only a bit more than you," he says.

Tom smiles back. "Right." And no one speaks for a moment.

"When you had this book, the manuscript, during the time you carried it to the priest—" Because Lily isn't sure what she's asking, she doesn't know how to continue.

But Nickolas seems to understand. "I have seen a healing by the faithful only once—in the *kellia,* days before I left with the manuscript." He looks at Lily, as if to be sure that he's answering her question.

She nods.

"A young monk was brought from Vatopedi. He was bound to a crude stretcher by leather belts. By the time I saw him, he was still, but the monks who carried him said they had strapped him down so tightly for fear he would snap himself in two—he bent double, then backward, but always completely silent. My uncle said, 'l know this demon.'" He looks at Francine and says something in Greek.

She smiles at him and turns to Lily. "Nickolas is concerned you won't be able to believe him. He says this sounds too absurd in English. But it makes sense in Greek."

"I believe him," says Lily.

"The monks brought the manuscript to the room," he continues. "My uncle put one hand on the text, and one hand on the young man's head, right here—" Nickolas places three fingertips down the center of his forehead, vertically, so the bottom finger rests just between his eyebrows. "I cannot describe the ritual itself—because it is impossible, because I only remember in images, not words—but when my uncle finished, the young man was no longer bound and began to weep, and a wonderful smell of mown hay and lilies filled the room, and my father, who had been dead for many years, put his hand on my shoulder and pointed to a set of gates which swung open and we moved freely back and forth, between two worlds, between that room and heaven." He looks directly at Lily. "Is that what you wanted to know?"

"Yes," she says.

"But the simple truth is this," says Nickolas. "The book contains the words of Jesus, recorded during his lifetime, and for me that is—"

A sharp buzzing sound cuts off Nickolas's words. No one moves, until Francine says, "Oh. The cell phone," grabs it and answers, mercifully stopping the noise.

Lily watches Francine talk, but she's too far away to interpret what she hears. Francine's voice is calm, but purposefully calm. Something has happened, that's clear. In a few minutes, Francine sets down the phone and says, "That was Samantha. They've taken her. They say they'll trade her for the last set of photos."

FRANCINE STANDS IN THE CORNER OF THE ROOM, BEhind Nickolas. Their faces are expressionless. Tom and Marty are talking together, and Lily sits quietly, letting the news sink in.

"How did she sound?" Lily finally asks.

Tom and Marty turn to look at Francine.

"Weird," says Francine. "Sort of calm. Not what you would expect."

"What are we supposed to do?" asks Lily.

"Get the photographs from the bank tomorrow at nine. Then wait for the next call, on this phone. They'll tell us where to bring them."

"Can you get to the photographs?" asks Lily. "Will the bank let you in?"

"Yes," says Francine. "We rented it together. I have a key, and my signature is on the contract."

"Did she say anything else?" asks Marty.

"They told her if we called the police they would kill

her. They said she wouldn't be hurt—that they would go away and leave us alone—if they got the photos back. She said she believed them, that we should do what they said."

No one speaks for a few seconds. Then Nickolas says, "They won't make more trouble than necessary."

More silence.

"We need to report this," says Tom. "We've got to get the police in on this."

Marty looks at him for a few seconds, then says, "Come on. Be honest. Are you gonna tell me that the police will definitely bring her back alive? Samantha believes them. Nickolas believes them. Why would they kill her once they have the pages?"

"But she knows about it," says Tom. "She's seen it."

"We all know about it," says Marty. "Are they going to kill all of us?"

"They would," says Nickolas. "If they had to. But they won't if they don't have to."

"There," Marty says to Tom. "Okay. Who do you think has a better chance of doing this successfully—us, or the so-called professionals?"

"It's probably time for me to step out," he says.

"Yeah," says Marty. "Good idea. I, on the other hand, have no loyalties."

"You could lose your license," says Tom.

"I'll get a new job," says Marty. She turns to the rest of the group. "I say we go with Nickolas's instincts. And if we can get her back alive, we do that first. Then we report it."

"Why should we report it at all, if we get her back?" asks Francine. "There won't be anything to report. The copies will be gone."

Marty glances at Lily, then at Tom, before she says,

"Let's take it one step at a time. We'll do what they say, get Samantha back, and then decide on the follow-up. Okay?"

Francine looks at Nickolas and nods. Lily watches the two of them, waiting for more reaction, but nothing happens.

"What do you want to do?" Marty asks Tom. "Because we need to make some plans here. In or out?"

Lily doesn't look at him. She doesn't know what he should do, and though she wants him to stay with the group—which, over the last few hours has turned into something more than a collection of people; their shared knowledge has made them into a single thing, some kind of unit—she doesn't want to influence him.

"Fuck it," he says. "I can get another job, too. What's the plan?"

THE PLAN IS SIMPLE. MARTY WILL FOLLOW FRANCINE to the bank and then stay behind her throughout the day.

"They may have you go a few different places," says Marty. "To test you, or to shake anyone following you. I'll do my best. I'm gonna go right now and get you a cell phone. It's not traceable, and if you hit the call button, it will dial me direct. Then I'm gonna be outside all night, probably in my car, maybe somewhere in the building. You don't worry about that. If they say anything about someone following you, don't pretend. Say you'll call me off. I'll still be there, trust me."

"Why don't I go with her?" asks Lily.

"No," says Francine. "They said come alone and don't call the police."

"Everyone's watching too many movies," says Marty.

"What should I do?" asks Lily.

"We need someone by a land phone. Do you work tomorrow?" she asks her.

"What's tomorrow?" asks Lily. "I've lost track."

"Thursday."

"I'm at the center. But I don't have to be."

"Do you have privacy there?"

"None," says Lily.

"Then stay home. If anything goes wrong, Francine or I will call you. If anything goes seriously wrong, I'll call the police. If you don't hear from me by the end of the day, call here, but don't leave a message. Don't talk to anyone else who picks up. If there's no one here, call me at home. If you can't get a live person you know, just wait until you hear from us."

"I don't care about being implicated," says Lily.

"Yeah," says Marty. "But we might end up needing the police. How likely is it that you were involved in this thing and Tom didn't know anything about it? Might as well keep you two out of it, if possible."

"Oh," says Lily. "Right."

"If you need us, call us," says Tom to Marty. "Then you and I can go into the catering business together."

"Yeah," says Marty. "People would pay me to stop cooking." She stands and stretches, then points to Tom and Lily. "Why don't you two stick around until I get back with the cell phone?"

"Do you think they know you're here?" Lily asks Nickolas.

"I have been extremely careful. I'm almost sure I wasn't seen. But, then, they seem to know things they have no way of knowing."

"Would they want to hurt you, specifically?" she asks.

Nickolas stares at the lamp in the corner. "I'm sure they would like to kill me," he says. "But they won't do that until they have the photographs. And perhaps they won't do it at all. At least, not right away."

35

THE DIGITAL CLOCK READS 4:07. LILY ISN'T SURE WHY SHE'S awake. Tom is next to her. She sits up straight but doesn't know what she heard—doesn't know if she heard anything at all. She listens to the silence, the wind, the sound of a truck or bus on Commmonwealth. Tom rolls over but doesn't wake up.

When the buzzer sounds—announcing someone at the downstairs door—she reaches the intercom panel in her front hall within seconds. She presses the TALK button and half speaks, half whispers, "Hello?"

At first, she can't understand the voice coming from the panel. It's a woman's voice, but so faint and indistinct the words slur together into nonsense.

"Who is this?" Lily asks.

"Samantha," says the voice. "Please come..." and then Lily can't make out the rest. She unlocks her own door, leaves it open behind her, and runs down the stairs. For some reason she doesn't want to take the elevator. Instinct tells her to be as secretive as possible.

When she reaches the dim lobby, she sees a figure slumped against the glass wall in the vestibule. For the first time, Lily pauses. What if Samantha is not alone? What if someone else is waiting for Lily to unlock the door? But she can't see anyone else, and she's afraid to wait any longer. She doesn't know what's wrong with Samantha, but if it's serious, Lily needs to get help right away.

Lily opens the inner door, and, as she does, she sees a car pull away from the curb and turn on its lights. She reaches out toward Samantha, and the woman leans into her arms, then collapses. Lily drags Samantha inside, shuts the inner door, and looks out into the night, through the glass doors of the vestibule. Nothing else is moving.

She picks Samantha up, draping the woman's left arm around her neck, putting her own right arm around Samantha's waist. "Can you walk?"

Samantha nods, and then says something that sounds like, "I can try."

Lily gets them as far as the elevator bank and then sees that one of the elevators is on its way down. Should she avoid being seen? But how, and where will she go? And too late to worry about it now, because the elevator has reached the ground floor. The doors open and Tom steps toward her. When he sees Lily, his face relaxes. Without a word, he puts his left arm around Samantha's other side and together they take her into the elevator. She is shivering, and, as the elevator rises, she begins to cry.

. . .

SAMANTHA IS ASLEEP ON THE BED, WRAPPED IN A wool blanket. She wouldn't take off her clothes or get under the covers. She was disoriented and terrified and didn't seem able to answer questions. She couldn't eat anything, but she drank two full glasses of water. Tom and Lily couldn't understand most of what she tried to say, but they understood enough to know she was not in any pain and refused to go to the hospital. When Tom insisted she see a doctor, she asked for help getting to the bathroom, then locked herself in, so Lily promised they would let her stay in the apartment, at least for the moment.

Lily stands on one side of the bed and Tom on the other, looking down at Samantha in the light from a lamp on the bedside table. Samantha's mouth is red and swollen, her lips raw-looking.

"Should we do anything else?" she asks.

"We should make her go to the emergency room, but I don't want to set her off again."

Samantha says something in her sleep, and her right arm appears from under the blanket, her hand in a tight fist. When Samantha is quiet again, Lily leans over and looks more closely and sees three small puncture marks inside Samantha's right forearm.

"Look at this," Lily says, and points.

Tom comes around to her side of the bed. "They must have given her something—maybe sodium pentathol—although that's the stuff of old spy movies."

"A lot of this is the stuff of old spy movies," says Lily. "I keep getting the feeling that most of these guys are men who never grew up, who watch too much television and imagine themselves on some sort of holy grail assignment."

"For now," says Tom, "I think I'll just take them seriously. I need some coffee."

They leave Samantha and go into the kitchen, where Lily puts on water for tea and Tom starts the coffeemaker.

"What time is it?" he asks.

"Almost five," says Lily. "We need to tell Marty, right?"

"Yeah," he says. "That may not be easy. If she's stashed away somewhere she doesn't want to be seen, or heard, she won't be able to answer her phone. At least we can get in touch with Francine. Then she can tell Marty when she goes to pick Francine up. I guess we'll just get everyone to come here. Is that all right with you?"

"Sure," says Lily. "It's not as if we've got anything to hide, at this point. They must know where Samantha is."

"That's the question, isn't it?" asks Tom. "What do they know? And how did she get here?"

"I have no idea. I saw a car pull away from the curb when I let her in. But I couldn't see anyone in it. I guess—"

"What?"

"Maybe someone in the group had a change of heart, didn't feel right about what they're doing. Do you think that's possible?"

"Possible. Not likely, from what I can tell. But she definitely didn't get here on her own."

"We'll find out when she wakes up. Do you have Francine's number?"

"Yeah," he says. "I got all three numbers from Marty— the cell she gave them, Francine's own cell, and the phone in the apartment. But let me try Marty first. Then she can decide the best way to get them over here. If she doesn't pick up, we'll call Francine." He returns to the bedroom and comes back with a piece of paper and the telephone handset.

The water boils, and Lily makes herself a pot of tea. When she's done, Tom leans on the counter and shakes his head.

"You can't get her?" she asks.

"No," he says. "Why don't you call Francine?"

"Okay. Give me the numbers. Which one should I try first?"

"The apartment phone, I guess. Then the cell phones."

Lily takes the phone and the numbers and sits on the couch. Five minutes later, she's called all three numbers twice, and gotten no answer. "That's weird."

Tom comes into the living room with his coffee and a cup of tea for her. He sits next to her and puts the cups on the table in front of them. "Nothing?"

She shakes her head. "Where would they be?"

He shrugs. "It doesn't make sense."

"Do you think they're okay?"

"I don't know. But I'm beginning to think I ought to go over there and check. Are you all right here?"

"I'm fine here. I'm not sure it's such a great idea for you to go over there alone, though."

He nods toward the bedroom. "You can't leave her in there on her own. There's no telling what kind of shape she'll be in when she wakes up. And we need to know what happened. You stay here and find out as much as you can. I'm going to see if I can find Marty—or Francine—or someone."

"Be careful," she says.

"You, too."

She kisses him on the cheek, then on the lips. "Don't get hurt."

"No problem," he says. "I'm a—"

"I know," says Lily.

.   .   .

LILY SITS UP, HER HEART POUNDING. SHE HAS FALLEN asleep ON the couch. She doesn't know why she's on the couch. She was dreaming about drugs, being drugged, someone forcing something into a hole in her forehead. Out of the corner of her eye, she catches a motion in the hallway. She stays still, listening. Suddenly a small woman with white hair and a white face, wrapped in a brown blanket, appears in the hall.

Lily gasps, then sees that it's Samantha.

"I'm sorry," says Samantha.

"It's not your fault," says Lily. "It's just that I had fallen asleep—"

"No," says Samantha. "I mean I'm sorry, in the larger sense. I'm sorry for getting you into this."

"What time is it?" asks Lily, because she can't think of anything to say in answer to Samantha's apology, and she's now the one who's feeling disoriented.

"Almost six," says Samantha.

"Are you all right?"

"Better," says Samantha. "Shaky. I must have been a wreck when I arrived."

"We were worried," says Lily. "Tom wanted to take you to the hospital, but you . . . refused."

"Did I? What did I say?"

"You locked yourself in the bathroom."

Samantha laughs—it's a surprising sound—and sits down on the armchair across from Lily. She seems more alert and calmer, maybe even a little calmer than usual. "What a bad girl. But then, I've always been extremely invested in having my own way."

"Are you all right?" Lily asks.

"I seem to be fine. Groggy. Still a bit confused. Maybe

even a little giddy. But I'm remembering more."

"What happened?"

"I'm trying to sort that out. Last night, I got ready to meet you all at Francine's. I went out the back way, through the basement. I was going to take the Red Line to Davis Square and walk. But the lights went out in the basement, someone grabbed me, taped my mouth, and then—I don't remember. I woke up in a bathroom. I was tied to the toilet, sitting on it, in a corner of a hotel bathroom. I'm not sure how I knew it was a hotel. Something was wrong with me—I couldn't get my bearings. I couldn't think. That was the most frightening part. Every time I tried to get my mind to work, it would slide out from under me." She looks at Lily with tears in her eyes. "I was so confused."

Lily nods. "Do you want some tea, some coffee, something to eat?"

"No," says Samantha. "I want to figure this out. I would doze off for a while, then someone would tear the tape off my mouth and ask me questions. There wasn't much to tell, of course. I told them about the set of photos in the safe-deposit box. But they can't get to them. I don't think they're up to robbing a bank."

"How many were there?" asks Lily.

"I only saw two. A large man and a smaller one with a scar down the side of this face."

Lily nods. "Yeah. I know him. But how—"

"Did I get here?" Samantha loosens the blanket from around her shoulders and shakes her head. "It's so fantastical, I'm not sure it happened. But it must have, because I'm here."

"What?"

"William."

"Who's William?"

"My husband."

"Your husband was at the hotel, with the other men?"

"I kept thinking I heard his voice. And then, because it all seemed like a nightmare, I thought I was just dreaming about him. After the last time they asked me questions, they gave me another shot and I passed out. When I came to, William and I were walking down a long hallway. I remember the pattern of the carpet—big blue diamonds on a maroon background. I counted them. I can't remember how many there were.

"We walked to a car in the parking lot. I was freezing then, but the cold cleared my head a bit—enough for me to ask him what he was doing there. In the car, he told me the whole story. I wish I could remember the details. It's as if they're in there," she hits her wrist against her forehead, lightly, "but I can't get them out. I do know he talked about Edgar, about Edgar rescuing him after I left. William had some sort of breakdown—I had heard about it from friends—and then Edgar and his family took him in."

"What's Edgar's last name?" asks Lily.

"Edgar Proctor. His wife was the one who saved me when William had me locked in," she says. "I seem to be doomed to be imprisoned in a bathroom. What a grim fate."

"Edgar Proctor," says Lily. "He was—" and then she remembers that Samantha knows nothing about Nickolas, nothing about his plan with Francine, nothing about Athos and the uncle and the priest. Nothing about *The Book of Light*. "I have a story to tell you. And then, between the two of us, I think we can make some sense of this."

"I do hope so," says Samantha. "I need my sense back. I had a moment in that bathroom—the one in the hotel. I thought, I am only my mind. I have nothing else. If they make me lose my mind, I have nothing."

Lily looks at the small woman across from her, wrapped in a brown blanket, knees clasped to her chest, and feels, for the first time since the day Samantha walked into her office, a wave of pure affection.

36

SAMANTHA STANDS AT THE SINK, LOOKING OUT THE kitchen window at the building next door. "All those people leading normal lives," she says. "I've spent many years feeling superior, and now it seems like a stupid mistake."

It's clear she's still taking in what Lily has told her—that Francine knew Nickolas in Oxford. That Edgar Proctor was Nickolas's teacher, and William's link to the manuscript. That, after Edgar's death, Nickolas and Francine planned to substitute Samantha for Edgar, to use her in order to get the manuscript published. That Nickolas is here, hiding in Francine's attic. That they knew they were risking their own lives, and the lives of everyone else involved.

"I guess feeling superior is always a mistake," says Lily. "Though it never stops me."

Samantha turns and looks at her. "Did you ever think about me, after seminary?"

"I remembered you, if that's what you mean."

"I know you remembered me," says Samantha. "But did you—you were important to me. Our friendship was important to me. I didn't keep in touch, but I was determined we'd be friends again someday. That's one of the main reasons I took the job at Tate, to be in Boston."

Lily can feel Samantha's eyes on her. "I'm not sure what to say."

"We don't have to talk about this if you don't want to. But it's my fault you're involved—you, and Tom, and Marty, for that matter. I thought if I drew you into the drama of my life, my big secret . . . I'm sorry."

Lily is touched by the repetition and the sound of Samantha's voice. There's a new note of vulnerability. "I'm a grown-up," says Lily. "And I'm pretty sure I knew that—or suspected that. You wanted something from me, and I wanted something from you."

"You mean the manuscript?"

"Yes," says Lily. "I've always struggled, you know?" She glances up at Samantha. "Faith has never been easy for me. But when I began to understand what the manuscript was, what it meant, I felt something shift for me."

"I know," says Samantha. "I've felt it, too—in me, I mean. It's as if the manuscript reveals our fears, making them clearer, but also less important, less real." She smiles and shrugs. "I'm not being very articulate. But I do know what you mean."

"I'm not sure I can be your friend," says Lily.

"Yes," says Samantha. "I'm not sure anyone can."

They're quiet for a few seconds. Lily notices it's a comfortable silence. As she starts to ask Samantha another question, she hears Tom's key in the lock. He walks in, and then Marty follows.

As soon as Lily sees his face, she knows something else has happened. "What?"

"Francine and Nickolas are gone."

"THE PLACE WAS EMPTY," SAYS MARTY. SHE SITS ON the couch with Tom, across from Samantha in the armchair and Lily in her father's recliner. "The attic, too. She left the two cell phones—her own and the one I gave her—side by side on the table outside the kitchen. Along with this." Marty takes the two phones out of her pocket and lays them on the coffee table, then holds up a small metal key with a red tag attached.

Samantha stares at it. "The key to the safe deposit box. She would have done it, then. She would have left me to them."

"What do you think they're going to do?" asks Tom. "I mean Francine and Nickolas. Where do you think they'll go?"

Samantha shakes her head. "I have no idea." She looks at Lily. "Why leave now? When she was the only one who could get into the box—I don't understand."

Lily looks at Samantha. "They must have another copy of the photos. They may even have more than we do."

"How do you know?" asks Tom.

"It's the only thing that makes sense," says Lily. "Remember when we were talking in Francine's bedroom, and Marty said we'd return the photos and report this all to the police once we got Samantha back alive?"

Tom nods.

"Francine started to object, and then she looked at

Nickolas. Neither of them said anything else. I thought that was weird, at the time, given how committed they both were."

"I'm not following you," says Tom.

"I am," says Marty. "They would never have let us give back the photographs if they were the only copy."

"And if we did that and then told the police—it's over. Nickolas knows these guys will kill him as soon as they have what they want. Francine and Nickolas knew then, in that moment, they were going to leave with whatever it is they have," says Lily. "They wanted to do it through you," she says to Samantha. "To introduce the book to the world through a respected scholar. But if that didn't work—"

"I was expendable," says Samantha.

Lily doesn't answer her.

"Yeah," says Marty. "You were expendable. Sorry."

Samantha looks out the window. "I need something to eat," she says. "And I'm remembering more. I want to try to get this straight. I want to know what's happening."

TOM MAKES EGGS AND TOAST FOR EVERYONE. SAMAN-tha eats and drinks two cups of coffee. While she's eating, she asks for a scratch pad and a pen, so she can write things down as they come to her. Once everyone's finished eating, they settle in the living room again, and Samantha begins to tell Tom and Marty what she's already told Lily, although Lily notices it's a richer, more detailed version.

"Was it a nice hotel?" asks Marty.

"No. It was more like a motel. In fact—didn't you say they were staying at the Days Inn?"

Marty nods.

"I think I remember the sign, when we went to the parking lot. That's where we were. I'm almost sure."

"How did you get to the parking lot?" asks Tom.

Samantha pauses and shakes her head, as if trying to grasp an image and failing. "First, I heard William's voice, but very close. Earlier, I had heard it, or thought I was hearing it, far away, from another room. But then he was talking directly to me, very patient and kind, sort of, 'Come on, old girl. We'll get you out of this.'"

"And did you just walk out?" asks Tom.

"There wasn't any ruckus. We were quiet. He was being very quiet. We didn't take the elevator. He half-carried me down the stairs. Then we went out into the cold, into the parking lot, and I saw the sign, and we got into a car. And he began telling me a story. It seems to me he talked the whole time."

"But you can't remember what he said?" asks Tom.

"Some of it. A bit more of it." She takes a sip of coffee and looks at the pad on her lap. "He said that Edgar had taken him in after I left. I knew he'd had some sort of breakdown. I'd heard through friends. He and Edgar became close. That's how he learned of the manuscript. But I can't . . . He said he had no idea I would be involved. Although, I must say, it's impossible to take his word for anything. He was always a consummate liar."

"So, if he and Egar became close, he probably knew Nickolas," says Lily.

"He didn't mention the name—or, at least, not that I recall. I'm sorry this is so frustrating."

"It's all right," says Marty. "Take your time. If they gave you sodium pentathol, you were probably in and out. Stuff will come back—maybe."

"I wonder why he brought you here," says Lily.

"He said it was safer, that they wouldn't be watching your place anymore. That they had gotten what they wanted."

"He knows a lot about these guys," says Tom. "And he seemed to have freedom to come and go. He knows where Lily lives. Do you think—"

"He was working with them," says Samantha. "That much *is* clear. He told me something about my car—that he had been the one to destroy it. But destroying the car was one thing, he said. He couldn't watch me being destroyed. I can hear his voice saying that. But I'm getting..." She leans back and closes her eyes. Then she opens them and stares down at the paper on her lap. "I remember getting here. He walked me into the vestibule and said, 'I'm going to have to leave you here. I can't wait.' And I asked him what would happen, and he smiled and said, 'They'll kill me if they find me. I'm going to try to prevent that from happening.' And that's it." She shakes her head and shrugs. "There's nothing else. That's all I can remember."

The pale gray light in the living room window grows stronger, suddenly, as a weak sun rises over the building next door, shining through a thin cloud cover.

"We have to figure out what to do," says Lily.

"She's right," says Marty and glances at her watch. "It's almost seven o'clock. They said to be at the bank at nine."

"But will they come, now, with Samantha gone?" asks Lily.

"I think so," says Marty. "They still don't know exactly what's happened. Maybe William took Samantha and headed out of town. That would make sense. As far as they're concerned, we might not know any more than we did last night. They're not going to call to say they've lost her. And this is their only chance to get the pictures. They'll be there." She looks at Samantha. "What time does the bank open?"

"I'm not sure. Eight-thirty, I think."

"We've got to get there before nine," says Marty.

"Why?" asks Samantha.

"Because now that you're safe, we've got some leverage, and I have an idea. I want this over fast and clean. And I want us to end up with insurance. And I think I know how to do both."

37

LILY AND SAMANTHA WALK DOWN GARDEN STREET, past Christ Church, toward Mass Ave and Harvard Square. The sidewalks are crowded. Lily looks at her watch. Eight-thirty-two. There was a lot to do before they went to the bank. Samantha didn't have her ID. It was in her purse, and she didn't know where her purse was—probably back at the motel. She had to go home to get her passport and an earlier driver's license. She also had to write a letter that Marty outlined for her. And Marty had to get in touch with a friend.

The air is milder. The sky is a soft gray and there is no wind. "Do you think we're supposed to be chatting, as if nothing were wrong?" asks Samantha.

"For whose benefit?" asks Lily. "It's not like the people on the sidewalk care. And anybody watching us on purpose knows something's wrong."

"Good point," says Samantha. "Thank you for coming with me."

"It wouldn't be right for you to have to do this on your own. You've gone through enough." Lily didn't add that Marty was worried about sending Samantha alone. She was afraid Samantha wouldn't be able to remember all the details of the plan.

From then on, they walk in silence. They cross Church Street and Lily sees the bank, halfway up the block on the right. They pass the Walgreen's and then the deli where they'll wait afterward. At the door to the bank, Samantha pauses.

"What time is it?" she asks.

"Eight-thirty-eight," says Lily.

Lily can see the white circle of the sun over the trees of Harvard Yard. Her breath makes a pale mist in the air. She looks up and down the block. She doesn't recognize any of the faces. She's in a kind of limbo—she has no real hope that things will go smoothly, but no idea about what will go wrong. Samantha opens the large glass door. And then Lily realizes she's not breathing and takes a gasp of cool air before the door closes behind her.

She follows Samantha into the lobby and down a flight of marble stairs. They turn right and find a woman, maybe Samantha's age, with thick white hair pulled back into a bun, seated at a long wooden desk. She smiles at them as if they are arriving at a party. "Good morning," she says. "Can I help you?"

"Yes," says Samantha. "I need to get into my box, but I have a bit of a problem."

The woman nods sympathetically.

"I had my wallet stolen," says Samantha. "So most of

my regular ID—driver's license, credit cards—was in there."

"Do you have an account with us?"

"Yes," says Samantha.

"And did you have a bank card in your wallet?"

"Yes."

"Have you notified the bank?" asks the woman. "Or would you like me to do that for you now?"

"I'm in a bit of a hurry," says Samantha. "If you would be willing to do it while we're inside—?"

"Of course," says the woman. "But I do need some form of positive identification."

"I have my box key and my passport," says Samantha. "I also have a current out-of-state driver's license."

Samantha hands the woman the passport and license. The woman studies them for a few minutes, then excuses herself and walks through a door behind her desk.

"What do we do if this doesn't work?" asks Lily.

"It will work," says Samantha. "I've got ID and the box key. They've got a record of me back there. It will work."

Lily watches the small gold-and-white clock on the woman's desk—on Mrs. Langston's desk, according to the nameplate. Five minutes pass. Finally she appears, smiling.

"Sorry for the delay," she says. "Will you follow me?" She crosses the marble floor, her footsteps silent, and opens a steel door in the wall. They find themselves in a large room lined with metal drawers, each with a numbered plate and two locks. Mrs. Langston walks across the room to a small drawer halfway up the wall and inserts a key in one of the locks and turns it. Then Samantha puts her own key in the second lock. Once the drawer slides open, Mrs. Langston takes out a box and hands it to Samantha. "Would you like a cubicle?" she asks.

"Yes," says Samantha. "Please."

Mrs. Langston shows them into a small room with a table and two chairs. "Be sure you let me know when you're ready to leave."

Once the woman is gone, Samantha opens the box and removes three brown legal-sized envelopes. She opens them, one by one, takes out the three photographs, and lays them side by side on the table.

"I don't know if I can do this," says Samantha.

Lily looks down at the photos. She can make out the texture of the scroll, the stitching down the edge of two of the pages. She finds the Lord's Prayer, and the words of forgiveness and judgment. Then she says, "We have to."

THEY LEAVE THROUGH THE FRONT DOOR OF THE BANK. Samantha has the envelopes under her arm. They walk into the Walgreen's next door and copy each of the photographs on the machine at the back of the store. Then they leave and enter the deli, which is packed with people getting their morning coffee and croissant. Marty is standing by the door, dressed in a pair of baggy jeans and an oversized suede jacket, with a black wool hat pulled down over her ears. Lily hands her the envelope holding the new copies, and Marty disappears into the crowd. Lily shoulders her way to the counter across the front window, bringing Samantha along behind her. There are no stools, so they stand next to each other, looking out at the sidewalk.

"Now what?" asks Samantha.

"We wait to see if the phone rings," says Lily. Slowly,

she takes it out of her pocket and holds it in her hand, as if she was thinking of using it.

"And what do we tell them?" asks Samantha.

"We tell them the truth," says Lily.

"Why would they believe us?"

"What choice do they have?" asks Lily.

"But how—"

"Let's just wait and see," says Lily.

Lily hears a buzzing sound and then realizes it's her own cell phone. She answers. A man is talking, but his voice is low, and she can't hear what he's saying. "Wait a minute," she says. "Don't hang up. I can't hear you."

One of the men behind the counter starts yelling at her. "You can't use that in here. See the sign?" He points to a large white piece of cardboard over the door with a cell phone crossed out.

"Hold on," she yells into the phone. "I'm going outside where I can hear you. Don't hang up." She can't keep track of Samantha and hold the phone and make her way through the crowd, so she leaves Samantha on her own.

On the sidewalk, she leans against the window and holds her left hand against her left ear. "Okay," she says. "I can hear now."

"I believe Mrs. Henderson has three envelopes under her arm," he says.

"That's right," says Lily. "She does."

"You don't have to yell at me," says the voice.

"Sorry," says Lily.

"I believe, too, that Miss Loetterlee and Brother Nickolas have left."

"Yes," says Lily. "Apparently."

"Do you know where they have gone?"

"No," says Lily. "They acted independently. They left without telling any of us."

"I understand," says the voice.

"Where do you want us to leave the envelopes?" asks Lily.

"First, put the photographs into one envelope."

"Okay," she says.

"There are pay phones across from the department store at the end of the block. Do you see them?"

"Yes," says Lily.

"Go to the phone at the far right and make a call. Lean the envelope against the wall of the box. Walk away. Do not look back. We won't bother you again."

"I have to ask you something," says Lily. She has to buy Marty as much time as possible, so she can get as far away as possible before they know what's going to happen.

The man hesitates. "Yes?"

"I'll return to this spot," says Lily. "But could you please call and confirm that you have the envelope, that this is over?"

He hesitates again, says, "Yes," and hangs up.

Lily puts the phone in the pocket of her parka and goes back to the deli counter.

"I'm not going to tell you everything now," she says to Samantha. "I don't have time. But it's working fine. I have to put all the photos in one envelope and take them down the block. It should take five minutes, max. If someone bothers you, or tries to get you to go with them, scream. This is a crowded place. You're safe here."

Samantha's face is blank and terrified. Lily takes the envelopes from her, puts the photos into one of them, then hands the other two empty ones to Samantha. "Hold on to these," says Lily. "Wait for me. I'll stand in front of you, on the street." She points to a spot on the sidewalk, and Samantha nods.

Lily leaves and walks toward the bank of pay phones. When she gets there, she's not sure if he means the phone on the far right facing the street or facing the department store. She chooses the one on the far right as she faces the street, goes to the phone, and leans the envelope on the small counter, against the wall of the box. She picks up the receiver, dials her own number, stands there for a moment, hangs up, then turns away.

Before she's past the department store, she hears someone calling out. She can't turn around. She keeps walking, slowly. She feels someone tap her on the shoulder.

A young man with long curly hair and a black book bag slung over his shoulder stands next to her. The book bag looks heavy. His face is flushed with exertion.

"You left this in the phone booth," he says. "Or whatever they're called these days." He hands her the envelope.

Lily stares at it, then at him, before she realizes he's just a student with a good heart. She says, "Thanks. Thanks a lot."

He smiles at her, hesitantly, and walks back the other way.

Now she's standing in the middle of the block with the envelope in her hand. When the cell phone rings, she can't remember where she put it. She checks her pockets and finds it.

"Do you see the newsstand across the street?" asks the voice.

"Yes."

"Wait five minutes, then cross the street to the stand. There is a stack of *Boston Daily* newspapers on the right-hand corner of the front shelf. Put the envelope down next to that stack, pick up a magazine, read it for a short time, then put down the magazine and return to the deli. Do not turn around."

"But you'll call," says Lily. "To let me know you have it."

"I'll call."

She sits on a bench by a tree. An old man with a guide dog sits next to her. He has a sign around his neck, but she can't read it from where she sits. She checks the digital clock. After five minutes, she walks to the corner, crosses the street, puts down the envelope, thumbs through a magazine, and leaves.

This time she makes it back to the deli without interruption. Through the window, Samantha's face is white. Lily nods to her and leans against the wall next to the window, the cell phone in her hand. She can feel time passing, as if she has a clock inside her that ticks away each second. She wills herself not to turn around. She wills herself to stay still, in that one spot, her back to whatever is happening down the street.

When the phone rings, she almost drops it.

"We have the photographs."

"Listen to me," says Lily. "An additional set of photographs is now at the office of a lawyer. He has four letters—one signed by me, one by Samantha Henderson, one by Marty Angel, and one by Tom Casey. Each letter says the same thing. If any of us should disappear or meet with a violent death, the other three—or any remaining survivors of the group—have the power to instruct him to open the envelope and mail the photographs to a prominent Biblical scholar, whose name and address are included in the letter—a young man, who should be alive a long time. If nothing happens to us, the photographs remain with the lawyer, or with his partner—both of whom are also young and healthy—unopened, until the last one of us dies."

Lily listens to the silence on the other end. She can hear breathing, and someone else speaking in the background.

"Don't move," says the voice. "I will call you."

Lily hangs up and waits. Now she can watch the seconds pass on the giant digital clock above the Square. In six minutes, the phone rings again.

"This is not a wise decision on your part," says the voice.

"Maybe not," says Lily. "But it's done."

"How do we know one of you won't change your mind or hasn't already changed your mind? One of you may have a copy still."

"We don't. There's nothing left. And none of us, individually, has access to the copy in the office. It has to be agreed upon by all surviving members of the group."

A brief silence follows, then he says, "Please tell Mrs. Henderson that it will be best if she forgets any of this ever happened. If she writes about the book, even speculatively—we will know."

"I'll tell her," says Lily. "She'll understand."

"And of course," says the voice. "That is true for you, Ms. Connor, as well. And for Ms. Angel and Mr. Casey."

"It's very unlikely any of us would be willing to risk our lives for a book," says Lily. "Even this book."

"Yes," says the voice. "Few people are."

EPILOGUE

1.

THE FIRST MONDAY IN DECEMBER, LILY SITS IN THE chaplain's office watching airy snowflakes drift past the window. The hill beside the library is coated, the steps slowly disappearing as the flakes continue to fall. Everything's quiet. In a few minutes, hundreds of students will begin trailing out of classrooms for the last time that semester. Tomorrow reading period begins. But right now, before the grounds crew clears the steps and students head for the library to begin studying for exams, it's as if she has the campus, and the snow, to herself.

The moment feels like a heightened version of the last three weeks. Nothing has happened. She's spoken to Samantha once, on the phone, and they both stuck to the facts, as if they couldn't bear to talk about the resonance of those facts. No one has heard from Francine or Nickolas, or William. The manuscript is gone. And if Lily didn't continue to feel a slow shifting in herself—as if, in her life, she was sitting in front of a window through which she viewed the world, but someone, or something, had moved her chair—she would begin to doubt her own story.

Two piles of books take up a quarter of the desktop, half of them books about Q. At first, she had been afraid to take them out of the library, to bring them into the office. Then she realized the Order couldn't know what she was reading. Of course, the reading didn't really help. Because *The Book of Light* wasn't in these texts. So she moved on to a study of the Orthodox Church, a study of mysticism, a study of light, a study of Athos. She won't do anything dangerous. She isn't interested in publishing or pursuing. She isn't interested in danger.

She hears footsteps on the stone floor outside her office and turns around. A young, dark-haired man in a black parka stands facing her, hesitating to come in all the way. "You left me a message, right?" he asks.

"John," she says. "Thanks for coming." She walks around the desk and shakes his hand. "Do you have a minute?"

He nods.

"Sit down," she says. "Do you mind?"

He shakes his head. He looks tentative and confused, and who can blame him, she thinks. He unzips his parka, and a couple of drops of water, melted snowflakes, shake onto the floor. He sits in the chair she offers, and she pulls her chair out from behind the desk, so she's facing him.

"Our last meeting, about the Christian Movement, didn't go very well. I owe you an apology," she says.

"You mean you've changed your mind?" he asks, looking more bewildered by the minute.

"No," says Lily. "I just—I sounded pompous and certain, and it's been bothering me. You and I are trying to do the same thing—live decent lives according to our faiths. That's not easy, and at the very least it requires humility. No one has all the answers."

"That's what Jim says."

"Jim is a lot better at this than I am."

"Not necessarily," he says. "This is the first time I've ever had an adult on this campus call me in to apologize, for anything. And there have been things to apologize for, trust me."

"Like what?" asks Lily.

"Like the time my ethics professor read my paper on relativism out loud and then spent half the class talking about how wrong it was. He even used the term 'Christian fundamentalism,' so everyone would know who wrote it."

"Did you report him?" asks Lily.

"No. By that time I knew better."

"And there have been other things, too?"

"Lots," he says. "Look. I know homosexuals are discriminated against. I'm not stupid. I know that's not right. But my faith—which is a big part of who I am—tells me homosexuality is a sin. So what am I supposed to do with that?"

"I don't know," says Lily. "It's a problem for me, too."

"What do you mean?" he asks.

"There are many things the church calls sins that I see as—what?—reality, being human, what people do, who people are. Sex between homosexuals is one of those things. Sex outside of marriage is another. Well, sex in gen-

eral, really. And then there are other things the church re-
fuses to even name—or sometimes supports—that are, I
believe, the root of evil."

"So how do you call yourself a Christian if you don't
abide by the teachings of the Bible? I mean, why do you
even bother?"

"Because," says Lily, "I do try to abide by the teachings
of the Bible."

"The ones you think are important," he says.

"Yes," she says. "That's true. The ones I think are important."

"Like what?"

"Like not judging others."

He looks at her and starts to smile. "Nice work," he
says. "I get the point."

He shakes his head, still smiling. "You think if we kept
talking long enough we would find one thing we agreed
on?"

"Probably," says Lily. "Are you a baseball fan?"

"Yankees," he says.

"So that wouldn't be it."

THE NEXT DAY, LILY BRINGS A SMALL BOX AND SOME
empty grocery bags to the office at Tate. Jim is due back
from Virginia on Monday. She puts the books on her desk
into three of the bags and carries them down the steps to
the library. The snow has melted and the world looks gray
and drab, the trees dark against an empty sky. Once inside,
Lily unloads the books onto the long front desk and then
pauses in the hallway to look at the titles of new acquisi-
tions, lined up on shelves along the wall.

Someone walks by behind her and then pauses. "Hi."

Lily turns and sees Annie Kim, her short hair pulled back with two white barrettes, her eyes sunken and ringed with circles. "Hi," says Lily. "I've been thinking about you. How are you?"

The girl shrugs. "Okay."

"Not very convincing," says Lily, and smiles. "You want to talk?"

"No," says Annie. "Thanks, though."

Lily sees two chairs in a corner of the lobby and points to them. "Can we sit for just a minute? Do you have time?"

Annie shrugs again and follows Lily across the room.

"So," says Lily. "Things aren't going so well?"

"They're okay. It's not the school's fault. I just think maybe this isn't the right place for me."

"Could be," says Lily. "That happens. Have you thought about what you might want to do instead?"

"No," says Annie. "My parents want me to stay here. So I guess I will, at least through the year. Then maybe I'll try to transfer."

"Can you tell me more about what's wrong?" asks Lily.

The girl gazes off into the space above Lily's head, as if she's hoping a more interesting answer will materialize. "It's regular stuff. You know. I'm not really making friends. My roommate's like—she just wants to study, all night, every night. She doesn't talk. And a lot of people around here don't like the Asian students. I'm not that smart, you know? Sort of average. And there's this thing that all the Asian students are really smart and work all the time. But I'm not like that, and there's no place for me to be."

"I don't think Professor Henderson would mind my telling you that she thinks you're smart," says Lily.

"She's great," says the girl, brightening for a minute. "Is she okay, by the way?"

"Why do you ask?"

"She seems sort of sick, like she's got a really bad cold or something."

"I haven't seen her in a while. I thought I might call her today," says Lily. "What about mentioning your name?"

"She's been really nice, and she's given me good grades. But I don't know her that well, and anyway—"

"It's more than that," says Lily.

Annie nods. "My parents are also getting a divorce. It seems stupid that I'm so unhappy about it. I'm not even living there anymore. When I go home for Christmas, my dad will have moved out."

"Do you have brothers and sisters?"

"No," she says, and shakes her head. "I'm an only child."

"First of all," says Lily, "it isn't stupid to be upset. Your home has been your world, all your life. Now that world is dividing, and it won't be there when you go back—at least, not in the form you know. And, second, don't you think that might have a lot to do with what's going on this term?"

Again, the young woman nods, but she doesn't speak.

"Does going to church help?" asks Lily. "Do you feel better when you do it?" When she sees Annie's face—half horrified, half guilty, she quickly adds, "It's not a trick question. I mean, I'm not asking in order to trick you into admitting something. I really want to know the answer."

"When I was little," Annie says, "and going to Sunday school, I always loved when we got brought into the main church, after the sermon. My father would stand me on the pew between him and my mother, or sometimes he would put me on his shoulders, if we were way at the back. Everyone seemed so glad to see me. I can remember the faces of the people in front of us, turning around to smile.

They always sang one of the children's hymns—'Saints of God' or 'All Things Bright and Beautiful.' I still know the words to those hymns, and I still get tears in my eyes when I hear them. I usually can't sing them, because then I really start to cry. I think I cry because I was so happy then, at that moment. No matter what had gone on between my parents all week—and the truth is, they've never gotten along very well—it would be wiped out. They would be singing and smiling, too. And for years, I thought that's what the Holy Spirit was—like, the Spirit rallies we have here now. I thought the Holy Spirit just meant feeling really good in church, like everything fit together, everything was whole."

"That's what I mean," says Lily. "I just didn't come up with the right language. Shouldn't faith be able to bring us to that moment, when everything feels whole and complete? Even when the circumstances in our lives make it look as if everything's broken—like divorce, or loneliness, or resentment. You get on your knees and pray, and you feel the world becoming complete again."

"Yeah, but I don't feel that way now. It's like I know too much. I'm not going to get tricked again into thinking those feelings are real, or that they last."

"But what if they did?" asks Lily. "What if you carried those feelings with you after church, because of your faith? Well, not exactly those feelings. They have to be shaped and informed by adult perception, just as you said. But it seems to me these days that this is just what Jesus was saying—that God is with us through the worst of it, and whatever happens we still have the choices of love and forgiveness. And if we choose those things, we have the power to make things whole again, or to see that they are whole, that they've always been whole."

Neither of them speaks for a few seconds. Then Annie says, "You mean we can make ourselves feel that way whenever we want, feel better? Like healing."

"Yes," says Lily. "Like healing."

THE BOX IS PACKED WITH THE FEW THINGS SHE brought with her to this job: one of her prayer books; a sweatshirt to wear when the building was cold in the morning; a pair of slippers for when she was there alone; a couple of legal pads, one of them half-filled with names and numbers of colleagues at Tate; a picture of her father, leaning against the house—you couldn't see his eyes because of the shadow of his hat, but the smile was unmistakable; a spiral notebook for her own reconstruction of the manuscript—the pages she saw, as well as Q material proposed by her many sources. There are moments, as she's transcribing a text, in which she senses that it is at this point the touch of light would appear. She leaves blank spaces between brackets, like the professionals.

As she puts on her parka, she remembers what Annie said about Samantha and starts to pick up the phone. But she doesn't pick it up. A couple more days, she thinks. I just need a little more time.

2.

ONE WEEK LATER LILY SLIPS INTO THE MONASTERY chapel and finds a seat on the back row. She is late for the service. She has just had a two-hour meeting with Bishop Spencer, who is always, himself, late. There was a lot to talk about. She is able to catch the end of the hymn before

the reading of the gospel—"O Come, O Come, Emmanuel,"
the classic anthem of Advent. Then she sits in the dim corner
and listens to the reading. "In the fifteenth year of the reign
of the Emperor Tiberius, when Pontius Pilate was governor
of Judea, and Herod was ruler of Galilee..." And she's back
in Samantha's workroom, listening to her explain the eccen-
tricities of Aramaic script in the Herodian period.

She pays attention again in time to hear, "Every valley
shall be filled, and every mountain and hill shall be made
low, and the crooked shall be made straight, and the
rough ways made smooth; and all flesh shall see the sal-
vation of God."

Like healing, Annie said. Yes, Lily said to her, like
healing.

As Lily stands in line for Eucharist, she notices the back of someone's head, an older woman with
cropped white hair and a black turtleneck. Samantha is
here, taking Eucharist, too. This is the first time they've
seen each other in almost a month. Lily left a message last
week, and Samantha left a message the next day, but nothing came of it. Lily has admitted to herself that her own
hesitation has to do with a kind of selfishness. She doesn't
want to talk about the manuscript—the reality hasn't
dimmed, but she's still in the middle of changing, and she
doesn't want to risk trying to describe it. She's afraid that
putting language to what's happening will trap it all inside
the limits of the language. She and Tom rarely mention
Samantha or Q or even Marty, something Lily finds strange
when she thinks about it, but for which she feels grateful.
Maybe Tom is changing, too. She'll have to wait and see.
It's hard to imagine how he could be a better person, but,

then, she is beginning to see that her imagination is sadly limited.

When Samantha finishes, she walks around to the side of the aisle and as she looks for her seat, their eyes meet. She looks startled and a little leery, at first, then she smiles and sits down. At the end of the service, Lily waits until the altar candles are out before she stands to look for Charlie. She's going to have dinner at the monastery, and afterward they'll have a chance to talk privately. But Lily sees Samantha waiting, with her coat on, near the door. She picks up her parka and goes to talk with her.

"How are you?" asks Samantha.

"Strange," says Lily.

"Yes, I know. Me, too. I'm going away for a while, and I would like to talk to you about a couple of things before I leave. Do you have time . . . ?"

"Where are you going?" asks Lily. "What about Tate?"

Samantha smiles and shakes her head. "They're not very happy with me, but I'm taking the semester off. I called it a family crisis, and, in a way, it is. Francine was my family—Francine and William, however twisted that may seem."

Lily feels a little current of electricity at the sound of those names. "Sometimes I think all families are twisted. You haven't heard anything, have you?"

"I'll explain tomorrow. If you can come. Can you?"

"Yes," says Lily. "What time?"

"In the evening, if that's all right. I have a lot of last-minute things to do, running around."

"Did you get a new car?" asks Lily.

Samantha laughs. "No. I'm renting one. I—I don't miss it."

Lily sees Charlie coming toward them. "Around five, then? Or six?"

"Five is fine," says Samantha. Then she turns to greet Charlie. "I was just telling Lily I'm going to be taking a sabbatical next term, so I won't be here for a while. But when I return, I hope to become a regular. I feel so at home in these services. They remind me of the first Anglican services I attended, in England, when I converted." She says good-bye and leaves.

Lily catches Charlie staring after Samantha. "What?" she asks.

"She seems different. Did you notice?"

"I think so. Calmer, maybe. Is that what it was?"

"I don't know. I never thought of her as much of a churchgoer."

"People change," says Lily.

AFTER DINNER THEY WALK ALONG THE RIVER. THE ground is covered in frozen snow. Charlie talks about the monastery, about the election of a new superior, about a trip he's planning with two other brothers to their mission in Nigeria. When he finishes, there's a pause, and Lily can hear their boots squeaking.

"I haven't seen you forever," says Charlie. "Where have you been?"

"Finishing up at Tate. Jim's back, so that's over. And catching up at the center. I got way behind there."

"You've been trying to do an awful lot at once," says Charlie. "I love the Women's Center, and I love Barbara, but you need—"

"I know. I just met with Spencer for two hours. I've heard this one."

"We're right, though."

"I know that, too. I'm going to take a break from the center. I just talked to Barbara. We need to hire someone to do full-time fund-raising and membership drives—the nuts and bolts. We've got a great volunteer who wants the job. Once she's trained, I can step out and let Barbara and her run the show for a while."

"What's a while?" asks Charlie.

"At least a year."

"What will you do?"

"Spencer has a job for me at a parish in the South End."

"St. Margaret's?"

"Yeah. Do you know it well?"

"Pretty well. I think it's a great place."

"That's what he says, although he's been wrong before."

"I know," says Charlie. "But this is a good match." He puts an arm around her shoulder. "I want to say something like, welcome back."

"I think I'm supposed to be slightly offended and say something ironic, but—thank you."

"You're welcome. How's Tom? What else is going on?"

"Tom's good. We're doing really well. I love him a lot."

"I hardly ever hear you say that. Are you thinking about getting married?"

Lily smiles and shakes her head. "I have no idea."

"I hardly ever hear you say that, either."

They walk in silence for a few moments. The streetlights along Memorial Drive shimmer across the water.

"I wanted to talk to you about something else," says Lily. "I've been in touch with my mother."

Charlie stops walking. "So, say that again."

"I've been in touch with my mother. I called her, and left a message, and she called back."

"How was it?"

"Weird. Unsettling."

"How did she sound?"

"Sober. She said she's still in AA. And nice, I guess. Like a nice person."

He stands with his hands in his coat pockets, looking at her. "I'm so—I've prayed about this, you know?"

"You have?" she asks.

"Yes. You and your mother are in my prayers for healing. Sometimes I put you on the monastery list. I don't put her name, but I always add my own petition. So, what's next?"

"I'm not sure. I want to hear her side of the story. And I want to tell her—I'm sorry for judging her so harshly all these years. I'm not sure I've had any right to do that."

"Wow," says Charlie. "This is—where did this come from?"

"It's a long story," says Lily.

"A long story involving Samantha and Q and a lot of secrets?"

"Yes," says Lily. She opens her mouth to explain, then closes it. Finally, she adds, "I'll tell you everything, eventually, but right now I'm freezing. Walk me to the T. Let's make small talk."

"Jeez," he says. "I leave you alone for a few weeks and all hell breaks loose."

3.

The following evening Lily comes up out of the Porter Square MTA station. The sky is the clear colors of a winter dusk, azure near the horizon, almost black at the top of the dome. The wind has picked up, and Lily stops to zip her parka before crossing the street to Samantha's apartment building.

Lily pushes the intercom button in the foyer and gets buzzed in. On the ride up in the paneled elevator, she tries to breathe deeply and calm herself. Being in the building takes her back to earlier visits—that first evening she and Charlie and Tom showed up for dinner; the day Samantha's car was destroyed; standing in the bedroom with Marty, Tom, Samantha, Francine, the smell of pizza mingling with the fear and confusion. What did I think of Francine, Lily wonders, and where is she now?

After Lily knocks, there's a short silence, then she hears someone undoing the locks, one by one, at least three of them. She doesn't remember Samantha having that many locks. The woman standing in the entryway resembles Samantha only in the most general way—a small woman in her sixties with cropped white hair. But this woman looks even smaller, and older. She's wearing what appear to be a pair of blue pajama bottoms and a black turtleneck under a red sweatshirt. Something about the colors makes Lily assume Samantha hasn't looked in the mirror yet today.

"Thank you for coming," says Samantha. "It's good to see you."

Lily follows her into the living room. The air of precise arrangement is gone. Most of the furniture has been pushed back against the wall. The floor is covered with books and papers—as Lily looks more closely, she sees that some of the books are the same ones she has, herself, been reading. She sees, too, that even though her first impression was of a mess, the piles of books and notebooks and notes are carefully stacked, and as she looks more closely she can see they're stacked by subject.

"Sorry," says Samantha. "I don't have a workspace big enough for all of this."

Lily picks up one of the books and reads the title, then turns to Samantha. "You're not going to do anything stupid, are you?"

"I'm sure I will," she says. "But if you're speaking of publishing something about *The Book of Light,* then, no, I'm not going to do that particular stupid thing."

There's a moment of silence, in which Lily puts down the book and sits on the sofa.

Samantha sits next to her. "I've thought about calling you, to tell you some of this earlier, but I needed time to sort things out on my own."

Lily nods.

"I received a letter from William, shortly after he disappeared."

"And?"

"He told me his story, a sort of confession, I suppose."

"Can I see it?"

Samantha shakes her head. "Some of it is very personal, about me and him and our history. The tone is—interesting, unlike the William I knew. I found myself believing him without hesitation, not something I could ever have imagined. In any case, I can't let you read it, but I want you to know the part that concerns you and the others. That's only fair." She takes a deep breath and leans back against the sofa cushions.

"Interestingly enough, we seem to have known or imagined most of it. Edgar did take William in after I left. They became close. Edgar trusted him—enough to tell him about the manuscript. But, of course, as William regained his strength, his old, true self—that's what he called it in the letter, although I'm not sure it was his true self—but that side of him returned. He wanted the manuscript. He wanted to translate it and present it to the world as his own discovery."

"How did he get hooked up with the Order?" asks Lily.

"Edgar had told him about them, that they imagined themselves to be the keepers of the book. William tracked them down. And though he says he knew nothing of Edgar's death, he may well have been the cause. He couldn't bring himself to admit that, but I can tell, from his language, he was aware of the truth. He made himself useful to the Order, told them what little he knew about the plans to smuggle it off Athos and send it to Edgar.

"When Nickolas disappeared from Athos, they knew to search for him and the manuscript immediately. They were a few steps behind, because no one knew he was gone right away. But not too far behind. They followed Nickolas to America and, finally, to us."

"Did William come with them?"

"Yes," says Samantha. "He claims he knew nothing of my involvement, but when he found out, he saw it as a perfect opportunity to kill two birds with one stone—punish me for leaving him and get hold of the manuscript. The car was his doing. But he says that afterward, when he looked at what he had done, he felt sick at heart—that's his own phrase. He was tired of destroying things."

"So why did he stay with them then?"

"Oh, I don't think his ambition waned. He wanted to get

his hands on the book. I suspect two things happened. First, he saw that was highly unlikely, that the Order was a more thorough and efficient watchdog than he had imagined. And, second, he saw me tied to a toilet in a motel bathroom, and heard them talk about killing me if the photographs weren't returned."

Lily watches Samantha for a moment, then says, "In a way, he risked his life for you."

Samantha returns her gaze, then she reaches behind the row of books on the bottom shelf and hands Lily a brown envelope, like the ones in which the photographs had been sent. "This came two days ago," she says.

"What is it?" asks Lily. She's afraid to open it. If the envelope contains another photograph, the whole play begins again. She doesn't think she can begin again.

"It's not part of the manuscript," says Samantha, "if that's what you mean."

The envelope feels light, almost empty. Lily holds it upside down and shakes the contents into her right hand. Two small newspaper clippings fall out.

The first is a single wide paragraph, the whole clipping no more than four inches by two inches:

TRUCK-CAMPER COLLISION KILLS 2, NO SURVIVORS

Sweetwater—An Arkansas trucker and an unidentified man were killed when the truck veered into oncoming traffic on Route 101 yesterday morning and slammed into a motorhome. The crash closed Route 101 for about six hours. State Police have identified the trucker as Stratis Nisyrios, 24, of Little Rock. Investigators say his empty milk tanker truck drifted into southbound traffic just north of Exit 22 around 4 a.m. The driver of the motorhome has yet to be identified. The resulting fire destroyed the contents of both vehicles. Police traced the motorhome to Jay Lawrence of Falmouth, Kentucky, who said a couple bought it from him for cash. He described the woman as small with red hair. The man was medium height, stocky build, dark hair. Texas State Troopers ask that anyone with possible information about the couple contact them immediately.

The paper gave the number to call—a hotline that guarantees anonymity.

The second clipping is smaller, probably one-sixth of a single column in a small-town newspaper.

POLICE SEEK IDENTITY OF DROWNING VICTIM

New Waterford—Police are still seeking the identity of a man who was reportedly thrown overboard last night on the ferry from New Waterford to Channel Port. Michael Toffey, an 11-year-old traveling with his family, had climbed to the upper deck, officially off-bounds to passengers, and claimed he saw two men on the deck below. According to the youngster, "The shorter man picked up the taller man by the legs and just dropped him headfirst." He reported the incident to his father, who alerted the pilot. A head count was taken upon arrival in Channel Port and there was one passenger missing. The boy could not describe either of the men, other than their

heights. Gulf Patrol and Channel Port police ask
that anyone with possible information regarding
the incident contact them immediately.

No phone number is given in this one.

Lily reads both clippings more than once. Even after
she understands them, she keeps reading, as if the texts
might shift before her eyes and yield more information.
Eventually she raises her head. "What about Francine?"
she asks.

Samantha shakes her head. "I haven't heard from her. I
have no idea. Her mother called last week and said
Francine had written to say she was going away again on
research and would send her an address when she was
settled. Her mother's in a home. She doesn't know what
day it is. What could I say?"

"What *did* you say?"

"I told her I didn't know where she was. That she left
suddenly. I told her I would let her know if I heard anything."

"When did these come?" asks Lily.

"Ten days ago."

Lily looks at the postmark on the envelope—Halifax,
Nova Scotia. "Why didn't you tell someone?"

"Because I needed time to think about the right thing to
do. That, by the way, is an interesting exercise in itself."

"What?" asks Lily.

"Trying to determine the right thing to do, what's best
for the greatest number of people involved. I suspect
you're used to it, but for me it was a challenge."

Lily reads both clippings again, then puts them and the
envelope on the coffee table. "What did you decide?"

"I sent information through the mail to both places—the

state troopers and the police in Newfoundland. I used storebought stationery and an old typewriter that's been sitting in the spare office since we got there. I wore gloves. I left Boston and mailed them from two separate cities."

"That's pretty thorough," says Lily. "Now what?"

"There's nothing else to do. I assume the authorities will contact Nickolas's family. William has no family, and he's retired, but presumably he has friends who will want to know—and a few ex-wives."

"And Francine?"

Samantha shrugs. "We wait."

"Do you think she's alive?"

"There's no way to know, is there? But judging from my experience of her astonishing resources and capacity for—what would you call it, camouflage?—I believe there's a good chance she is."

"Are you angry at her?" asks Lily.

"Not anymore," says Samantha. "I was very hurt, you know. In the face of everything that happened, what seemed most salient to me was the fact that I had been betrayed. But over the past few weeks, I've begun to lose interest. Which, I should add, surprised me. It's as if my former habits of thought aren't available."

"I know," says Lily. She picks up the two clippings, then replaces them in the envelope without reading them. "Do you think the Order found the manuscript?" she asks.

"They did, or they will, eventually. They have only one goal and no conscience. That's a good formula for success." Samantha picks up the envelope containing the clippings and slips it back into the bookshelf. "I should have offered you something. Do you want a Coke, water, something to drink?"

Lily realizes she was waiting for the offer or even expecting a bottle of wine to be out on the dining room table, with glasses, and cheese and expensive crackers and some kind of smoked fish.

Samantha watches her face and says, "I'm not drinking wine at the moment. I hope to stop altogether. Of course, I plan to stop on my own, without help. But I have decided if that plan fails, and there's no reason to think it won't fail, since it always has before, this time I'll get some help."

As soon as Lily hears this, she realizes the same thing is true for her. She will call Marty and go to an AA meeting with her. But she isn't ready to say it out loud, yet. After a moment, she asks, "Where will you go?"

"To get help?"

"No," she says. "On your sabbatical. What are your plans?"

"I would rather not say. I'm sorry to be so secretive, especially after all the secrets we've endured. But I think I need to be out of touch with everyone, at least for a while." Then she smiles, just a slight lift of the corners of her mouth, and says, "Even you."

Lily looks at Samantha's face, quickly, to see her expression. It's neutral. "I'm sorry about that conversation in my apartment, about our friendship . . ." she begins.

"Don't be ridiculous," says Samantha. "It was absurd for me to bring that up then—or probably any time. I'm an old woman—well, older—and I've never learned to take care of myself. If I can do that, then, perhaps, later . . ."

"Yes," says Lily. "Do you think they'll come back?"

"The Order? They might, although I don't see why. As long as we stay quiet, they have nothing to gain. And if something should happen to one of us, they risk everything."

"Are you still afraid?" asks Lily.

"Yes and no. Sometimes I imagine I'm being followed. But it isn't true. It's vestigial. And, in general, I'm so much *less* afraid than I used to be. Do you understand?" Samantha asks, and looks directly at her.

"I do," says Lily.

ON THE SIDEWALK OUTSIDE THE APARTMENT BUILD-ing, Lily realizes how seldom she thinks about the Order. Maybe the power of the threat is still too strong. The wind has died down, and the stars shine clearly in the cold. But it's not just the threat, she thinks. Somehow, the Order was the least interesting part of the whole experience. They exist out there somewhere, like all the other cruelty and stupidity in the world, alongside the pleasure of breathing in sharp winter air and walking, almost unafraid, down a quiet street.

As she stops to zip her parka, she glances up at Samantha's apartment—six tall windows across the front of the building, three floors up. What she sees surprises her. She counts the floors to be sure she has the right place. She does. As she watches, she sees Samantha's silhouette moving from window to window, lighting a small, electric candle on each windowsill, so that the row of dark empty spaces is transformed.

ACKNOWLEDGMENTS

Thanks to Martha Bushko, Gail Hochman, and, especially, Dennis McFarland for their time and help and wisdom.

THE TENTMAKER
MICHELLE BLAKE

"A wonderful debut: amazing,
graceful, satisfying."
—*San Fransisco Chronicle*

The author's acclaimed debut, introducing
Episcopal priest Lily Connor.

"Shove over Brother Cadfel, and make
room for Lily Connor in the vestry."
—*Chicago Tribune*

"Amazing."
—*San Fransisco Chronicle*

0-425-17668-1
Available wherever books are sold or
to order call :
1-800-788-6262

(ad # B406)

MICHELLE BLAKE

EARTH HAS NO SORROW
A LILY CONNOR MYSTERY

In this sequel to the critically-acclaimed
The Tentmaker, Episcopalian priest Lily Connor
seeks to find a friend who may be a victim of
a viscious hate crime.

"Shove over Brother Cadfael, and
make room for Lily Connor in the vestry."
—*Chicago Tribune*

"Richly textured...Blake neatly juggles
the theology and the police work."
—*Boston Globe*

0-425-18523-0

Available wherever books are sold or
to order call: 1-800-488-6262

B896

LOVE MYSTERY?

From cozy mysteries to procedurals,
we've got it all. Satisfy your cravings with our monthly
newsletters designed and edited specifically for fans of who-
dunits. With two newsletters to choose from, you'll be sure to
get it all. Be sure to check back each month or sign up for
free monthly in-box delivery at

www.penguin.com

Berkley Prime Crime

Berkley publishes the premier writers of mysteries.
Get the latest on your
favorties:
Susan Wittig Albert, Margaret Coel, Earlene
Fowler, Randy Wayne White, Simon Brett, and
many more fresh faces.

Signet

From the Grand Dame of mystery,
Agatha Christie, to debut authors,
Signet mysteries offer something for every reader.

*Sign up and sleep with
one eye open!*

B112